BLACK JACK

Rani Manicka

Black Jack

Published by Rani Manicka
First published in paperback 2013

Copyright © 2013 by Rani Manicka

Cover Design by Spiffing Covers

ISBN: 978-0-9576812-0-0

Other Novels by Rani Manicka

The Rice Mother
Touching Earth
The Japanese Lover

Rani Manicka is the prize-winning author of the international bestseller, The Rice Mother. Her works have been translated into 26 languages. She currently divides her time between Malaysia and the United Kingdom, and lives with the two loves of her life, Rick and an indescribably naughty German shepherd puppy called Tyron. Find her at http://www.ranimanicka.com

Previous Praise For Rani Manicka

The Rice Mother

'You'll struggle to find a more powerful, moving read this year.' **GLAMOUR**

'Powerful.' **SUNDAY MIRROR**

'Emotionally satisfying, complex books like this are hard to find.' **HEAT**

'You'll love Rani Manicka's first novel.' **NEW WOMAN**

Touching Earth

'Woven with the beautiful intricacy of a spider creating its web, Touching Earth uses exquisite, lyrical writing to present us with the harsh realities of heroin addiction, prostitution and innocence lost.' **HEAT**

'High on atmosphere and tension, this is another powerful novel from the author of The Rice Mother.' **WOMAN & HOME**

The Japanese Lover

'A seductive tale of forbidden love' **STYLIST**

'This unconventional love story is told with great imagination. Vivid, complex and full of color, it's a fabulous read.' **CHOICE**

For my beloved Ty,
'Run free, my love. One day we'll meet again.'

For our struggle is not against [human beings], but against the rulers, against the powers, against the world forces of this darkness, against the spiritual [dark forces] of wickedness in **outer space**."

-Ephesians 6:12 [the uncensored citation translated from Greek

ANNUIT COEPTIS

(He looks favorably upon our work)

Schooner Klaus stood with his nose slightly raised: a bi-pedal wolf sniffing for prey. Yet, his was no wolf brain fighting for survival in the wilderness; inextricably bound by the dark, sweet call of warm blood. Dressed in high-ranking military uniform and shaven-skulled, he stood in the control room of one of America's top secret military bases. His thickly muscled, hulking form appeared curiously immobile in the bluish glow emanating from the wall of soundless television screens. A green light on the console flashed.

'Yes.' His voice was unexpectedly silky, hypnotic almost.

'They're ready for you, Dr. Klaus,' a disembodied voice informed.

Only his eyes, gray and cruel, shifted. To the largest screen on the wall. To the image of a naked, gagged child secured to a metal table in a metal room. Her fair hair was plastered to her head, and her thin body covered in cuts, bruises, and burns. There was an IV in her left arm, a leather strap across her forehead, audio phones over her ears, and electrodes attached to her fingers. Her terrified, pleading eyes were darting desperately around the six men who had arranged themselves on either side of her.

But staring straight ahead the men displayed the only objective they had ever made known to her, day after day, week after week. To subject her to excruciating pain. And to this effect they used jellied acid, long needles, electrified probes, and other unspeakably horrible instruments that they found on the shelf underneath the table she lay upon. Every session ended with the substitution of the leather headband for a metal one so that the electroshock torture could commence and continue until blessed blackness came for her.

She awakened inside a metal cage too small to stand or lie in, with a blinding headache from the electroshock treatment, and her body hurting so bad she felt certain she was dying.

'Ma. I want my ma,' she had begged in the beginning.

She may as well have been invisible. Not one uttered a word. Food pellets and water were shoved through a slot, the portions barely enough to keep her alive. There was no toilet: she had to urinate and defecate in her pitiful position, and afterwards sleep in her own mess. Hardly had she slept when the door opened and men wearing rubber gloves yanked her out by the arms and dragged her down a corridor to a room with a concrete floor. There a cold-water hose was directed at her cowering body. No soap. A rough towel.

Then it was back to the metal table.

One day they threw an armless teddy bear into her cage. It stank of excrement, but in the freezing darkness she reached for it. 'It's all right,' she whispered to the helpless thing. 'I'll be your friend. My name is Dakota. What's yours?' She hugged the silent bear tightly, but when she was awakened it was gone. The loss was so traumatic, she did not even gasp when the icy water struck her body.

Being only seven, she could not understand any of it. But her nakedness, the lack of sanitation, the constant cold, the disturbed sleep, the mutilated bear, and the complete lack of human interaction were all aspects of a carefully controlled, extreme trauma program. Even the meager food portions were not chance cruelty. Sugar and protein deprivation starved any rebellious tendency, and the severe limiting of her water intake increased her brain temperature, which disorientated her, and induced hallucinations.

Since there were no windows or clocks there was no way for her to tell day from night. She began to imagine she had been in that terrible place for years. She used to dream of her father coming to her rescue and her return to her mother's soft, yielding arms, but the memories of her previous life when she had worn mittens and a red coat and had run free in a snow covered field were leaving her fevered brain. A handful left, and even those were fading fast. She was already so weak she could hardly stand unaided, but with the instinct of an animal caught in a mangle, she understood; the men would never stop until she was dead.

So it would have surprised her greatly to know that Schooner Klaus, observing her from his concealed position, saw not a helpless child enduring a slow, torturous death in a steel trap, but an unbelievably dangerous and unpredictable creature—one capable of killing and injuring his team. Perhaps even him, in unimaginably bizarre ways, using nothing more than her mind.

Otherwise, she would not be on his table to learn the meaning of real fear.

Her journey to him had begun with a local newspaper story in Kansas. It claimed a child had stood at her bedroom window, and with psychic force alone held back a rabid Rottweiler from her pet, a wolf cub, until her father had arrived, shotgun in hand. A whole hour later! Even if he allowed fifty-five minutes for small town hot air it remained an astounding feat. Field operatives had been dispatched.

They had been casual in their approach, but not in their detailed report: Celtic ancestry, RH-negative blood group, able to finish other people's sentences, and numerous accounts of shopkeepers who suddenly developed an irresistible urge to rush out with candy for her as she passed their shops. But most intriguing of all was her nickname—the Locator—an allusion to her uncanny ability to find lost things and people.

In truth, he had not needed the report. He had had only to look at the first long-range photograph of her, eyes gazing fearlessly out at the world, to know instantly: she was special. There would be no hanging about for months while she learned to psychically restrain hamsters dying of thirst from partaking of their water sprouts. That she might even be 'the one.' Her participation in the agency's program had become a foregone conclusion.

Her disappearance had been easily accomplished. An unmarked vehicle. An empty swing. A lone, travelling pedophile, perhaps? He imagined the one-street town's people, stupid rednecks, kicking the dust, shaking baffled heads and muttering, 'Damn shame, what happened to the Locator, but why take the wolf cub?'

Thursday's Child Has Far To Go

Nursery Rhyme – Monday's Child.

The woman sat at the window and stared unseeingly out. Her fair hair, which was considered her best asset, lay around her shoulders, uncombed and greasy. It had not been washed since the girl's disappearance. Her eyes were red-rimmed and her mouth was slightly open. There was a sheen of sweat on her upper lip. In her lap her fingers clenched and unclenched incessantly.

Outside, nothing moved in the hot, heavy air. The golden cornfields were still and full of secrets. She felt as if she had been sitting there for a very long time. She did not cook, she did not clean, she did not do the washing. Neither did she water her vegetable plot nor feed the chickens. She only sat by the window, waiting.

She heard the sound of her husband's truck pull into the dusty dirt track that led to their home. The engine died. His heavy boots were loud on the wooden porch. He was in a hurry. He pushed open the front door and appeared as a shadow in front of her. She did not turn to look at him.

His voice was a whisper. 'They found the body of a girl. They think it might be her.'

Her body stiffened. She took a deep breath. It's not her, she wanted to say, but she did not.

'We have to go into the city to identify her, Ma.'

She hated it when he called her ma. It made her want to claw at his face. She was not a ma. Not anymore. The girl was gone. No need to call her ma. She stood up silently and made for the front door.

'Aren't ya gonna change?'

The woman didn't answer. Instead, she twisted her neck suddenly and glared at him. The ferocity in her eyes made his mouth close uselessly. He dropped his eyes. She continued on her journey and he followed dejectedly. They climbed into the old truck and he started the engine. They did not exchange a single word during the two-hour journey into the big town. The man did not know the way and twice he had to stop to ask directions. The woman never took her eyes off the road ahead. It's not her. It's not her.

The truck stopped outside the morgue and the woman opened the door and climbed out. Her bones ached. She closed the car door and began up the steps. Her husband joined her. Their steps matched perfectly. He felt empty. He held open the door for her and she walked through. The interior was air-conditioned. The woman shivered. A young woman sitting behind a counter lifted her head and looked enquiringly at them. Her lips were painted red. They walked towards her. She buzzed for someone to come and see them. A young man appeared through a side door and introduced himself as Mr. Whittman. Mr. Whittman was very polite, but he only addressed the man. For the woman refused to look at him. Dry-eyed she stared at a patch of wall.

They were led into a corridor. There were chairs lined up against the wall.

'This way, please' the young man who had been dealing with them said, indicating a door. He put his hand on the handle and, turning it, went through. The man made to follow, but the woman shot out a hand and caught his forearm. Her grip was steely.

Surprisingly, considering she had hardly eaten for weeks. She looked up at him wordlessly, and then she went past him and through the door. The man crumpled into a plastic chair. He buried his face in his hands and tried to stop the tears. But they would not stop.

The woman found herself with the young man in a tiny, dim enclosure. The wall facing her held a large glass window. There was a room beyond the glass. It was made of metal and brightly lit by fluorescent lights. There was a table in the middle of it and an elderly woman was standing next to the table. There was a tiny body on the table. It was covered with a bluish grey cloth. The woman's lips began to tremble uncontrollably. The girl was the right size.

'Ready?' the young man asked. In that small space he could smell her unwashed body.

The woman nodded.

He in turn nodded to the woman standing by the table. Gently, she began to raise one end of the cloth covering. The first thing the woman saw was the girl's blonde hair. She spun away from the sight. In the dimness the young man could not see her face, but she was grinning. Grinning like a mad woman.

That child on the cold slab was not her baby.

> All the King's horses and all the King's men
> Couldn't put Humpty together again.
>
> —Humpty Dumpty

Dakota's eyes rolled frantically from one implacable face to the next, begging and begging. How could she know that they had no say in her fate? That they were the most expandable of the twelve that made up her torture team. So many of them had left in body bags that they were nicknamed 'targets'. In the event that a psychic child was capable of retaliation it was always one of them who suffered the consequences. Their orders were specific and ruthless. They were not to stop until they were given the signal, and they could never move away from the metal table no matter what the circumstances. If for any reason at all they disobeyed either of these two cardinal rules, they would be shot in the head by the Dead Man.

The Dead Man, a superb marksman, sat in a concealed booth to the right of the door. His instructions were chillingly simple: if anyone in the torture chamber moved away from his assigned post or behaved in any way out of the ordinary, he was to shoot them dead. The only person he was not authorized under any circumstances to eliminate was the psychic child. That task was the sole responsibility of the two armed guards located outside the chamber. Their orders, in the event that the small strobe light located on the wall just above the door flashed red, were to open the doors without entering it, and, no matter what they saw, regardless of what anyone else was doing, kill the child.

Unseen by her were also the ECT (electro-convulsive therapy) technician, responsible for controlling the electrical part of the torture, and a highly trained medical person who monitored her vital signs and accordingly administered the optimum dosage from a selection of psychoactive drugs. With subtle changes he could greatly enhance her pain or bring on impressions of confusion and extreme terror. He was also in charge of administering the nerve receptor blockers that made it impossible for her to faint or black out to escape the pain, no matter how horrific it became. At the end of each session he provided the 'blackness' by injecting a quick-acting sedative directly into her carotid artery by order of the Eye in the Sky.

Safely located in a separate room a short distance away, the Eye was the unquestioned leader of the team. He alone had access to the fail-safe button and absolute life and death rule over the child's life. A trained psychologist, he monitored the chamber's activity via closed-circuit TV, and the brain activity of the psychic child via remote EEG. His commands were issued through electronic reader boards. Schooner Klaus sat down, his movements precise and fluid, and into his voice activated console said, 'Begin.'

On the screens above his head, his team came alive. The gag was removed from the child's mouth, the biotech injected her with the necessary chemical cocktail, the ECT man turned his dials, the six targets reached for their specific instruments, and the girl began to scream. Schooner Klaus had a headache and he found it more unpleasant than usual to endure her hoarse screams, but it was as vital to her to experience her own reverberating screams, as was the sight of her spasmodically jerking body on the mirrored ceiling.

Fifteen minutes passed with the girl's futile shrieks and moans, and Schooner Klaus staring at her impatiently. Fisting his right hand, he tapped it lightly against the rim of the table, a supremely aggressive gesture. Her brain was surely on fire with all the drugs and, yet, she lay there squirming and trying to outwrestle her steel manacles, as if she was without options.

'Fight back, you little bitch,' he urged softly.

His eyes drifted away from the screens. The clock told of the passage of another four minutes. His head throbbed. He switched the microphone off and slumped back. Why did she not strike back? If she did not retaliate soon she would die in the process like so many before her.

Then... At twenty-two minutes her sweat-soaked body convulsed horribly and became still. He sat forward and watched eagerly as her eyes turned in their sockets. To stare at him!

'Impossible,' he exclaimed. The cameras were minute and so skillfully concealed amongst other equipment that they were undetectable even to professional sweeps. But those large, empty eyes were boring into him. She had 'located' him! He jerked back and stood suddenly, his chair skittering away on the smooth floor, a creature of fear. But nothing happened, and he realized that months of torture had turned her gaze weak and harmless.

He bent toward the mic, his eyes no longer anxious, but shining with excitement. 'The men will only stop if *you* stop them. The same way you stopped the rabid dog.'

She frowned. A memory, not yet lost. Sleeping on the sunlit porch. A pink tongue on her face. Shadow.

11

Her father's voice, 'If I see one teeth mark on your face, young lady, that wolf's going right back to where he came from.' Her voice full of laughter, so confident, 'He won't bite me, Daddy. He loves me.'

Schooner Klaus willed her to act. 'Come on,' he whispered.

Suddenly, movement on the other screens. His eyes darted to them. Two of the targets had downed their tools and were coolly untying the girl's hands. She had gone for two. A thrill of pleasure coursed through him. Not taking his eyes off her face, he signaled the Dead Man.

The Dead Man responded instantly and with great efficiency. Both renegade targets crumpled where they stood. The other four stared ahead stonily. None dared look at the fallen. True, they had undergone the rigorous de-sensitization process and been injected with all kinds of drugs to deaden the evolutionary instinct of self-preservation, but even so, by God! With fear in their throats they clutched their shining instruments and rued the day they had ever thought to enter that hell-hole. Within minutes the standby targets assembled outside the door came in, to take the places of the dead.

Dakota's hands were rebound.

Schooner Klaus leaned forward until he was inches away from the middle screen. She looked an ill little thing in that monstrously clinical room, but he suffered neither shame nor pity.

'Go on, show me what else you can do,' he taunted.

As though she had heard his challenge, all six targets as if of one mind turned away from her and buried their faces in their hands.

Schooner Klaus took a startled, delighted breath. Impressive. No, not impressive; extraordinary. He alerted the Dead Man. 'All,' he ordered callously.

With their faces still covered they died. Not one had tried to run or defend himself. The Eye in the Sky did not spare a thought for the men he had sacrificed. They were not important. What was important was that the child understood that no matter what she said or did, the torture would carry on. She must conclude that all resistance was useless and passively submit to her fate. Blind, unthinking obedience—that was what he needed. He barked for more back-up to stand by. From their quarters men heard the buzzer and poured into the rubber-tiled corridors, perhaps to their death.

The girl was grizzling softly when the six new targets arrived at the door. They stepped over the corpses to take over where their predecessors had stopped. When the girl saw the implacable faces arranged around her, different and yet the same, she stopped crying. She had lost heart. She knew then—her enemy was too great to defeat.

Schooner Klaus sent a directive to the ECT controller.

The tech knew the girl's brain was close to frying, but displaying neither emotion nor hesitation he increased the voltage. The girl convulsed uncontrollably. Her mouth frothed and her eyes rolled up into their sockets. They remained white for so long Schooner Klaus felt a tinge of apprehension. Had he gone too far? But like blue stones, they slowly dropped into place to stare blankly at the overhead lights. Years of practicing on hundreds of children brought in from Mexico and other poor South American nations had taught him the meaning of that glazed look.

She had lost and he had won.

The Hypercube

(The perfect double prison)

'Put her down,' Schooner Klaus commanded the biotech.

The trauma had become so unbearable that her child's mind had said, No, this isn't happening to me, and escaped to a place without fear or pain. Monstrous details that should have mattered terribly no longer did. The taste of the rubber plug jammed between her teeth, the feel of the steel clamped to her skin, the smell of her burning flesh and hair. They collected harmlessly in glass jars while she floated free. Pain had become pleasure.

While the sedative was being administered, Schooner Klaus dabbed lavender perfume onto his wrists. It was no shallow affectation—in future, he would be able to make her dissociate with nothing more than a whiff of the scent. He stepped into a pair of specially made rubber boots and walked into the deserted corridor. He entered the torture chamber where the bright headlights had been dimmed and stood for a moment looking at her small, still figure. He registered and savored a victorious sense of cold possession. It had been a spectacular battle of wills: he had gambled the thing he believed to be his most precious find, and he had won.

He had shattered her mind. Now his intention was to further split it many times more and to mold each fragment into a personality in its own right, capable of thinking, feeling, and functioning by itself. Each one would have its own name, memories, behavioral traits, emotional characteristics. Separated by amnesic barriers, they would all be unaware they were sharing a body with 'others'. And all of them unavailable to the core personality or the 'real Dakota's' conscious recall. Her inner world would become a labyrinth full of strangers who could only be called forward and controlled by him or someone to whom he gave the appropriate access codes.

The other programmers and handlers owned the obligatory three-ringed notebooks and laptops with all the access codes and triggers for their slaves, but he had been trained in the oral method. He had it all memorized, especially the secret back door codes that he never revealed to anyone.

He was not a squeamish man and he stepped easily into the growing puddles of blood, to lean over her. Her eyes were open and staring at the ceiling. He removed her earphones. His nostrils flared. The smell of her. Blood, sweat, a sour note—vomit, fear and something else… A child thing… His thing.

The first alter to be programmed utilizing the thirteen by thirteen grid was always the protector persona.

'She looks like you,' he whispered. 'But she is not you. We will always strap you down and hurt you. But *she* will come forth and hold all your pain. Her name is Merica.' He paused for a moment to let the formal, unique name he had given the protector persona sink in. 'I am now speaking with Merica, the one who holds all the pain. You are Dakota's protector. From now on your only task is to keep her safe. If she disobeys us, you must do whatever necessary to stop her. 'Or…' He touched her face with an electrically charged ball wrapped in salt water. Dakota's body convulsed violently. 'We will hurt you. Don't ever forget. Do your job well.'

He lightly pressed his fingertips behind both her ears, and administered another low dose of electroshock to lock in the command. This 'feel the pain' sequence would be repeated again and again until Merica could be 'trusted' to take over the function of Dakota's prison guard, the insistent voice inside her head that her twisted logic would call 'her protector'. For the rest of her life Merica would keep not only the girl and later the woman isolated and pliable, but, more importantly, also her programmer and owner from capture or retribution. Merica would resist any recollection even in the hands of the most qualified therapist.

The next persona he sectioned off was a weak thing, hardly human. It had no courage. Its heart, he told the girl, had been ripped out and sealed in an Earthen jar. 'Now give all your feelings of wanting to hurt us to it,' he commanded. In this way any desire for retaliation or revenge against her tormentors would no longer be accessible to the dominant personality, but held by that sorry, stunted creature. It too was given a formal, unique name—Eylon.

In this manner anger was channeled into another alter and told it that it was not human, but a chained, wild creature. Only he had the keys. Only he could access that frothing beast. Over time that creature would be stoked, nourished, given legs, hands, wings, heart, mind, soul, and be set against any that would try to help her.

Week by week with faultless precision he created

many other alters. Almost all, permanently crippled, or taught to view themselves as hateful and hated. Some were frozen as little children; others blind, mute or deaf.

Hope, he told her, led to wanting, and wanting was very bad, the cause of great suffering. 'Friends will always hurt you. Boys will hurt you. You must remain alone. Don't ever let anyone touch you. Or...' He held open both her eyelids and squeezed a few drops of chemical irritant into her eyes. While she writhed with pain the lights were switched off to simulate blindness.

'See what wanting does? Now you are forever blind.'

Wanting was christened Cromag.

'Your job,' he told Cromag, 'is to keep her from wanting. If she wants, take it away instantly. Replace it with doubt and discomfort.' Cromag would spend the rest of her existence, isolated, blind and in terrible pain; nevertheless ferocious in the performance of her job.

Another personality was created to house curiosity. 'Never,' he spoke firmly, 'let her have questions. Questions belong to us. Do not look for answers. Answers do not belong to you. They belong to us.' Holding her by the throat he injected an irritant into her larynx. The pain was so severe that the girl temporarily lost her voice. 'You will never again be able to speak,' he lied, and instantly that alter became mute. Another poor mute was given the task of remembering Dakota's past. 'If she remembers she will die. Do your job well.'

When all the traits that were thought to be detrimental to his control of 'the real Dakota' had been locked away into a truly impressive myriad of alters, it was time to invoke the personas that would control access to her psychic abilities. It was vital that she have no access to her own powers in her daily life. He referred to the first such alter he created as 'the powerful one' or 'the one who holds your powers'.

'I am talking to Shekina,' he said, using the imprinting gesture of rubbing her forehead just above the bridge of the nose. ' You hold *all* her psychic powers. She must never be allowed to use these powers. These powers belong to you. Only you. If she tries to use them you must stop her. If you fail to stop her, we will hurt you.'

He hurt her.

Then, he created a secondary alter called a key, so it would be impossible for her to either intentionally or accidentally access her own gift without this trigger alter. This gatekeeper he named Timu.

'When you hear Timu you will know it is we who want you to use your powers. You will use your powers only as we tell you to. Do you understand?'

'Yes.'

Death to the weakling, wealth to the strong!

—Book of Satan 1:1

One day the door of Dakota's dank prison opened and a huge man enveloped in a cloud of lavender perfume approached her cage. Even though she had been programmed not to remember his face, for a bewildering moment, she was unaccountably terrified by the juxtaposition of his imposing military figure and the familiar smell. But then he smiled and it was an indescribably wonderful smile. It lit up his entire face and he seemed beautiful to her beyond anything she could imagine. There was no doubt in her child's mind: her troubles were over. He was some sort of policeman who had come to save her.

Schooner Klaus unlocked the cage and told her that he had come to take her away from that horrible place. After the abominable cruelty she had experienced she felt insanely grateful to him. When he gathered her nearly skeletal body into his clean, sweet-smelling arms she clung pitifully to his strong neck and emitted a low, frightened howl.

'I know, I know,' he soothed gently. 'But everything is going to be all right now. You have been a good girl and you deserve good things from now on.' With infinite tenderness he carried her down the bare corridors and into a rather odd room.

The walls were purple, and from the black and white tiled floor sprouted three pillars of different heights, none of which quite reached the ceiling. Although she

21

had the impression that there were no windows, yellow drapes drawn shut made it seem that there were.

On a black stone platform in the middle of the room stood a marble bath with clawed feet. He carried her to it and she saw that it was half filled with fragrant water. Gently, and with kind words, he lowered her into it. The water was deliciously warm. He took off his jacket with all its gleaming medals and rolled up his shirtsleeves. With a washcloth he proceeded to wash her. He unclenched her fists and examined her fingers, blue with needle marks underneath the nails that ran from tip to root. She heard him sigh sorrowfully. For some time she remained with her eyes lowered, but as his soft, reassuring voice kept on repeating just how incredible it was all going to be henceforth, she turned an adoring gaze up to him.

He lifted her out of the bath and enveloped her in a thick towel. She put her cheek against the soft material, and unconsciously made the contented sound of a dog when its master bends to scratch its ears. There were polka dot panties and fine clothes laid out on a black velvet chair. He dressed her in them. In a daze she ran her palms down the front of the dress and smoothed it over her legs. This was her first time in clothes since she had woken up caged.

She was taken to a playroom. There were many toys in a big, lidless wooden box, and another child was sitting on the floor playing with a train set.

'Tom is the same age as you, Dakota. Would you like to play with him?'

The little boy was fair-haired like her and seemed unsurprised by Dakota's appearance in the playroom. Dakota wanted to join him, but, feeling shy and tongue-tied, she hung back behind Schooner Klaus.

'Go ahead,' Schooner Klaus encouraged kindly. 'I'll be right here if you need me.' He moved to a table nearby and sat down. Paying no more attention to the children he began to shuffle some papers on the table.

Tom had neither smiled nor spoken, but he was silently holding out a green and black train compartment toward her. With timid steps she went to sit in front of her new friend. But no sooner had she settled down, when the door burst open and a large man barged in. Dakota was instantly immobilized with fear. Everything about him reminded her of the coldly remote six that stood around the metal table. Worse, he appeared to be in an uncontrollable rage.

She scrambled up and tried to run to Schooner Klaus, but the man was lightning fast. His iron fist closed around her forearm tightly. He would have dragged her out of the room, too, if Schooner Klaus had not looked up from his papers and said in a calm, firm voice, 'There must be some misunderstanding here. You must want some other child.'

But the man was adamant. She was a runaway and must return to the metal room with him. Dakota began to cower with abject terror.

'Let's discuss this outside,' Schooner Klaus suggested reasonably.

They left the room. Dakota lay frozen on the floor, where the man had tossed her, for what seemed an interminable time. Finally, the door opened and Schooner Klaus walked through it. He seemed concerned. The man loomed at the door with crossed arms. Schooner Klaus knelt on one knee beside her so he could whisper into her ear. He told her that the man had orders to take her away and kill her, but that he had managed to convince him it was not important which child died, only that one did. And Dakota, well, Dakota could decide whether it was she or another child that did.

'Perhaps Tom could take your place?'

Dakota went white.

Schooner Klaus shook his head regretfully. 'I know,' he soothed, 'but it was the best I could do.'

Dakota looked at Tom. Unaffected and uncurious about what was going on he had quietly gone back to playing with his train set. In a daze it occurred to her that she had not yet heard him speak. Perhaps he could not. He seemed strangely solemn and unappreciative of his own good fortune, living in that brightly lit, colorful room full of toys. She had done nothing wrong, and yet she had to die. It seemed terribly unfair. She thought of the metal table and began to shake her head. She couldn't, she simply couldn't go back. Her heart was pounding in her chest.

'Well?' Schooner Klaus prompted.

She uttered her first word since being out of the cage.

'Tom,' she whispered.

Barely had the word left her lips when the man strode into the room, grabbed Tom by his head, and, with a knife that he pulled out of his pocket, slit the poor boy's throat. From ear to ear. Blood gushed out of the gaping wound as he kicked and writhed. Dakota stared in shocked horror. When eventually Tom stopped jerking, the man calmly wiped his knife, put it away, and left. In the dead silence, Dakota thought she heard the sound of wet gurgling coming from the boy's throat. She felt numb and cold and very frightened.

'There, there... You did very well, my pretty, little butterfly,' Schooner Klaus praised, gently patting her on her back. She turned her stunned gaze toward him, and found him smiling and approving. She had done well? She felt confused. Perhaps, the boy had not been 'good' in some way. He *must have* deserved it. And yet... Schooner Klaus held out his hand in front of her face and she bent forward and put her wretched lips to the big, black stone clawed within his ring.

He took her hand, and hand in hand they went out of the door, down a long corridor, up in a lift, and through a metal door into bright sunlight. She turned her face up to its warmth. She thought, it's all right now. All is well.

A long, black car with tinted windows pulled up alongside them and they got into the back seat. The car pulled out of the front gates of what looked like an ordinary office building. Dakota realized tears were flowing down her cheeks. She felt horrible. Her small fist closed around Schooner Klaus's index finger. Looking down at her he understood precisely her reaction. Symbolically she had lost her innocence. The distinction that one was the victim and the other the perpetrator had been erased. This was, in fact, the beginning of self-loathing. He allowed her to hold his finger.

'I've spoken to your parents,' he said, as he fished in his trouser pocket and brought out a grape-flavored sweet. He unwrapped it and put it directly into her mouth. 'They love you very much, but they said that I should keep you for a bit.'

'Don't they want me back?' she asked, but the sedative was quick-working and she laid her head back sleepily. He patted her on the top of her head and whispered, 'Of course they do, but go to the safe place now, my little butterfly, over the rainbow. It's time to forget everything.'

To induce retrograde amnesia before she actually fell asleep he extracted from his jacket pocket a stun gun that could have passed for a fountain pen, and electro-shocked her in the muscled area below the shoulder blades. Since human memories do not become coherent for about twenty-four hours after they are imprinted, shock-scrambling them while they are still stored in the short-term memory section of the brain destroys them. When she awakened she would remember nothing.

As she slid into his lap he stroked her hair and smiled. By the time he was finished with her she would be transformed into a biological robot, unschooled to read, write or execute simple math, but capable of performing any act, no matter how depraved or barbaric. Devoid of any moral or ethical standard, and stripped of all human compassion, she would be the force behind Project ABADDON.

'Seven for a secret,
Not to be told;
Eight for heaven,
Nine for hell
And ten for the devil's own sell!'

Nursery Rhymes – One for Sorrow, 1840

The man came out of the shower and dressed quietly in clothes that he fetched from the laundry basket. They were unpressed and crumpled, but they were clean and smelled faintly of the lavender detergent the woman had used. Barefoot, he left their bedroom and walked along the narrow corridor to the little one's room. He opened the door and stood as if frozen at the threshold. Again that desire to bawl like a baby. Again that rage that he had been turned into this helpless, useless creature.

Again that terrible, terrible, terrible fear for her.

His eyes moved around the room. It had become a shrine. Silently, he gazed at the gay paintings. The little bed with its multi-coloured quilt that his mother had made for the girl. The wolf's drinking bowl. The little fairy princess musical box.

He closed the door softly and walked towards the musical box. He picked it up in his large clumsy hands and carefully turned its key. Then he opened it and watched the fairy princess turning round and round to the tinkling music. He had always found these things eerie in a way he could not explain. They made the hair at the back of his neck stand. This one was no exception. With his knuckle he tapped the lid and it slammed shut. The room fell silent again.

He went to sit on the narrow bed. He had sat in this very place so many times while her small body was tucked up inside it. Listening to bedtime stories.

'Last one. Pleeease, Pa.'

He switched on the small bedside lamp and switched it off again. Then he let his calloused hands caress the surface of the quilt. He leaned back until his body touched the bed. A sigh escaped him. He lifted his legs and curled his body into an awkward, ill-formed ball. He felt so lost. so alone. He was startled when the door opened suddenly.

His wife was standing at the doorway. 'What are you doing?' Her voice was shrill with shock and anger. She advanced into the room.

He jack-knifed into a sitting position. 'I'm clean,' he explained, defensively, guiltily. 'I showered first.'

It stopped her cold. She looked at him and for the first time he saw just how frightened she was. He lay back down, and moving closer to the wall, made a space for her.

She hesitated. 'I'm not clean,' she muttered.

'She won't mind,' he said hoarsely.

With a small sob she went to lie beside him. He held her thin body close.

'Why? Why her?' she asked. It was a question that went around and around ceaselessly in her head until she felt she was going mad. Why her baby? Every time she saw a child. Why her?

'We'll find her, Ellen. We'll find her.'

'All the posters are still up, aren't they?' she sniffed. 'The kids haven't torn them down?'

'Yeah, they're all up.'

'My heart is broken, Pa,' she whispered.

'I know, Ellen, I know,' he said sadly, and for a while he simply lay listening to her crying softly. He had never heard her cry before. Once, when she found out that her mother had died, he had watched tears flow helplessly down her cheeks while she carried on sitting at the table eating her dinner, but she had never allowed herself to sob openly.

'I'll never stop looking for her,' he promised into the tangle of her unwashed hair as she carried on with her heart-wrenching sobs.

January, 2012

National Security Agency (NSA)

If it moves, enslave it. If it doesn't, steal it. If it resists, kill it.
If it is no longer useful, destroy it.

—Steven J. Smith

Dakota lay sedated in her underground dorm, deep beneath the sprawling one hundred square mile confines of the NSA's Marine Base Quantico. The complex had its official name, naturally, but she and the others like her knew it simply as 'the Black Hole'. The name derived not only from its main multi-story, black glass building, but was also an allusion to the many who went in and never came out.

Although she recalled being taken to the ops room almost daily, she had no conscious memory of what she did there or how to access her own psychic powers, except the once, when she had dreamed that she had been to the roof of the black glass building and seen large satellite dishes, oversized cooling units, and, as far as the eye could see, in every direction—pitch black forests. Traveling through the building, she learned that the above-ground floors were mostly office space.

All above board; all legitimate.

In fact, there was absolutely nothing above ground to even remotely suggest the secret world underneath that only the initiate had access to. A complicated maze of underground hallways connecting hundreds of secure dormitories, all stacked one on top of another, and tied together with elevators that required a magnetic strip and an access code to operate and never traversed more than one level. Of ops rooms with state-of-the-art psychotronic computers and well-scrubbed, freight-sized elevators, down which came marine security teams with 'shoot to kill' instruction in the event of 'incidents' involving the psychics.

Aware of the risk she was taking, for it was lethal to be caught where one shouldn't be, she had let her mind drift into walk-in freezers, large, well-stacked dry goods storage rooms, and the large central kitchen where all their food was prepared. But below the kitchens she instinctively understood she *must not* go. Her floor and above housed mostly other benign data collectors like her, but farther below lived the Delta teams— assassins. Some were considered so dangerous they lived in self-contained units and interacted with no one but their specially trained chaperones and handlers. They were killing machines.

She had lived in that place with its blast-proof doors, on-site crematorium, and uncarpeted floors (tiles were very forgiving of 'wet work') for two years now. Her transfer there had been accomplished under cover of night from a secret military/NASA installation at Offit Air Force Base, Nebraska. It had occurred to her that she could remember almost nothing of her many years in Nebraska, other than brief flashbacks of sitting with one eye taped shut while watching a reel of film run so fast it was almost a blur; working with puzzles and pulsing lights under the supervision of men in lab coats; a single, slide-like memory of floating in a sensory deprivation tank; and a disturbing one of a 'blood trial'—earning stripes—where she was in an octagonal cage in a forest. There were spectators outside the cage and she was facing a crouched, snarling wolf. She recognized the wolf. It recognized her. She must have

34

killed it. Any attempt to remember more fetched only blinding headaches.

At fifteen, she was the youngest inhabitant of the maze. The rest she'd heard were between the ages of seventeen and thirty. She knew only a few by sight and a handful—those that had been involved in missions with her—she knew by name. Even then, no meaningful friendships had emerged from any of them. They were as aloof and disconnected toward her as she was toward them. At any rate, mingling and lingering were not encouraged. There was not even a communal dining room. All meals arrived on trolleys to their quarters, and everybody ate alone.

Dakota was pulled out of her chemical slumber by her chaperone, a tall, statuesque, mysterious woman in her mid twenties. Miss Monroe lived in, was on call 24/7 and seemed to have no discernible family or friends. She wore at all times an emergency alarm device that if activated would summon down an armed Marine killer team. In the two years that Dakota had known her she had never seen Miss Monroe smile or make eye contact with *anyone.*

Miss Monroe broke the top of a glass vial and pulled the clear liquid in it into a syringe. Her other hand reached below to pull the waistband of the girl's pajama bottoms down a few inches. With practiced efficiency she swiped a cold disinfectant swab on the girl's exposed skin and eased the needle into her flesh. The drug was a stimulant to counteract the sedative she had injected into the girl the night before. Dakota shielded her eyes with one hand and turned groggily to her side.

A few minutes after Miss Monroe left Dakota sat up and stretched. Her bedside clock said 8.10 a.m. but it could have been midnight for all she knew. In the maze day began whenever your chaperone woke you. She padded into her spotless bathroom, where she used the toilet, brushed her teeth, and showered, all under the gaze of a surveillance camera. Wrapped in a towel she stood in front of the mirror. A ghost looked back. She undid her long, golden braid, combed it and re-plaited it. Then she dressed in a pink tracksuit that had been left neatly folded on a chair for her. It had a butterfly monogram on the left breast. Next she went into the kitchenette and helped herself to a glass of orange juice.

Wandering into her living area she switched on the TV. Without it she would have been intolerably bored, but, in fact, it was not there for her entertainment. All visual media in the maze was access controlled and functioned primarily as a conditioning/reinforcing tool. Each psychic had his or her programs expressly selected for their specialty. Hers was designed to keep her mentally infantile, compliant, and locked in a fantasy world of all things extra-dimensional and other-worldly, especially alien life forms. She was never allowed any movies or programs that portrayed rebels, world affairs, or dealt with any subject matter that could cause her to think or begin to question her strange and lonely existence.

That day she had been a given a Disney animated movie, a cartoon, *The Wizard of Oz* with Judy Garland, an episode of *Star Trek,* and a specifically adapted documentary about angels. She immediately selected *The Wizard of Oz*. Like those of all trauma-trained slaves her brain stem had been scarred to develop a photographic memory, so she knew every frame of the film by heart, but for reasons incomprehensible to her she was unable to resist its lure even after hundreds of viewings.

She began to watch the movie and almost immediately her programming triggers kicked in and she lapsed into flat state—a non-thinking trance. It was only when the thick metal door opened and Miss Monroe walked in with her breakfast that she was brought around. Miss Monroe put the tray on the low table in front of Dakota and held out the morning's medication, vitamins, minerals, and the cocktail of drugs necessary to counteract the long-term liver and kidney damage caused by the strong and often lethal doses of psychoactive drugs she was forced to consume daily.

Miss Monroe left when she had downed her pills. Dakota unwrapped the plastic utensils and ate. The food was hot, very good, and highly nutritional. Afterwards, she leaned back into her armchair and was soon lost in another trigger-induced stupor.

Again, it was the arrival of Miss Monroe, this time with lunch, that roused her from her hypnotized state. There were more pills to be taken. These were metabolic buffers designed to alleviate some of the debilitating physical side effects of the drugs that would be injected into her body during her afternoon mission. Dakota finished her entire meal knowing that it would be her last for the day—after her afternoon drugs she would be unable to hold down anything solid for six to twelve hours.

When the time arrived, Miss Monroe came for her.

PROJECT ABADDON

[The demons and workers from hell have] a king over them, which is the angel of the bottomless pit, whose name in the Hebrew tongue is Abaddon.

—Revelations 9:11

They walked quickly down a long, central hallway, always silent, always deserted. It had many branch corridors that led off to more dorms, all secured with thick doors requiring magnetic strip cards and access codes to operate.

Outside one of the briefing rooms, Miss Monroe passed her into the care of another purposely expressionless man. He was 'a suit'. Suits, called so because of the way they dressed, were mission coordinators and the leaders of their respective teams. They were always male, psychic, and lived on-site. One of their specialties was to feel intrusions into their mind. They had been through a very rigorous mind control process that had left in its wake a dangerous bloodlust in them. All were hard-wired to kill on command. Each concealed a gun with a silencer on his person, and had the clearance to kill both the psychic and himself in the event that either was compromised.

As a means of bonding their relationship, Dakota's suit had given her permission to call him by his first name, Teddy. She considered it an odd privilege. Not only did he refer to her as 'the subject' when speaking with the other team members, but she had specific and rigid instructions never to look him in the eye.

Teddy smiled politely and held open the door of the briefing room. It was bare, but for a rectangular table and some chairs around it. There was a glass bowl of candy bars on the table.

They sat opposite each other. 'Take one,' Teddy invited.

'Thank you.' She put a sweet in her mouth. It was laced with memory-enhancing drugs.

Teddy opened the laptop into which he would log information throughout the session. It contained a detailed and complete profile of her as well as the list of command codes and keying gestures that would elicit different responses from her.

'How are you today?'

Her breathing had become slower and deeper, but her eyes remained open and alert. 'Fine. Thank you.'

'Good. Any questions?'

'No.'

'Shall we begin?'

'Yes.'

Teddy moved so fast he was holding open the door for her before she was out of her chair. In silence they proceeded to a nearby ops room where the actual mission would be carried out.

The ops room was built like a vault. There were computer banks to the front and rear. A back room led off from it, where two men could sit and view the proceedings. In the middle was the 'trip' seat, a reclining, padded seat that looked very much like a dentist chair, only much bigger. It faced a large screen. Dakota climbed into it. It was very snug and curved around her like a cradle. She put on the pair of headphones that lay by the side of it and leaned back. A device around the back of her neck held her rigid while the biotech activated the four metal clamps on her arms and wrists that pinned her to the machine. When Teddy had loaded the targeting coordinates into the psychotronics console, he turned toward her and applied the keying gestures and said the code words that would call forth Dakota's most powerful alter, Shekina, to come to the front of her mind and hold her body.

Shekina's arrival was heralded only by a change of expression in the girl's eyes—superior confidence and unconcealed disdain for Teddy. She despised him.

Like a robot he uttered the exact same words he had every day for the past year and a half. 'Today your instructions are to remote view this time next week on the vector coordinates you are given. Is that clear?'

'Yes.' Her job was to drag data out of her trip into the future.

With Shekina in full command, Teddy called the other team members into the room. The comm tech, an ex-computer hacker with a criminal record, tasked with monitoring her heartbeat and, whenever targets were involved, theirs too; and the biotech, who proceeded to attach the EEG headband and the heart monitor wires. Then he inserted an IV needle into the permanent internal IV catheter in her arm and started the drip. With a syringe he pushed the first dose of psychoactive drugs into the IV line.

Almost immediately her body became anesthetized and heavy, in direct contrast to her mental state, which was greatly heightened. Only her judgmental machinery remained untouched. She would break through into her mission exactly as she had been before the drugs.

In her drug-induced hypnosis, Shekina heard Teddy say, 'Abandon amazement. Pay attention. Look at everything.'

The lights went down and brainwave tones were played through her headphones. Vector coordinates appeared on the screen and she was told to focus her mind on that location.

Long.: 66°33'6, 60"S

Lat.: 99°50'24, 84"E

The image of the cabalistic tree of life was projected onto the screen and she began interfacing with the computer, putting her entire concentration on the sephirot or circle at the top of the tree until it morphed into a Tibetan mandala-like geometric shape that she had been told to think of as 'the flower with the thousand petals'. The flower began to spin, faster and faster until all the different colors raced into each other. Thousands of details per second, but her photographic memory missed nothing. She kept her eyes on the spinning object until she felt absorbed by the vortex.

By monitoring her EEG Teddy knew with near-mathematical precision when to depress the button that sent an electric shock coursing from the trip seat into her body. The shock had the effect of propelling her awareness at tremendous speed through the vortex. She heard the sound of ripping Velcro and a whoosh, and she was through the flower membrane. The transition did not feel like a mental impression to her, but an actual physical sensation. Once past the membrane she was able to go anywhere. At incredible speed she flew over land mass and sea toward her vector intention.

In seconds, she was in the freezing, bleak landscape of the South Pole. To get her bearings she let herself float for a moment in the deep blackness. The moon was very bright and there were lots of stars in the sky. She had been looking at them every day for a year and a half with no result, but that day a blinding white light, like a falling star, suddenly lit the night sky. It was traveling at fantastic speed. It was not in her sight by accident and it was intelligent. Without any fear she began chasing it. Incredibly, it appeared to slow down to let her catch up with it.

She entered the white light and found herself in a bright, white room with no walls and no visible source of light. There was a strange, low hum, like that a machine or computer might make. When she looked down she saw that the floor was littered with objects, which at first she thought were Fabergé eggs. Jeweled, intricate, complex, and incomprehensibly marvelous… Then she realized they were, in fact, alive and waiting to hatch. But they could not do so without the help of human endeavor. They needed to be 'sung' into existence. She reached down and touched one of them, and heard a whisper in her head. 'When the time comes you must give her to him.'

'Give who to him? And who is he?' she asked, but before the egg could answer, she heard the sound of men's voices shouting urgently, 'Wake her up. Quickly, or it will be too late.' Then she was violently flung out of the white room, back into her trip seat and gasping for breath.

> "Who'll dig his grave?"
> "I," said the Owl,
> "With my pick and shovel,
> I'll dig his grave."

—'Who killed Cock Robin?',
Tommy Thumb's Pretty Song Book (1744)

Teddy was looking down anxiously at her. 'What the hell happened?'

'You stopped breathing,' accused the panic-stricken bio med. He was holding a syringe of emptied adrenalin.

Her body felt leaden and her head throbbed. Shekina turned her eyes away from their enquiring faces.

'It's here,' she said.

'What's here?'

'The being you are looking for.'

'Did you make contact?'

'It knows I am looking for it, but it will not let me look at it.'

'How do you know it's not a Gray or just another alien life form?'

She closed her eyes. 'It is stronger, bigger, and far more powerful than anything I have encountered before.'

'Which star system is the entity from?'

'I don't know.'

'What happened in minute twelve? I lost you.'

'I was inside some construct it had created for me.'

'A construct?'

'A white room with eggs in it.'

'Eggs? What kind of eggs?'

'They are waiting to hatch. But the environment is not right.'

'Hatch into what?'

'I don't know.' Even a shrug was too much for her. She turned the corners of her mouth downward. 'Sorry.'

'That's it? Can you *try* to elaborate a little more?'

'It needs us. Events and things have to be put into place before the eggs can hatch.'

'What events and things?'

'I don't know.'

'Did it or the eggs communicate an intent?'

She paused. 'The eggs seemed neutral, but, like I said before, the one that is carrying the eggs is too powerful for me to even look at.'

'Quick recap: you were taken into a white room, shown some eggs, and then shut out... Nothing else?'

For the first time since she had been created, Shekina decided she did not want to comply. She would not tell him about the mysterious instruction to 'give her to him'. She did not yet understand it, but knew intuitively that its meaning would be revealed to her in time. She shook her head slowly.

The suit walked away, frowning. There was something different about her. He crossed off the idea that she might be lying. Power alters were hard-wired to tell the truth at all times. He could see from his console that the other data collectors were still remote viewing, as if nothing of import had happened. She must have picked it up briefly as it came into the Earth's atmosphere, a supernova bolt of pure energy. Obviously, they were not under attack or anything like that, but...

'Release her,' he said and the bio med quickly set

about unhooking her. When both the bio med and the comm tech had left the room, Teddy walked back to Shekina and through gesture and code brought Dakota back into dominance.

'Are you all right?'

'Yes.'

He pressed the button to summon her chaperone and Dakota lay back with her eyes closed, too weak to move. The drugs would wear off in a while, but for the moment even her head was too heavy to lift off the leather. She longed for the soft dim of her dormitory where Miss Monroe would gently put her to bed, and she could sleep undisturbed. When Miss Monroe arrived, Teddy lifted Dakota and put her into the chair that Miss Monroe had wheeled in.

The door closed quietly behind them. Teddy got in front of his computer and sent out an encrypted code.

"Who will dig his grave?"

The reply was so instantaneous that Teddy let out a low whistle.

"I," said the Owl.

For some moments Teddy's finger hovered over the send button as he reviewed the events of the last hour. Clearly much depended on the outcome of this file. Had he done anything wrong? No. Could he have done better? Not that he could see. He hit the button and leaned back into the chair. Come what may.

Schooner Klaus studied the computer transcript with meticulous care and watched the video of Dakota's session twice, pausing and rewinding many times. Finally he stopped his video player and stared at her frozen face, his eyes hard. Something was not right. He stroked the smooth stone on his ring and contemplated his next move. He must inform the network. He rifled through some papers in his safe and extracted a mobile phone. He connected it to a power source and waited for it to start up. Then he punched in a set of numbers and holding it to his ear stood looking out of the window. He counted the rings. One, two, three...

A voice gruff and thickly Semitic rasped, 'Yes.'

'The girl says *he* is here.'

There was a long pause. A German aria was playing in the background. Schooner Klaus did not recognize it. The pause stretched. Schooner Klaus imagined the fragrance of Vermont Brie and eggplant fondue, though he had no idea what Kite drank or ate or even looked like. Kite's power was real, yet he moved in the highest circles simply as a faceless, nameless, crestless codename—abode unknown.

Kite had waited for and anticipated Schooner Klaus's words for years, and now that Venus was spinning as an upside down pentagram, his lord had come. When finally he spoke, his horrible voice throbbed with urgency and excitement.

'I want to see her. Tomorrow night, in Virginia.'

'Yes, Sublime Master,' Schooner Klaus crooned obsequiously.

Poor Pearl, she had no time to play,
The merry game of childhood;
From dawn to dark she went all day,
A-wooding in the wild-wood.

—Gerald Massey,
'The Legend of Little Pearl' (1981)

Dakota fought her way out of the clinging web of synthetic sleep the next morning to find Miss Monroe standing a few feet away from her bed. Her chaperone was wearing a long evening gown and high heels. Not only was her dark hair decorated with jeweled clasps, but she was also wearing make-up. Without her deliberately imposed dowdiness she was quite the beauty. She gestured toward the low table where three glossy cardboard boxes had been set.

'They're for you. Come and open them,' she invited softly.

Dakota hesitated. Both surprises and gifts caused her intense anxiety. Invariably: the fear—someone's going to get hurt. Real bad.

'Don't worry,' Miss Monroe assured. 'They are not gifts. You cannot keep them.'

Dakota left her bed and went to lift the lids off the boxes. Inside layers of tissue was a stunning blue party dress; in another box a pair of sparkly shoes and skin-colored tights; and in the largest box a soft, deep blue, woolen coat.

'You are going to a very special ball today.'

'Like Cinderella?' Dakota's voice was barely a whisper.

'Like Cinderella,' Miss Monroe repeated. 'Call me when you're dressed and I'll help with your hair.'

Dakota finished her toilette and changed as calmly as possible. But the rustle of silk against her skin was undeniably exciting. She looked at herself in the bathroom mirror. Her eyes were sparkling. Like Cinderella.

'I'm ready, Miss Monroe,' she called.

'Very pretty,' Miss Monroe complimented from the door.

'Thank you,' Dakota said shyly. Never before had Miss Monroe offered such a personal remark.

Miss Monroe came into the small space. From her evening purse she pulled a semi-transparent, blue sash. Its ends were decorated with tassels of glass beads. She tied it around the catheter in Dakota's arm. With a comb she gathered a small section of hair from above Dakota's forehead, then expertly braided and secured it with an elastic band. From her evening purse she fetched a butterfly clip to adorn Dakota's hair.

'Miss Monroe?'

'Yes.'

'Why do I always have to have butterflies on me?'

The question was so unexpected that Miss Monroe could not prevent her unguarded eyes from rushing to meet Dakota's in the mirror. There she found not the empty, doll-like expression she had come to associate with the girl, but something so naked and defenseless she had to struggle to extricate herself from its appeal. She dropped her gaze to the girl's hair. There was a metallic buzzing somewhere inside her head. She felt the blood rushing to her face. Butterflies. They lived in her own quarters too, and on her underclothing, unseen by others but ever present… Why? She turned her face away from the girl. Upset. She was upset. Pretend; pretend the girl has not touched you. She snapped her purse shut. The sound was loud in the tiled room.

'You know, you are *never* to make eye contact with me. It is against the *rules*. Take this as your last warning. Don't do it again, or I will report you. Have I made myself clear?'

'Yes, Miss Monroe.'

'Come. If we don't leave now we will be late.'

It was night when they landed on someone's private helipad.

'Ready?' Miss Monroe shouted above the noise. She appeared very distant.

Dakota nodded.

A uniformed chauffeur drove them down a road that wound in a leisurely manner through lamp-lit woods. Their journey ended at the steps of a Gothic mansion guarded by stone gargoyles. One of the doormen showed them through a marble hallway and into a grand room with a mahogany split staircase that had once stood in a Scottish castle. A silent butler appeared to relieve them of their coats and lead them into a massive ballroom full of music and elegantly dressed people. Dakota gazed at the glittering chandeliers in amazement.

'Champagne, ladies?' offered a silky voice behind them.

Thorns will overrun her citadels, nettles and brambles her strongholds. She will become a haunt for jackals, a home for owls.

—Isaiah 34:13

Dakota smelled him before she saw him—lavender. A child sang a rhyme in her head.

> Lavender's blue, diddle, diddle,
> Lavender's green;
> When I am king, diddle, diddle,
> You shall be queen.

Hooked in the mouth she turned toward the scent. A bald stranger was standing a foot away. He smiled suddenly, an indescribably wonderful smile—it lit up his entire face—and Dakota experienced such an incredible rush of fear and hatred for him that every cell in her body screamed, 'RUN'. But the lavender had had the same effect on her that the roar of a tiger has on a man—the sound reverberates in his chest and paralyzes him. Dakota stood frozen.

'Schooner Klaus,' he said, extending a hand toward her. With his other hand he made a quick gesture, thumb, middle finger and pinkie touching lightly and the other two fingers extended—the horned hand—a hypnotic induction symbol for slaves. Instantly, Dakota's mind dissociated. Her moment of utter terror and loathing became an insignificant incident, a distant memory. Willingly, she put her hand into the one he proffered. His clasp was cool, very brief, and somehow familiar, even though she was certain she had never met him before.

'Hello, Dr. Klaus,' Miss Monroe said.

Dakota looked at Miss Monroe. She was a transformed woman, gazing adoringly up at the stranger. A waiter appeared with a tray. It held a single glass. Completely ignoring Miss Monroe, Schooner Klaus took the glass by its tall stem and put it into Dakota's unresisting hand.

'Our host told me,' he said, 'your name, but he didn't tell me what a pretty butterfly you are.' He smiled again.

Dakota looked blankly at the quickly rising bubbles. 'I don't know who our host is.'

'Come, I'll take you to him,' he offered, and led her away from Miss Monroe.

They went through the crowd and down a short, carpeted passageway. It ended in front of a set of tall double doors. He opened them, and she stood at the threshold of a cavernous, dimly lit study, decorated sumptuously in green and gold. The floor was highly polished, antique dark wood and the air smelled of cigars, leather, and burning wood. There was no host to be seen. Schooner Klaus motioned for her to enter. She stepped into the room. Behind her the heavy doors closed and the sounds of the party died. Schooner Klaus gestured toward a large, green leather chair. He himself moved away from it and leaned against a nearby desk. He sipped his drink and surveyed her over the rim of his glass.

'Do you know that the name Dakota, in occult

Kabala, carries *significance?*

The green leather was cold against her skin. She shook her head.

'It's an uncanny system where each alphabet has been assigned a numerical value, and when the alphabets in a word are added up they act as a method of divination. Your name, for example, suggests a fate rich with certain demonic qualities or the raising or creating of something, or my favorite, a door…' He trailed off.

Demonic qualities? Door? To where? Shhh… Remain uncurious. Only troublemakers ask questions. She was silent and so was he, but he was watching her carefully. The fire crackled. The champagne glass was cold in her hand.

'Does the name Shekina have a meaning?' she asked suddenly.

But for a slight narrowing of his eyes, Schooner Klaus did not show how deeply shaken he was by her question. 'Shekina?' he repeated softly. 'Why do you ask?'

'In my dreams a woman comes to tell me I must find Shekina. Twice now she has come.'

'A woman? What does she look like, this *woman?*'

'She is brown-skinned and has long, black hair that she coils at the nape of her neck.'

Schooner Klaus stared at the girl. This was utterly without precedent. The breaking of amnesic barriers and the leaking of alters into the consciousness of the dominant personality never manifested until the age of thirty or thereabouts, when most mind-controlled slaves were 'disposed of'. She was only fifteen. He wondered if it was because she had gone through the process too late. Historically, the key of David had to be given to slaves between the ages of two and four, and the mind shattered and rebuilt before the age of seven.

Whatever the reason, it was a terrible prospect. No time could be allocated for reprogramming her while they stood at the cusp of something the world had never seen before. The prospect that she could gain access to her own powers and become dangerous to an unpredictable degree loomed before him. He could only hope that it would happen at the end of her usefulness. When disposing of her would be of no consequence.

'How interesting. Shekina is the name given to the soul of the Ark of the Covenant. Ancient accounts describe her as glowing energy that confers illumination to the prepared initiates, but who can also bring destruction and waste to hundreds of opponents in one single act of concentrated violence.' He smiled pleasantly.

No help there, but something familiar about that smile. 'Have we met before?'

His expression did not change. 'No,' he said, and brought the lip of his glass to his mouth.

He was lying, but only troublemakers pursue that which is hiding. No curiosity, no pain. She turned her eyes away from him. Her gaze latched upon a painting. A fluorescent green, inverted pentagram painted onto a matt, black background. The five-pointed star was missing an arm, but it radiated a presence, a violence, that was palpable.

'Do you like it?'

'No.' She had seen such a symbol before. Somewhere. Where? She tried to remember and felt a headache coming on. She stopped trying to recall the memory.

'That's an inverted pentagram. Some call it the mark of the beast; a symbol that demons cannot resist. When they see it they must congregate around it.' Schooner Klaus's voice was melodious, persuasive; inviting her to see beauty where she had found none. 'They know the space inside is the void, a pit where they will be fêted and enticed to contract by those in the know. Blood sacrifices in exchange for a sorcerer's bidding. You make deals with them. A goat, a child, a million soldiers wearing an agreed-upon symbol.'

She stood and walked toward it. Up close, it was hideous. 'Why is one of its arms broken?'

'It was deliberately left that way. It represents a pact not yet fulfilled, a job unfinished. They have already had their blood... Does it frighten you, Dakota?'

'No.'

'Good. I like courageous little girls. Come over here,' he called. Placing his glass down he walked toward a nest of low couches facing the stone fireplace.

Obediently, she turned and followed him. He went around a low table, and, putting it between them, stopped and smiled. She could see their reflections in the large, ornate mirror hanging over the fireplace. She seemed very small and pale. And the thought: I shouldn't be here.

'Drink,' he ordered.

The bubbles hit the back of her throat and made her catch her breath. She did not care for the taste either, but she drained it to its last drop. He took the empty glass from her slack hand and set it on the low table.

'Sit.'

The Seconal in her drink worked very fast. She sank back into the sofa behind her, her head dropping slowly onto her shoulder. The tips of her hair touched her knees and shone golden in the firelight. Her eyelids fluttered. The last thing she heard was the sound of the glass beads at the end of the blue tassels crunching underneath Schooner Klaus's shoes. He had come around to stand over her.

He sat on the low table in front of her slumped figure and, reaching forward, touched her behind both ears. 'I call awake Timu, who is unaffected by Seconal. Bring to the forefront Shekina. Shekina, I command you to take the body now.'

The girl's eyes opened. Bright and alert. 'Hello, Commandant,' she greeted quietly.

'Hello, Shekina.'

> "Who Killed Cock Robin?"
> "I," said the Sparrow,
> "With my bow and arrow,
> I killed Cock Robin."

—'Who killed Cock Robin?',
Tommy Thumb's Pretty Song Book (1744)

'There are hidden eyes watching us, Commandant,' she warned.

'Don't concern yourself. It's only Kite, Rook and Fish.'

She looked into his cruel face. A voice in her head said, beware nursery rhymes—they aren't what they seem.

'You bury things. Are you Owl, Commandant?'

One corner of Schooner Klaus's mouth lifted in admiration. He had taught her well.

'If I have been brought into a room with Owl, Kite, Rook, and Fish, who am I?'

His lips twisted. 'Don't disappoint me now. There is only ever one role for you.'

'Sparrow?'

'But of course.'

'And Cock Robin, who is he?'

'It does not matter who or what Cock Robin is. What matters is that you will come face to face with him. He could be a life form so terrifying and malevolent that even the sight of him will kill or drive insane ordinary human beings. However, your exhaustive training has seen to it that even in a situation of direct conflict you will display nothing but valor in the performance of your job. Can I count on you?'

'Always.'

'Good. Now, about the being from your data collection trip yesterday. If, as you inferred, it needs humans to do something for it, then it must require contact with one.'

'It does.'

'So why not you?'

'Incompatible vibrational frequency.'

'Are you not able to change your frequency?'

'No.'

'Why not?'

'The frequency bridge to him is a purified heart.'

'A pure heart?' He frowned. 'Are you sure?'

'Absolutely. The human, whoever he or she is, must possess a very high vibration. Like a monk, a priest, or a holy man. Perhaps even a nun.'

'Understood. When the being gets in contact with that someone, will you be able to identify that person?'

'No.'

'Why not?'

'I can only remote view those that are of similar or lower responsibility than me. Unless he or she gives me permission I cannot go there or I will self-destruct.'

Schooner Klaus thought for a moment. 'Will you be able to contact someone connected to this person, if he or she is of a lower vibration?'

'If significantly lower, yes.'

Schooner Klaus smiled. 'Good. Then, that is exactly what you will do. You will find the bad apple. Tomorrow you will begin to look for this worm-infested fruit and you will not stop until you find him or her. Is that understood?'

'Yes, Commandant.'

'Anything else you want to tell me?'

She shook her head.

'Can you tell what I am thinking, Shekina?'

She stared into the orbs of gray—they were like wet glass, so easy to slip on—and saw a brick wall as long as it was high. Immediately, as she had been hypnotically instructed to do, she gave up and turned her back on the wall. 'No.'

'Good,' he said, and yet he regarded her critically. She had been programmed to be too morally and socially superior. The project needed a different approach, a softer alter. 'When you do find the holy person, I don't want you to interact with that person. I want you to slip away and let Winter take the body. Winter, and Winter alone, must deal with that person. Are your instructions clear?'

'Yes.'

'You understand, of course, that Dakota must be protected from all this. She is weak and not as clever as you. It would only upset and confuse her. You know how much she has already suffered. No need for more.'

Shekina nodded in agreement.

'Good, now go back into the mind,' he said, and made the keying gesture to send her away. He let a moment pass, and then he touched the girl in the hollow of her throat. 'I call Winter to come to the front.'

The first thing Winter did was cross her legs and fluff her hair, her movements those of a woman supremely conscious of her sexuality. Smoothly, as if she had done so hundreds of times, she reached forward and lightly rested her hand on Schooner Klaus's knee.

Ignoring the small white hand on his person, Schooner Klaus looked at her sternly. 'Listen carefully to your instructions.'

Winter took her hand away from his knee and put it primly in her lap.

'When Shekina instructs you to hold the body your job is to make the man or the woman you find before you fall deeply and hopelessly in love with you. Be outwardly shy and innocent, but do whatever is necessary to achieve your objective. If you fail all the sand will fall into the bottom bulb of the hourglass and you know what that means. The end of Dakota. And when it is the end for Dakota it is the end for *all* of you. Do you understand what is expected of you?' he asked sternly.

'Yes, Daddy.'

'Remember also that your contribution is a matter of national security not just for any one country, but for the survival of the entire human race. Your role is a holy mission, a crusade of utmost importance. Are you ready to give up everything, even your life, in the performance of this duty?'

'You know I'd do anything for you, Daddy.'

'Good girl. When I pull your strings, you will speak my words. There is no room for error.' He stroked her forehead gently. 'Now go back into the mind.'

Next Schooner Klaus used his finger to write on the forehead of the sleeping girl, a code—so secret it used the Enochian alphabet.

'Key, come forth,' he invited softly.

Key came. Her eyes were a void, for she was not human. Key was a stage three reporting alter, created through such terrible torture that she had left the body to hover over it like a mist. Totally invisible to all the other alters, she played a very important role. She was the watcher of the entire system. There was nothing that she did not know. Created to have excellent rapid recall, she alone knew every alter and kept a record of everything that had happened to Dakota's body. In the unlikely event that Key was compromised there were six back-up alters who could be accessed by more secret codes known only to Schooner Klaus.

The procedure was very strict. 'Hello,' said Key, and waited for the standard response format, which was 'Hello, Princess'. If ever that did not come, she would instantly disappear.

'Hello, Princess,' said Schooner Klaus. 'Who is the brown-skinned woman from Dakota's dreams?'

'She comes when Dakota is asleep so I am unable to monitor.'

'You are certain she is not a previously unknown alter Dakota might have created while in the sensory deprivation tank?'

'No such alter exists.'

'Thank you for your help. Return the body to Dakota now.'

Schooner Klaus took a syringe from his pocket and placed it on the low table. Then he took a few steps toward the one-way mirror over the fireplace, bowed deferentially, and left the room. Outside the door Miss Monroe was waiting.

'Her medication is on the table. Take her back as soon as she wakes up,' he said. Always, his voice reminded Miss Monroe of ink being poured into a glass tank, of elegant swirls and coils. 'Goodnight, Dr. Klaus.'

He looked at her strangely. Something about the way

she had bade him goodnight. A lost memory broke free: his mother bending down to kiss him, her mouth soft on his cheek. 'Goodnight, beautiful Klaus,' she whispers.

He had been so small. So innocent.

Schooner Klaus turned resolutely away from the memory and made his way toward the other end of the mansion where a masked ball was in progress. Here, all depravity and excess were not only encouraged, but celebrated. He would drink a cup of blood and temporarily forget about the dangerous brown-skinned woman until dawn.

The Brown-Skinned Woman
London, England

Bumi awakened on her sofa bed, distressed, having dreamed of her dead father. He had been sitting on the steps of her childhood home in Calcutta, looking unwell and unhappy, but no one else other than her had appeared to be able to see him. He had vanished when she had tried to hug him.

It was still dark outside, but she could see by the blue light that came from under the door of the boy's room. Hooking her feet into her bedroom slippers she moved soundlessly to her cramped bathroom. There she switched on the little electric blow heater, and while the room warmed up, stood looking at herself in the mirror above the sink. Two years shy of forty, and already abandoned and alone.

Once, many years ago, at a banquet held in the manor where she had worked, an English lord had lifted his wine glass to her in an ironic salute. An offer of sorts, but certainly not, 'Correspond in secret. I am in love.' Immediately she had averted her eyes to the wallpaper, a Liberty pattern with peacocks, peonies, and pheasants. Better to be a wild bird in the falcon's beak than to leave the servants' quarters through that small, unadorned door of shame. As she cleared away his dinner plate, her gaze had been pulled to his fat, be-ringed fingers, drumming on the pristine linen.

She had understood that haughty gesture too.

She had been born in India, after her mother had decided that six children were enough and vowed that she would not lie with her beekeeper husband again, unless one of the wild monkeys that roamed the outskirts of their village entered their house through the front door. Two days later a bold monkey did just that. Three generations of her husband's family had lived in that house and never witnessed such a thing. The baby's arrival became an eagerly awaited, celebrated event, a miraculous gift from the monkey god, Hanuman.

She was named Bumi Devi, Goddess of the Earth. Her childhood had been a life cherished and untroubled by cares; running as wild as the monkeys, refusing to eat unless hand-fed, and sleeping with the safety of her parents' bodies on either side of her. Then one day, when she was ten, she had looked out of a window, and seen the telegraph lines outside her home closely packed with still, silent crows. And every one of them was turned in her direction. Frightened, she had rushed her mother to the sinister sight, but by then they were all gone.

'An ill omen,' her grandfather had muttered, scratching his withered leg, but who could have imagined that the birds had come to call her beloved father to the next world. That Wednesday he had dropped to the floor with a heart attack.

She would never forget that day when the neighbours came to break her mother's glass bangles. The symbolism behind the wonton destruction was clear. Not even the temptation of adornment should a widow be allowed. At the funeral her mother wailed, 'Take me too, take me too.' And Bumi had put her lips on her father's cold, stiff cheek for the last time.

Her brothers took over the hives, but unsuccessfully. They had never learnt to brush the bees aside with their bare hands. Life became hard. One by one her brothers married and brought their wives to live in the small house. Her mother and her took to sleeping on a mat spread on the porch.

Bumi was twelve when her third brother returned from Bombay with his new bride, Renuka. Renuka spoke English. She had learned it while working as a servant at the great house of a Memsahib. The first words Bumi learned from her were: 'It's too bloody hot in this bloody country.'

Then at seventeen a marriage broker had come a-calling. A London based accountant desired an odd thing—an 'unmodernized' bride who spoke some English. She fit the bill. A week after the wedding they had traveled to England. The black cab had stopped outside a two-story, semi-detached house converted into two one-bedroom flats. He had put his key into the door and gone ahead of her, up a creaking wooden staircase to his rented abode. He had crossed the threadbare carpet, thrown open a couple of windows to let the musty odor out, turned to her and made a surprisingly prescient prediction. 'From this day on, this will be your palace.'

When he went to work she cooked and cleaned, and afterwards, walked up and down Hounslow's high street until it began to shut down. His footsteps would sound on the wooden staircase about eight. He would immediately put his briefcase away, divest himself of his office clothes and present himself at their dinner table. Often they ate in silence, neither having anything to say to the other. She knew she was not in love, but she was not unhappy either. As soon as the Home Office returned her passport stamped with a two-year working visa, the Earth Goddess had found herself a job as an office cleaner.

One day she had come home from work and found him gone from their tiny flat. There had been no note. Just a missing suitcase, a bare space where his clothes had been, and toiletries gone from the bathroom cabinet. But there had been no argument, nothing in his manner to suggest that he was in any way dissatisfied, she had reflected, bewildered. Again and again she had thought of that dawn before she had left for work; of how he had lifted one end of the duvet, called her back into their warm bed, and had his way with her.

For many months she had gone about in an uncomprehending daze, too ashamed to even tell her mother. She would open the front door and head straight for the bedroom with the hope that he would be there. His return as mysterious as his departure.

To pay the bills she had worked two, sometimes three jobs. Then, through ignorance, but no real fault of her own, she had become an illegal immigrant. Her temporary visa had run out. Fortunately, by then she had already secured permanent employment in the kitchens of Lord Carrington's manor. A year and a half later, when the housekeeper of his London flat left, she had been promoted to the post.

That was when she had got the boy.

The boy. She would never forget the sweet day. When she had given in to a whimsical desire on her way home from work and followed a rainbow. Well, it had led to a dead-end full of overstuffed black rubbish bags, but turning away, she had thought she'd heard a cry. Later she would come to realize that it could only have been her imagination. She had moved toward the sound.

Amongst bin bags of restaurant waste she had found a black baby sleeping inside a transparent plastic covering. She had glanced around apprehensively. Her illegal status had made her wary of any situation that involved the authorities.

Not a soul in sight.

She had squatted next to the baby. Pinned to its clothes had been a hastily handwritten note, the ink smudged, the letters large and ill formed.

> My name is Black Jack.
> Please help me.

Strange—a black boy called Black Jack. He was so incredibly still; she had feared he was dead. But he had opened his eyes suddenly and stared steadily at her through the plastic. Never in her life had she seen eyes such as his. Tilted upwards like a cat's, they were enormous with irises that glinted the way water inside very deep wells does. Looking into them she felt the same mysterious sensation she had once experienced gazing up into the night sky. A nameless, timeless, never-ending connection.

She had put her hand beneath the plastic and touched his hair. 'Oh!' She had expected it to be wiry. It was soft as a cloud. Her hand had wandered to his face. Poor mite was cold. On his chest she had found a small silver cross. A little Christian. When her index finger had skimmed across his palm, he had curled his tiny fingers around it so fiercely that her heart lurched. How could anyone abandon so beautiful a thing?

It had begun to drizzle and drops of rain fell noisily on the plastic sheet, the sound breaking the magic. A stray thought. What if his real mother changed her mind and came back for him? Hiding him in her clothes she had hurried away, to sit at the back of the bus, a thief. Heart racing, she had stared unseeingly out of the window and decided the story most likely to be believed for her sudden possession of a black baby.

As it turned out it was a problem she had never had to address.

Even warmed and fed, he had neither made a sound nor moved a limb of his own accord. How could it be? She had heard his cry and felt his tenacious grip. But those feats were gone, left amongst the rubbish and her imagination. Poor sod had been unable to laugh or cry, or even stretch his mouth into a smile. It had taken him a whole painful hour to drink half a bottle of milk.

Since medical assistance would have exposed her crime, she had detailed the symptoms that afflicted her boy to Lord Carrington and begged him to find the cure for the strange disease. His probing had led him to believe that it was probably a rare and incurable neurological disorder called locked-in syndrome. 'He will never walk, talk, play, go to school or have friends. I'm afraid to say he probably won't have a long life either,' he had warned gravely from the depths of his great armchair. But the rainbow, she was convinced, had led her to the boy for a purpose. She would be his savior. Somehow she would sort it out.

When even the paltry capability of sucking at a teat had frozen she had learned to feed him with soft tubes inserted down his throat. In a year the ability to blink or close his eyes, even when sleeping, had been lost. Food had gone in, waste had come out—but for his eyes that followed her around the room with huge curiosity, he was a living statue.

Instead of buying a cot, which might have alerted her curtain-twitching neighbors, she had ordered a sofa bed for herself and moved the boy into her bedroom. She had always worked long hours, but that hadn't mattered since he had needed nothing more than the television, left on one of the children's channels. To feed him she had hired a woman to come in six days a week, at first three times a day, eventually whittling down to just once. Heather was chronically sullen, but, being a benefit cheat herself, could be trusted not to inform on Bumi. She had no love for the boy, but the weekly cash was a lot to her, and she had turned out to be a constant in their lives. The years had passed. The boy had turned six, then ten, and twelve, and yesterday fourteen.

All the birds of the air fell a-sighing and
a-sobbing,
When they heard the bell toll for poor
Cock Robin.

—'Who killed Cock Robin?',
Tommy Thumb's Pretty Song Book (1744)

Bumi knocked softly on Black's door before turning the handle and going in. Black lay propped up on three pillows, his eyes turned toward her. He could say many things with those eyes of his. Yes, no, joy, sadness, interest, surprise, pleasure... That moment, he was smiling broadly at her. She approached his bed.

She used to mind him not being able to speak, but her experiences with the world had taught her that speaking was, in fact, the art of concealing one's real thoughts. The boy had never lied to her. Still, she was sometimes certain he spoke to her telepathically. Small things. Like, Hello. I love you, Mother. I'm cold, or I like this story you are reading to me.

She bent forward and kissed his cheek. The whiff of apple puree. Her hands—they were ugly, the knuckles grown large and shiny with hard work—stroked the cornrows on his head. They ended in colorful beads at his shoulders—her handiwork. Many years ago she had taken the Tube to a hairdresser in Brixton to learn how to braid his hair, so different from her own.

On the TV screen Richard Attenborough was explaining the evening habits of sea lions. Once when he was eight she had come home to find the TV on the National Geographic channel. Assuming it had been a technical glitch she had put it back on Disney, but the next day she had found it back on the Discovery channel. Her astonished eyes found his and found them a-sparkle with excitement. By will alone he had changed the channel setting. Enthusiastically, she had looked forward to other feats of mind manipulation, but many months later she had had to accept that that was the extent of his capability.

'How are you this morning, my love?' she greeted cheerfully. The large catlike eyes fixed on her, unblinking, intense, sad. In the silence inside her head she listened intently for a reply, but nothing. He had stopped responding to her for some time now. She understood: he was dying.

He had been dying since the day she had found him, but now she felt him hurrying away faster. Already he was hardly more than a twig in autumn. The thought of life without him filled her with such horror that even the sight of a single crow while going about her day caused her sleepless nights and nightmares for weeks afterwards. Her fingers caressed his arm. Stiff as a bone, crooked at the elbow, and curled inward at the wrist. Some drool ran down the side of his face. She dabbed at it with a face towel and smiled gently. 'I dreamed of your grandfather last night. He was sitting on the steps of our old home in Calcutta, looking well and happy…'

With great devotion, as if she was performing a sacred ritual, she began the twice-daily, hour-long process of carefully contorting and manipulating his dead limbs one by one out of his clothes, meticulously cleaning every inch of him, swaddling his bottom and redressing him. It was a source of great pride to her that so many years bedridden had not left him with a single bedsore. As she administered to him, she recounted all that had happened to her the day before, the people she had met, the things they had said, the gossip she had found inside the glossy magazines on Lady Carrington's coffee table, and what she had witnessed in the streets from the bus on the way home. And all the while those beautiful, cat eyes never left her face.

After removing the feeding tubes, she positioned his wobbly head on a thrice-folded towel at an angle to allow the collecting saliva to flow out on the towel and not his clothes. Then she lavished his face with butterfly kisses and bade him goodbye.

The air outside smelled of winter.

Bumi shut the door behind her and walked down the street, unaware she was watched by the man living in one of the rooms across the road.

When she passed out of his range he moved away from the net curtains and put his binoculars away. He rubbed his unshaven face thoughtfully. His relentless obsession had begun late one night when he had spied her leaving her bathroom without even a hastily tied towel. Casual enquiries down the shops and from his landlady had brought the information that she was husbandless and lived alone. True, he had never seen anyone else come out of her door, but he was not convinced that she actually did. For one thing he saw the blue light of the TV every day while she was out.

He had twenty minutes before he had to leave for work. He lay on his filthy bed, unzipped his jeans, and closed his eyes. First he savored that towelless body in all its glory. Then he saw himself erect and huge looming over her, grabbing her by the hips, throwing her on the bed, and doing to her what he had seen done to the shameless sluts on those special Internet sites he frequented. If she screamed he would gag her; if she resisted he would tie her. He was merciless with her. The bestial urge to have her even when he was limp and finished was so strong that he knew he must engineer a way to realize his needs very soon. Or it would eat him from the inside like a colony of white ants inside a dead wood.

Houston, this is *Discovery*. We still have the alien spacecraft under observation.

——Recording from the space shuttle *Discovery*

Until they were irrevocably lost to him, Black followed his mother's footsteps in the street below. Though he had never actually felt her hands on his numb skin or the kisses she rained on his face and hands, for the next ten hours he would desperately miss her presence. She was his whole world. Every day, he waited for the twilight hours when she would rise, and listened to the muted sounds of her movements around the small flat, until she appeared at his door beaming with goodness. Of late, though, he noticed her smile had become worn and forced, and that she herself appeared encased in a cocoon of barely suppressed dread. It saddened him greatly, but there was nothing he could do.

He was dying and she knew it.

Since he never slept while she was in the flat, he let his eyes blur on the ceiling, and with his eyes wide open he slipped off into sleep. The sound of a key in the street door awakened him. Feeding time, Black. Heather's heavy tread came up the stairs and headed toward the kitchen. She arrived at his side without any eye contact. He recognized the scent on her breath. Once his mother had put one, just one, fizzy drop on his tongue, and said, 'Coca-Cola, but it's bad for you.'

For the next twenty minutes Heather's corpulent face hovered over him, silent, efficient, and detached. She left the flat without having spoken a word, her thick shoes clunking dully down the stairs. The click of the street door closing behind her was a good sound. The carefree laughter of small children passing by floated up. A woman scolded. Their sounds faded away. He looked at the clock on the wall. It was 12.30 p.m.

He watched a documentary, but it was a repeat, and it didn't hold his interest. Visions of death, his own, kept intruding upon his concentration. His mother had taught him that humans reincarnated incessantly, but he had learned from watching the telly that other religions believed differently. He hoped she was right, for he longed for the chance to be returned as a normal human being.

The news came on. Automatically he transferred his focus to it. He had an insatiable curiosity about the world outside his room. Often, he watched the broadcasts put out by all the different channels—BBC, ITV, Channel 4, CNN, Aljazeera, Fox, MSNB, and sometimes even the foreign language channels that he could not understand. After the news he flipped through the channels without finding anything worth watching. The occupants of the tree outside his window, a pair of courting pigeons, were returning. He moved his attention to them. He loved watching them.

He was wondering if he would still be around in spring when their nest was once again filled with noisy chicks, when he experienced a strong fluttering inside his chest. It was something he had never registered in his paralyzed body before and it shocked and frightened him. Was this Death come to snatch him away? His eyes darted to the clock—at least three hours before his mother's return. He told himself that he was not afraid of dying or what lay beyond, but he must see her one last time. Innocently, he decided to wait for her return before he died. The panic ebbed away and after a while he realized he was not dying, at least, not just yet.

A cookery show came on. Food intrigued him. He watched the presenter bite into a peppermint profiterole, roll her eyes dramatically, and expel a long 'mmmmmm'. When she could bring herself to speak, she described the experience enthusiastically: delightfully refreshing, elegant, light... In his dreams he was often sitting up and eating, all manner of things—cakes, spaghetti, sandwiches, pizzas, fruit—but he always awakened no wiser about their taste or the sensations of eating. He didn't know the difference between juicy and chewy.

The winter night descended leaving the room illuminated only by the flickering blue light of the TV. Black eyed the clock: 3.29 p.m. A strange stillness hung in the air, but he was overcome with a sensation of disquiet. He wished again for his mother's return with the evening paper, for normality. An instinct warned him. Ever since the fluttering. Something was not right.

And he was right.

The TV flickered suddenly and became a silent, blue screen. A deadly quiet filled the room. He listened intently and heard only the blood drumming in his ears—where were the outside sounds? Fearfully his eyes skirted around the room. Inside his head a vibrant, beautiful voice said in perfect English, 'Don't be afraid. Friend.' Then the clear deduction: *It cares about me...*

He stared in disbelief as dry, black rain poured from the ceiling, and flashing, swirling vortexes and white orbs appeared in it. Within that whirlpool of pulsating energy a being began to materialize. At first he was only a transparent, shimmering wave of green, undulating like an interrupted two-dimensional broadcast on TV, but he very quickly gained density until it was no longer possible to see through him.

When he was completely solid the rain and the swirling stopped. A glowing, pale green, humanoid boy stood in his room. Black gazed at him in stunned wonder. His mother was shorter than Heather, and the being was shorter than his mother. Hard to tell, but perhaps the entity was his height. He had a large forehead, no eyebrows, enormous eyes (at least three times the size of a normal human being's), high cheekbones, a delicate nose, and a pointed chin. His neck was long and graceful and his straight, shoulder-length hair was the same color as his skin. He was dressed in a long, emerald green robe that was belted at the waist and smoldered like live embers. The edges were trimmed with some strange material that flowed and lapped around him like water.

But the most spectacular thing about him was his skin. It looked like polished jade or some similar stone, but not only did it glow with a peculiar luminosity, it also reflected its surroundings. Extraordinary thing in itself, but made stupendous by the never-ending, fantastically complex and colorful fractals that appeared and disappeared on the surface of his skin. The self-repeating forms appeared to Black's entranced eyes, marine-like—indescribably beautiful, jeweled seahorses. But on deeper reflection he had the impression of dancing dragons.

Impossible to see his feet, but his hands were shaped exactly like that of a human being, perhaps more slender. He secreted a scent that Black could not identify, but found pleasant nonetheless. In his head, Black heard again the bright voice reiterate, 'Friend.'

The reassurance was unnecessary. The boy being emanated such nobility, kindness, purity, compassion, and warmth that Black felt no fear. His presence was all around the room, uplifting. In fact, compared to the shining perfection and radiance of his visitor, Black felt himself to be no more than a shadow. He seemed more real than everything else in the room.

He came forward, the watery edge of his robe silent on the floor. When he was but a foot away he raised his left hand, probably some form of greeting, but in the reflective surfaces of his arm, Black saw, for the first time, his own reflection.

Why, Black! You're black.

He had *never* imagined—but his mother was Indian, who… Must not then be his mother. That horrible moment also brought understanding of why she had never once thought to bring a mirror to him. Pitiful. Twisted skeletal limbs protruded uselessly out of his blue Thomas the Tank Engine pajama sleeves. That large head that could not be set straight, and the horrendously drooling, half-open mouth...

'Hello, Black,' he heard in his head.

His baffled eyes drifted upwards. The being's irises, a deep green, were not round, but bled out into the whites of his eyes, which were not really white but a much paler shade of green. Caught in the being's gaze Black understood that he was safe, but utterly naked. That the being had total access to all his memories: everything he had seen, heard, experienced, felt, and every thought he had ever entertained even if it was only for a few seconds. There was nothing that the being did not know about him.

A thought formed in Black's head. He's not blue so he can't be Lord Krishna. Could he be one of the forever youthful 'boy gods' his mother spoke about?

The marvelous creature laughed, the dancing fractals in his beautiful face glowing brighter. 'I'm not a god! I was created as you were.'

Black formulated the question. Who are you?

'I'm a hyper-dimensional being. Your scientists might categorize me as a virtual visitor from the zero sum point, or what they assume to be the vacuum of the universe.'

An alien who speaks English.

'In the strictest sense I am not an alien. An alien is a stranger or foreigner from one's own dimension. I am not of your realm. I can only hold my physical embodiment for short periods in your world. And to be perfectly honest the only English words I know are the ones I found in your mind.'

What's your name?

'There is no word that adequately translates my name into English. The language of hyperspace is nonverbal. It is made of tone, archetype, and color. Even if I put it into your mind, it would sound garbled to your ears, and you would not be able to replicate it. It might be more fun if you simply found a name for me.'

For some seconds Black could only look at the being with what he now knew was a dull, open-mouthed stare. Then a truly lame idea—Green. He was instantly embarrassed, but all the fractals in the being lit up more brightly than when he had laughed.

'Green and Black?' he exclaimed. 'I like that. It's fitting… For now, anyway.'

Black felt a surge of pride and joy that the beautiful being liked his choice. What are you doing here, Green?

'The alarm bells are ringing for mankind. Not from now, but from far in your future. I am on assignment to find the purest human on Earth, and should he agree to serve humanity by facing a great challenge, it is my duty to help him learn big things and hand him the sword he will require in his confrontation with the dark hierarchy that threatens the future of mankind.'

Instantly, Black felt sadder than he had ever been in his short life. You've made a mistake. I'm not the one.

Green shook his head, smiling gently. 'Only the catalyst, and only during the year of the dragon in the rain, can attain the morphic field pure enough to enable me to step down into this reality. And only that soul will be able to perceive me. If you can see and hear me then you are the one.'

But I'm totally paralyzed.

'The body is a tool with which to experience a realm and express oneself in it. What if I told you that you are the product of a meticulous design? That your entire life has been a hidden initiation grooming you for this very moment. Do you think it is by accident that you have never met the real god of this dimension?'

Who's that?

'The god of money. While you cried that you had not been invited to sup at the banquet of the damned, your solitary existence earned you the distinction of never having harmed a living thing by thought, word, or deed. Likewise the world has not been able to sully you with its baser instincts and preoccupations. Without your useless body you would not be the holder of the purest, highest vibration of your kind.'

Black wondered if he should let Green know that he was dying.

Green smiled. 'That won't be necessary; all humans are in the process of dying. You must believe me when I say you are most suitable for the job at hand.'

I still don't understand what I can possibly do in my condition.

'Something very important, but a task that ultimately requires great sacrifice and loss.'

But I have nothing to lose.

'You have more to lose that you can imagine now.'

What do I have to lose?

'Impossible to speculate. There are unpredictable functions to the information fractals. The future and even the past are fluid and mutable.'

What happens if I fail?

'Then it will not be the first time. Every human attempt to improve this world has failed and served only to make the evil ones stronger, giving them more reasons to crush and oppress mankind. You will have to be very pure and very strong in the face of the ultimate evil.' He smiled suddenly. 'However, the chances you will succeed are very favorable indeed.'

What happens if I refuse?

'I leave and you carry on as before.'

Black didn't have to think. His entire life had been spent in joyless isolation. There was nothing he wanted less than to be left to carry on as before. Yes. I will help.

'In the next few days you will learn many important things. Some of them will cause you great grief if you do not keep foremost in your mind the most important knowledge of all—that physical incarnation is only the chrysalis in which one may transform. Will you do that?'

I will.

'Be ready for a most extraordinary adventure.'

An adventure? Black looked at the incandescent entity standing over him, at the mathematical formulas that repossessed themselves deep within his being and appeared as constantly moving, never-ending geometric patterns on his splendid skin, and experienced his first burst of unfretted excitement. It was a great feeling.

'Much more to say, but time to go. Same time tomorrow, Black,' Green said, and turned into something similar to a heat distortion in the desert, one that disappeared the moment his mother turned the door handle. He had not heard her key in the downstairs door or her tread on the stairs.

'What is it, my son?' she cried fearfully from the doorway. Her son's large catlike eyes were shining in a way she had never seen before.

> Not knowing a thing could not be done,
> they went ahead and did it.
>
> —Karate DoJo

Black watched the next day drag with agonizing slowness on his clock face: 2 p.m. Where are you, Green? At exactly 3.29 the dry rain came and Green's luminous figure appeared inside it. He stepped up to the bed, held out his long, narrow arm with its ever flowering geometric fractals, and said, 'Take my hand.'

I can't. I told you, I haven't any control over my limbs.

'And I told you, you are not your body. Now come out of that body,' he ordered firmly.

Thinking about it afterwards, Black could never quite make out how he did, but without any warning, just as if uncorked from a champagne bottle, he slipped out of the relentlessly oppressive weight of his body. Oh, but the sensation! The lightness. The freedom. The sheer delight of it. In disbelief he looked down at the twisted body lying so still in the bed, the eyes frozen open. He could have been dead. Only he wasn't. So what was he now? He looked down upon his new self. Barefoot and dressed in the same childish Pooh Bear pajamas, everything intact. He moved a finger. It moved!

He was so exhilarated by what was happening to him that it was some seconds before he realized that he was moving away from his inert body at considerable speed and would soon hit the ceiling. He put his hand out to stop himself, but his hand simply went through it.

'Quit messing about and come back down,' called Green.

How?

'Use the power of your mind. Think you want to come down.'

'Instantly Black found himself floating inches over his inert body.

'Upright on the floor as if you are standing upon it.'

Bubbling with excitement Black righted himself.

'Try to keep your feet from going through the floor. It looks better that way.

Black bounced upwards.

'Now take my hand.'

Black reached out and found that, though his hand had gone through the ceiling he could not only touch, but grip Green's hand. It was solid and warm.

'Your spirit body has substance,' Green explained, 'but because it is too subtle to be felt in the material realm your hand went through the ceiling. In your present state you will be able to grasp things from other dimensions but not of the third, which is too coarse.'

Black opened his mouth and tried to use his vocal cords. 'Hello,' he said and found he could. He had a voice—not the thick, strangulated sounds of someone who has never spoken in his life but a clear, finely modulated voice. 'Wow, this is brilliant,' he shouted, and began to laugh with the sheer joy that speech brought.

'We have much to do and less time than I originally expected. Nevertheless, first...'

Once again it happened so fast, Black did not even feel the transition from his room into the blackness of outer space. Green released his hand and he began falling, freewheeling through the vastness.

'Heyyy!' he cried out, alarmed.

'Let go. Have fun. You can't hurt yourself here,' Green said, and after completing a few cartwheels, spun like a Catherine wheel firework until Black was certain he must be utterly dizzy, but he wasn't. His bright, radiant form laughed and shot off in the opposite direction. Black began tumbling then soaring after him. He had never felt so happy or alive in all his life. He couldn't even blink; who would've thought he could fly? With an indescribable euphoria he projected himself forward at great speed. It was amazing.

Ahead Green came to a sudden standstill. Black found that he too was easily able to accomplish the abrupt stop. He parked himself right next to Green and grinned. Green tucked his arms to his body and raced head first toward a twinkling star. 'Look at me,' he shouted. 'I'm a shooting star.'

Black plunged down to join him, marveling at and reveling in the closeness he felt toward Green. Amazing how quickly he had lost his awe for Green. Replaced by an intense but old love. He was his only friend.

Green executed an elegant half-roll. 'Are you ready to begin your initiation?'

Black copied him and nodded.

Green made a circling motion with his hand and suddenly, a few hundred miles away, an incredible celestial orb came into view. It was full of gigantic structures, monoliths, pyramids, towers, crystalline domes, and steps leading to buildings with massive entrances.

'Wow! How did you do that?'

'It was always there. You simply needed to be

dimensionally shifted to perceive it.'

'What planet is that?'

'That's your moon.'

Black was astonished. He knew the moon as a gray and deserted entity. This was a full color, and obviously inhabited piece of real estate.

'There are many things that are hidden from humankind. But, for now, focus your attention on planet Earth and the area surrounding her.'

Black looked behind him. Many thousands of miles away Earth sparkled with breathtaking beauty; a blue and green jewel in the velvet blackness, all the details very clear. But as his focus sharpened he observed something very strange. The planet was glowing brightly and pulsating. In many places it appeared almost liquid. Every once in a while flares of dazzling light shot out. Sometimes they died down; sometimes they became even brighter and began to spread. It reminded him of a great forge where things were being shaped.

'What is happening to it?'

'Earth is not an "it", but a sentient being who is in the process of evolving into the highest, most magnificent aspect of her being. She is being blasted with cosmic beams of intense energy and information so that light will be reinserted into her. Pay attention to her surrounding.'

When Black did, he noticed that for many miles around Earth countless millions of beings were suspended. Some were very large, miles long, and had shape. Others were simply formless wisps of grayish smoke, but every one of them was glowing in various degrees of intensity with the same light that was coming from Earth. He had the distinct impression that they were all waiting for something to happen. That sense of anticipation was so great that he perceived their collective expectation as the crackle in the air of an audience waiting for the start of a rock concert.

'Why have they collected around the Earth?'

'They have manifested from nearby energy systems, although not necessarily from your time reference, to witness, as you rightly perceived it, a very rare and exciting performance. Such an event will also signal their own upliftment. All your ancient civilizations foretold of this end-time.'

'Oh! The Mayan prophesy. Is the world really going to end on the twenty-first of December?'

'The world is not going to end—there are too many interested parties to allow such a thing to happen. It is not a date, but a season. In Earth time, an eight-year process. An alchemical kingdom is about to be born where both Earth and human consciousness will drastically change. This change is an event that happens once in many tens of millions of Earth years. The best way I can describe it to you is as a convergence of a great deal of odds, which will then emerge as several probabilities and some possibilities. One likelihood may alter human consciousness to rapidly emerge from its limited time-space illusion into a unified energy system. But, as always, with extreme opportunity comes danger.'

'Danger?'

'Mass extinction is one, but the key danger is that Earth will become what you see in the futuristic, dystopian, police state music videos that your elite love to produce, and you occasionally watch. Where humanity has been turned into a micro-chipped, half-human, half-robot slave population. Watched by telescreens and controlled by faceless police in riot gear they no longer think for themselves, but have been assimilated into the hive and act in the 'greater good'.

Black had watched and enjoyed music videos styled on just such themes, but it had never occurred to him to think of them as the propaganda arm of a harmful agenda deliberately propagated by 'the elite'. He still didn't. It was just entertainment. And it looked good.

'There,' Green continued, 'are many moves afoot to sabotage the energy so that as many possibilities as possible remain unrealized. Your action, minute as it will be, is one of those random variables that may tip the odds in favor of humanity. Are you ready to begin?'

Black did not take his eyes off the waiting expectant forms, some of them so bright they hurt his eyes. 'Yes.'

'Before we move to a place better suited for our needs, I have to ask. Would you like to remain in your bedclothes or shall we find something more appropriate?'

Black looked down at his clothes. He had often wondered where his mother went to buy clothes with children's motifs in his sizes. 'Can I choose anything I want?'

Green nodded.

As soon as he thought of it, he was dressed in blue jeans tucked into a pair of cowboy boots, and an open-necked tan shirt.

'Very nice. Ready?'

Black nodded.

'Hold on,' Green said, and they were deposited on a bare, sun-torn landscape.

No man ever steps in the same river twice, for it's not the same river and he's not the same man.

—Heraclitus

Black looked around him in wonderment. 'This is amazing. All my life I have dreamed of standing in a desert.'

'Glad to please. Look to the west. We are not alone.'

On a sand dune in the distance a lonely figure stood motionless beside his seated camel. He had lived in that furnace all his life and knew both the terrain and its inhabitants intimately. But always it had new secrets to share—a boy who appeared out of nowhere. He left his camel and began walking toward the boy, his robes billowing around him, the slip-face of the dune singing under his feet.

'Can he see us?'

'No one can see me, but you will be tangible to the rare adept. The ones who see even that which casts no shadow.'

The man came to a stop six feet away from Black. He had a savagely beautiful face; deep-set, coal-black eyes and skin of pure leather. 'On the way to somewhere else?' he asked in a tribal dialect that Black shouldn't have understood, but did.

'I'm looking for an oasis,' Black replied in English.

The man pointed to the east. 'Half an hour on foot.'

'Thanks.'

The man shaded his eyes against the blazing sun and said nothing. A small lizard moved on the hot sand.

Black hesitated, feeling strangely reluctant to leave the desert wanderer. He had the strong sensation of wanting to touch him, in some way show kinship.

'Your hand will go right through him,' cautioned Green.

'Will you tell me something important about the desert?' Black asked instead.

The man shrugged, his old face creasing. The flurry of lines brought forth a deeply mysterious smile; it encompassed his camel, the white bones buried under the sand, the oceans he had never seen, and the stars he knew not the names of. 'She is unknowable. She could be Death wrapped in beauty or a goddess come as a dog.'

Black nodded. Yes. Some part of him knew that. In another life when his camels were his dearest friends, and a woman and five children lived in a tent with him. He turned away and began walking in the direction the man had pointed to.

The man's eyes remained fixed on the departing boy. He had left no footprints, but he knew the boy was not a jinn. Perhaps he was a fairy child. He watched him until he disappeared behind the shifting sands. He made a sound and his camel grumbled upright and made its way toward him.

'How come I could understand him?' Black asked.

'I delved into his mind, learned his language and translated it for you.'

'Did you do the same for him?'

'Yes.'

Undisturbed by any sensation of heat Black found the empty vastness of the desert beautiful beyond description.

'Green?'

'Yes.'

'Will you teach me how to get out of my body on my own?'

Green stopped and turned toward him. His emerald lashes swept down and his head shook sorrowfully. 'I was warned you would ask. I'm so sorry, I wish I could, but it is not part of the deal.'

'Don't worry, really it's OK,' Black said, and rested his hand on Green's arm. It hurt him to see his friend look pained.

'It's not that I don't want to, but if you travel without me you could come to great harm. You have many enemies. There is a much safer way for you to leave your body, though. It is stored in your memory banks as lucid dreaming.'

Black frowned. 'But I've never heard of such a thing.'

'It was in a documentary you watched two years ago, but it is no longer in your conscious memory.'

'What is lucid dreaming?'

'It is a method of waking up inside your dream, so you are conscious you are dreaming. In this way you can enter rich and detailed fantasy worlds where you can feel the sun on your skin, eat in the best restaurants, attend concerts, compose your own music, go anywhere you please, and meet anyone you want. And since physical laws need not apply anything you can conceive of you can do and be. You can even fly. It's quite fun, I believe.'

'Can I meet you there?'

'Yes. In this world you can also meet dream characters, who are other lucid dreamers. As you get better at it you will even be able to enter other people's dreams.'

'Tell me how it is done.'

'The first step will be to plan your dream in the greatest detail. Once you have done that, before you fall asleep, set your mental alarm clock to wake up after a few hours—you have used it before to catch late-night programs. When you awaken, firmly intend to wake up in your dream, and go back to sleep while hanging on to the thinnest strand of consciousness. To determine if indeed you are awake in your dream simply try doing something you would be unable to do while awake. In your case try to move your limbs or talk. If you can, you are lucid dreaming.'

A half-crumbling stone tower heralded the oasis. Here life began again: trees, children, men watering their beasts at the well, and women going about their business in thick, black robes. Their chipped nail polish gave Black a secret pleasure. A group of young boys were eating watermelon. Wistfully Black watched them throw the rinds to the camels, lick the juices off their dusty hands and run off to play. Green led them through a grove and they sat beneath a date palm.

'Ready?' Green asked.

'Yes, but I am really troubled about something. May we discuss it first?'

'Of course.'

'That incredible audience you showed me are waiting for an outcome that is so much greater than myself. How can I possibly be of any use in such an enormous galactic plan.'

'You are the door with the small open. Through you much can come. Like a cattle stampede that starts out only as a "stir". A few heads or even just one that agitates others in the surroundings to move, but that then goes further and further until the entire herd is moving in frenzy. You have been selected with great care. Put your mind to rest. You are not expected to fail. We must begin now. Soon the girl will find you.'

'The girl?'

'She is a bright shaman who has been turned, and is now a tool of the dark hierarchy. Beautiful, but badly damaged, she represents great danger to you.'

'Who are the dark hierarchy?'

'They are the ancient ones, inorganic, immeasurably powerful inter-dimensional entities. Unseen they come, unseen they go, for they exist not in the spaces you know of, but between them. They are the real rulers of your world. Their governance of humanity is from behind the scenes and solely by proxy, but it would be a grave mistake to think their grip is less than total and absolute. There is not a single step the human race makes that is unwatched by them. Their greatest desire is to enslave the souls of men, but men in their ignorance call them gods and prostrate themselves before them in exchange for Earthly power and material gain.'

'If they are so powerful, why do they have to hide? Why not rule openly?'

'Logic is successfully applied when one knows the real agenda. Earthlings don't. There is a very good reason why they remain hidden, and we will get to that very soon, but first we must lay the foundation stones of your understanding, as human beings have been lied to on a grand scale. You are only fourteen years old, and a lot of what I am going to tell you will be distressing to say the least, but your mastery of these matters is vital, so I urge you to pay the greatest attention and refrain from making any judgments until I have finished. Will you do that?"

'I will.'

'Earth scientists have been forced to conclude that on a quantum level matter doesn't actually exist. The real substance to your reality is created by a force that first brings to incredible vibration the particles of an atom and then holds that minute solar system in place for its lifetime. And atoms, by the way, are not objects or things either, but fluctuations of energy and information that exist as potentialities or possibilities. Do you understand so far?'

'I think so.'

'Cutting-edge science has also had to admit that the human brain is but a narrow band hologram generator. What would be the natural deduction from both these discoveries?'

Black shook his head. He felt overwhelmed and unable to think properly.

'If your brain is a hologram generator, then despite its apparent materiality, the universe you are living in is a sophisticated 3-D projection or a virtual reality. Your entire world is an illusion that is decided by the way your brain has been programmed to interpret the hologram. For instance, the human eye can decode or perceive nothing beyond a certain band of frequencies called visible light: a tiger, a tree in which it will be possible to hide from the tiger, and afterwards a river to drink from. All others, an infinite band of frequency ranges, are screened out. That is why the world that you see, hear, and experience is totally different from the one that dogs, bats, snakes or insects do, even though you are all in the same sea of energy.'

'But I'm not a hologram; I'm real and so is the world around me. And even though I can't feel it when people touch me, I know they can,' Black protested.

'Imagine a fan that is going so fast the blades appear to be a solid metal plate. If one threw a ball at it, it would bounce back. To a man who has never seen a fan in that kind of motion wouldn't that be irrefutable proof? You are a swarm of atoms, but your senses are too unrefined for you to perceive it. You were wishing just now for a taste of the watermelon the boys were eating, weren't you?'

Black nodded.

'Would you like a bite?'

Instantly Black's mouth filled with deliciously cool, sweet flesh. The juice welled up between his tongue and teeth and ran in a cold trickle down his throat. The sensation was incredibly real until it was abruptly over.

'*Everything* you experience starts off as an electric signal in your brain, which your brain then decodes into taste, smell, sound, sight, and touch. Whether it is the blue sky, the birds in it, the food you are eating, the time on your clock face, or the languages you use to communicate, it is all a constructed fiction.'

Black had seen a documentary about holograms. For a hologram to be maintained the broadcast had to be continuous or the image would disappear. Who...?

Green smiled. 'Well done. I cannot find a word in your mind to adequately describe it. For now, suffice it to say that you live in a simulated construction controlled by, let's call it... Ah! your favorite movie, *The Matrix.*'

Green paused to let the idea sink in.

99

'The Matrix is a perfectly well-oiled, unimaginably immense, vastly complex, and incredibly intricate program that weaves the web you live in. It is held in place and controlled by mathematical codes. In this field of information absolutely everything has been thought of and catered for. The maintenance, modifications, and necessary adjustments to it are most impressive. It is deceptive on a scale you cannot imagine, and so pervasive that there is no sanctuary from it. At every level the machine fools you. And it is run to forever perpetuate this deception. Always there will be the cycle of birth, growth, maturity, and death for the poor souls trapped in it. There is no escape for the ordinary human being from this time loop. Every turn they make brings them back to square one.'

Black was appalled. If those words had not come from a glowing inter-dimensional being he would have laughed at the ridiculous idea that he was trapped inside a grand cosmic deception. As the words had he floundered, like a turtle on its back. 'Are you trying to tell me that Earth is a prison?'

'It is, but only on one level. It is also a farm and a—'

'A farm?'

'That would bring us neatly back to your earlier question. Why the controllers don't show themselves? I know you will find this distressing, perhaps even horrifying, but the truth will be your shield. Humans are not at the top of the food chain.'

'We aren't?' Black blinked uncertainly. This was no country that he knew. Too absurd.

'For eons man has been shown stories and literature themed on the meme that humans are fodder for other beings, but he has never "got" it. It would seem the best way to hide an unpalatable truth is in fiction.'

'They eat humans?' Black stared at Green, aghast.

'Humans are not eaten, not on this planet anyway, but are harvested energetically for their electromagnetic frequencies, a much valued food in other dimensions. Humans have to eat food to gain energy; "they" have to eat energy from humans to gain form.'

'What is it exactly that they are eating?'

'The carbon-oxygen equation of every living thing on Earth naturally vibrates to produce this substance—there is no word for it in your vocabulary so I will refer to it as the resource. Animals, during their relentless fight for survival, when protecting their young, during courtship conflicts, and at the termination of their lifespan produce the resource, but humans are the unrivaled providers, in both quantity and quality. The resource is freely emanated by all humans when they experience love, friendship, greed, hate, pain, guilt, pity, disease, pride, ambition, ownership, possession, sacrifice—and on a much larger scale by wars, famine, religion, industry, nationalism, racism, trade, natural disasters, and so on.'

'That is terrible,' cried Black.

'Is it really? Every day you produce carbon dioxide as a waste material. Do you resent the trees and plants that use it to live? What will you do with it if the trees will not use it? You have no use for the resource; what if someone else has need for it and extracts it without harming you?'

Black shook his head. He felt lost and confused. 'It's still wrong to take without asking,' he insisted.

'You must get over this, quickly. There is worse to come. Here is what the resource feels and looks like to them.'

In his mind Black heard the sound of a train speeding toward him. It exploded in a heady rush, dense with impressions of musical cords, patterns, and color graduations, all the way from a thick red sludge to a milky white light. The sensations they roused inside him ranged from a feeling of great superiority and unlimited physical power to an intense euphoria that was impossible to describe. He felt an incredible craving for more when the high was suddenly over. He turned to Green with desperate eyes.

'No addiction for you,' Green said, and magically the all-consuming need was gone.

'Wow, so that is what we are being farmed for.'

'Yes, but it is not the finest grade that is most sought after by your present controllers, but the red sludge caused by fear and suffering.'

Black had a thought.

'Sorry, but your mother is included in "every living thing". Although the type of resource she produces is totally different from the type you do.'

'What's the difference?'

'Yours is a result of loneliness and yearning; hers comes from the highest emotion possible, tremendous love. The purest, most refined form.'

Black wanted Green to be wrong, but years of observing the world on his TV screen had secretly led him to the inevitable conclusion that Earth was an eat or be eaten jungle. That the first law of the system, the immutable rule, the underlying drive behind every action in the animal world, and even human existence, was survival at any cost. The true horror of survival meant that if the lion entertained any notions of honor, empathy or mercy, it must starve to death.

The entire system was set up in such a way that all creatures, plants and animals lived at the expense of each other. No life form was totally safe. Every species had at least one carefully chosen predator—except man. Now it seemed man had a very carefully chosen predator too. A parasite!

'That's right, Black. You enter this matrix either by choice or by trick, but once you are in it you must consume or be consumed. Parasitic patterns are an intrinsic design of the weave. Every participant is a predator and the process cannot be altered or changed as long as the Earth life is to continue.'

'Then why are all those beings waiting around Earth so eagerly? Do they want this horrible process to continue?'

'I understand that you are shocked and angry, but since we do not have much time please try to suspend any judgment until the end of our discourse, when it might be possible for you to see this in its proper perspective. Earth was never meant to be a prison or the factory farm it is today.

'It was a garden where all manner of souls came willingly to experiment, experience, express, and evolve. It was, and despite all they have done to it still is, a school beyond compare. For the crucible of human experience can confer an imitable greatness. Some of the brightest glowing beings you saw gathered around Earth were once human. But now it is time for you to return; your mother is back.' He paused to smile encouragingly at Black. 'And she has a surprise for you.'

> If you wish to enjoy a grander view,
> climb to a loftier height.
>
> —Chinese proverb

It was only when Black saw his mother approach him, a gaily wrapped present clutched in her hands, her face full of devotion and love, that the full horror of Green's revelations hit him. She dropped the present to the floor and rushed to him, her eyes sick with fear.

'What is it?' she begged, again and again, but he could only stare back. A despairing mute. That an occult brethren of darkness and not humanity was in control of Earth, or its own destiny was too fantastic to believe, yet… What if it was true, and all of humanity had been fooled and betrayed? A part of him was bewildered, and another petrified. In the end she had pulled up a chair to his bed, but despite her best efforts had fallen asleep sitting upright. He watched her sleeping and for the first time in his life he pitied her. She was being milked like a cow and she hadn't the slightest clue. Black turned his attention toward the TV screen. It had always comforted him, but that night he registered it as a blur of moving colors. Even the news could not hold his attention.

He remembered the prayers he had said during his lifetime, all his hopes of a miraculous recovery. Now he wondered: did God even exist? And if there was one what good was a god that let you be food for inter-dimensional predators?

All night long his mind roved restlessly. He didn't want to believe any of it, but so much of it made sense and answered his deepest worries. Until now there had seemed to be no point in human existence. One spent all one's life gathering love, money, and power, but no matter how rich, powerful or loved one was, always one died alone, and every single atom gathered from the Earth wrenched back. But now he could see that even the homeless tramp living on top of a rubbish dump was of great value to 'someone'.

In the morning his mother tried to call in a day off, but there was an emergency of sorts, a broken pipe having led to a flooded kitchen floor. There was cleaning to be done, and urgently. Besides, it was obvious there was nothing she could do for Black. She opened his present for him—to his surprise, finally, adult pajamas.

'I'll be home early tonight,' she said, and kissed him goodbye.

After she left a strange thing happened to him. The numb shock evaporated and in its place came, first, hurt like he had never thought possible, then a terrible, terrible rage. It was an emotion he had never experienced before, and its effect inside his frozen body was spectacular. It built up like a tempest, the air exiting his nostrils in a trembling rush. It galvanized him into a large and powerful force. His rage had a target: Green. Green whom he had naively trusted and loved was a cunning trickster—he had betrayed him—for what purpose he did not know yet. But the idea that greatness could be achieved from the experience of being planted in a garden and secretly harvested was ludicrous. Only a fool would believe it.

So what if the present controllers preferred red sludge to milky white? Both were manipulating humans to further their own needs. Whatever their secret plans, he wanted no part of them. Never would he contribute to the continued enslavement of humankind. He desperately wished there was some way for him to warn humanity, at the very least his poor mother.

3.29p.m. Green arrived and extracted Black from his body. Immediately, Black opened his mouth to begin his prepared tirade, but Green held up a silencing hand. Black noticed the sadness in his beautiful eyes. All the wonderful fractals on his face and body appeared not only more faded, but processed so slowly they seemed rigid or almost crystalline in nature. In his mind came an image of Green tumbling and soaring ahead of him in the velvet blackness of space, all the fractals glowing brightly, his eyes full of laughter. How happy they had been then. And just like that the spectacular fury he had been stoking for hours extinguished. The truth was he didn't want Green to leave him. He would miss him terribly. Green was the only friend he had ever had, and he loved him.

'You claim to love me, but you won't even hear me out,' Green said. 'If you no longer desire to keep your part of the agreement, that is your choice. This is the planet of free will. My duty is done even if you don't do yours. However…' He held his hand out to him. 'Before I leave there is something I want you to see.'

Black hesitated. He had promised to withhold judgment until he had heard everything, and there was also his insatiable curiosity that told him, what harm can come of one little trip? He reached out for the proffered hand, and instantly he was taken to the edge of a forest.

'Where are we?'

'Scotland.' Green turned to him. 'You have to be

psychically modified to enter. May I?'

Black nodded. He didn't have to wait long before he felt as if he was a deck of microscopic slices being very rapidly flicked, shuffled, and allowed to drop one on top of another. The sensation was painless and quickly over.

They stepped into the forest; its interior was dim and cool. He understood instantly that it was in a magical place. For it was exactly how he had imagined the forest Hansel and Gretel had been abandoned in would look. There were no dead leaves and his bare feet sunk into the rich, black dirt. A silver birch was growing next to him and he touched it. His hand did not go through it. 'Am I physical?'

'No, but you have been momentarily altered to be of the same frequency as this dimension so there is the illusion of physicality.'

Green pointed to a brilliant light radiating through the trees.

'What is that?'

'A unicorn.'

'Unicorns are real?' Black gasped.

'Of course. They hold the frequency of divine love for this world, and since they need an extremely high, pure vibration to do that, they have to keep away from humans. Would you like to meet it?'

'I would love to meet it, but I thought only virgins could.'

'Don't you qualify?'

Black had to smile. The anger was all gone. There was nothing left, but an enduring love for his only friend.

'The virgin thing is actually an allusion to purity. However, there is an etiquette in dealing with them.

Approach it slowly and stop when you are about six feet away. Go ahead; I will wait here for you.'

It was the creature's golden spiral horn that first became visible. The rest remained a vague shape inside the large, misty cocoon of light that radiated from it. About six feet away Black came to a stop. It was still not possible to see properly through the light. The unicorn lifted its head from the ground and rose slowly. Black gasped in awe. It was huge, perhaps twelve feet high, with a glowing, pure white body, a translucent mane and tail, and huge, purple hoofs. It was the most extraordinary thing Black had ever seen.

Slowly, it turned its head and looked at him. It was a moment he would never forget. The intensely beautiful, purple eyes radiated a magnificent love, truly not of this world and beyond anything he could ever have imagined. His body began to vibrate. He was mesmerized by the heavenly creature. He never wanted to leave it.

The unicorn did not speak telepathically the way Green did, but Black simply knew that it wanted him to come closer.

In a daze he stepped forward until he was near enough to touch the magical beast.

In the same way he been invited to come closer he was warmly welcomed to the forest and told that he was the oldest unicorn in service to humanity. Thousands of years it had lived there, and would do so for as long as necessary. Black gazed into the unicorn's enchanted eyes, and realized that in all that time the unicorn had gained no knowledge whatsoever, only wisdom.

Something shifted in the unicorn's eyes and he was privy to an image of himself lying on a bed in a white room, wearing a skullcap with electrodes that were attached to high-tech equipment. He had a hunch that it was not a hospital, but somewhere secret. Then: a split second image of a girl—her back was to him; she had long, golden hair, which hung in a thick, long braid down her back. Then she too was gone.

All we have is what each of us is prepared to give. Although, mind you, service is not the same as servitude.

Bending his great head, the unicorn dropped the tip of its horn into Black's palm. The sliver was no bigger than Black's fingernail. My gift to you. Black looked at the unexpected gift. It dazzled his eyes briefly before melting into liquid gold, which seeped into the skin of his palm. Black looked into the large, kind eyes. 'Thank you,' he whispered, and the unicorn neighed as a horse does, but it was the most musical sound Black had ever heard. Then it walked away, a serene giant.

Black felt Green appear beside him.

'He gave me the tip of his horn.'

'The pure and blameless may receive such gifts. When Earth was still a paradise, unicorns were not so shy. They lived openly amongst man. There was no spoken language then, but what you shared today with him. The Earth was different then too. It did not have an atmosphere so there was no decay or putrefaction, no electromagnetic field, no astral net cast around it. And man was not the puny thing he has become today, but a magical being. Bestowed with great powers and wisdom, he was the divine keeper of an astounding array of knowledge; a living library and a memory circuit for the mineral, vegetable, and animal kingdoms in Earth's biosphere. He did not need to eat to survive, even the thought of eating the flesh of another being to sustain himself could never have occurred. He ingested only divine life force emanations and retained intact memories of all his past lives, and all the forms he had taken. He could enter and exit his body with ease very much as you are doing now.'

'Are you referring to Atlantis?'

'Do not think that human history is only a few thousands of years old. History is another great fraud perpetuated on mankind. It was millions of years ago when physical reality was in accordance with divine will.'

'What really happened to us?'

'Perhaps that is best explained to you by one of your own kind. Same time tomorrow?'

Black nodded. He would hear Green out.

Auribus tenere lupum

(I hold a wolf by the ears)

He walked quickly into the minimarket, his body tense with anticipation, and waited impatiently for her. She was reaching for a carton of milk when he could bear it no longer. He walked down the aisle and brushed his body against her arm, firm, smooth—in his dreams—cinnamon before it was powdered.

'Oh, sorry,' he said.

Their eyes met. Hers, he was profoundly disappointed to note, unlike his outrageously vivid fantasies were a void of sexual knowledge, almost that of an innocent child.

'It doesn't matter,' she muttered, apparently unsettled by his bold stare, and turned away hurriedly.

'Wait, don't you live in the flat opposite mine?'

Bumi turned back slowly. Took in the thick, curly hair held down with a generous dollop of something greasy, the large, bulging eyes, the wiry moustache, the reddish tongue that flicked out to wet the puce lips that had been curved to appear as if they were smiling, but were not. And the great unwashed smell of him.

Without welcome in her eyes, 'Do I?'

He flushed badly, but his dark skin hid it well. 'Yes, yes, on Kessler Road. I rent one of the upstairs rooms in number 22, and you are in 5, aren't you?'

She looked at him cautiously, then. A neighbor, an unnecessary inconvenience. Of course, the window encrusted with pigeon droppings.

It couldn't have been more obvious, she was

uninterested, but he ploughed on determinedly. 'I sometimes see you going to work.' A pause. Another odd smile. 'I know the family downstairs, you see. We are old friends from Calcutta. My name is Veera.'

Bumi borrowed the stiff, formal tone Lady Carrington employed in her dealings with tradesmen. 'Well, nice to make your acquaintance, Veera, but I am late and have to rush.' She turned away. Without the carton of milk.

'You forgot to tell me your name.'

He saw her hesitate.

To be rude might bring worse consequences. 'Bumi,' she said, and before more could be gleaned, hurried away. Bothered, spontaneously recognizing danger.

He watched her go, her cheap coat flapping in the wind, and thought, she's hiding something. And his interest quickened. A hunter on the scent.

Bumi found her feet moving faster and faster. No milk for her coffee tomorrow morning. She felt disturbed. She had always managed to keep everyone at arm's length, but this one was different. Some deep instinct warned her to be careful, very careful. Something about his eyes. Too close together. Too full of sex and badness, as her aunt would say. He would not be quenched as easily as Lord Carrington's dinner guest. She fretted about the problem he posed all the way home, but when she opened the door to her son's room her fears became soap bubbles that touch something real and collapse into nothing.

She clasped her palms to her cheeks. 'Oh my God! Black, your hands,' she cried. 'They've straightened out.' As if unable to believe her own eyes, she grasped his hands in hers and examined them closely. 'It's a miracle,' she whispered, kissing them repeatedly and reverently. Suddenly she stopped and frowned. Her fingers left his hands and moved swiftly over his body. She raised an incredulous face to him and declared, 'I know you'll think I've gone mad, but with God as my witness, you're bigger now than you were this morning.'

And God said, 'Let US make man in OUR Image, after OUR likeness.'

—Genesis 1:26

The question is who are the 'us' and 'our'?

Black found himself standing on a sun-drenched, yellow and orange-brown landscape. Only a few shrubs dotted the rocky land. Black glanced down at himself. He was dressed in a long, loose-fitting, white tunic and trousers. In the empty sky above a lone vulture circled. Black gazed at it in fascination. 'Where are we?'

'Persia, Earth time AD 13. I brought you here to tap into the memories of your own species. In there,' he said, pointing to a rocky hill behind them, 'is one of the greatest human seers that ever lived.'

'Inside the rock?'

'Is a cave.'

'But there is no entrance.'

'That shouldn't stop you.'

He went up the pathway—it was full of loose stones, which he disturbed not—and walked right through the wall of rocks and mud that sealed the secret entrance, an experience that he had to admit, he thoroughly relished. Inside the air was neither damp nor dank, but cool and fresh. He followed the dim, narrow corridor of roughly hewn rock.

It opened out to a small enclosure, big enough for him to stand upright, but surely too low for the man who sat cross-legged in the light of a single lamp. Dressed in thick, white robes he was bent over his work, which was set on a low wooden table. His fingers were

117

extraordinarily long and tapering, and his feet were bare. There was a stack of leather-bound books on the floor by his side.

At Black's appearance he looked up, neither startled nor afraid. His beard was long and gray, but his face was rosy and youthful, and his eyes were calm and full of the music of the soul. He had found something special locked away in that cave. He laid down his writing instrument and gestured for Black to come forward. 'Welcome, welcome. We have been waiting for you, and I, Jahanbakh, am honored to be the one to receive you,' he said in Coptic.

Black stepped into the weak circle of light. 'Have you really been waiting for me?'

'Yes, really. What year have you come from?'

'2012.'

'That far forward. Well, well.'

Black looked around the sparse enclosure. Other than an Earthen jug and bowl next to him the small space was completely bare. 'How long have you been imprisoned here?'

Jahanbakh's eyes twinkled with amusement. 'It looks like a prison to you, but this humble hole in the Earth is where I have chosen to lay my eggs in safety.' He laughed like a child at the expression on Black's face. 'All human endeavors of a spiritual nature are eggs. They wait for the right environment to hatch and grow. I will remain here until I finish my part of this work.'

'What is it that you are working on?'

He pointed to the pile of leather-bound manuscripts. 'One day when the time is right these works will be discovered in clay jars and be called the Nag Hamadi scrolls. They are crucial to the survival of the human race.'

'Why do they have to be sealed away?'

'If they are not, we fear they will be intercepted, destroyed, or, worse, manipulated to serve the ones they seek to expose.'

'Will you teach me about the fall of man? Why he is no longer the magical being he once was?'

Jahanbakh exhaled a long breath. 'Ah, you want to know about man's greatest foe: the Archons.'

'The Archons?'

'The primordial ones. Long before the sun, the planetary system, Earth or man was formed, they arose in the depths of the cosmos. A phantom species of inorganic cyborgs, they were spawned of elementary matter. Created in error these first androgynous entities resembled aborted human fetuses with oversized heads, huge eyes, and spindly limbs. These grotesque neonates, in their own bizarre way, were alive and aware, and through the fractal process of endless, self-repeating generation they emerged as a massive horde or 'legion'.'

'Are these neonates you speak of gray?' Black had once seen a documentary about the true-life stories of people who claimed to have been taken and tortured by creatures of a similar description. They had referred to them as the Grays.

Jahanbakh frowned. 'Possibly. They are often pale in appearance and come in the night to abduct souls, but their appearances on Earth must be by necessity sporadic and brief since they are not designed to inhabit an organic environment. Their original habitat was inside the thread-like tunnels extending from the core of the constellation of the Hunter.'

Inside his head Black heard the translation. *Hunter* =

Orion.

'But as more and more of these shadow beings came into matter, a second variant appeared, an aggressive reptilian humanoid. One of them, a terrifying, lion-faced, serpentine-bodied beast, upon first opening his eyes, falsely perceived the limitless quantity of matter around him as his own creation, and arrogantly declared, "It is I, who am God, and there is no other power apart from me."

'Endowed with the formidable powers of his divine beginnings, this fierce reptile-like mutation rapidly dominated the embryonic order and assumed the role of overlord. The entire Archon colony came alive under his demonic fire. But spiritually blind and fiercely territorial, he refused to obey the place from which he came. This caused the entire species to be cut off from the divine nutritive energy source from which they issued. Unable to generate their own energy the formidable shape-shifters had to become parasites in order to survive. Mind parasites.'

'Mind parasites?'

'Yes. Messengers of deception. They descended upon dying worlds like swarms of locusts and consumed them by forcing the invaded population to devolve to lower and lower states of vibration. By chaining those souls in the darkest of conditions of fear and slavery they secure themselves the energy of the invaded populations, not only to sustain themselves, but to enlarge their empire based on their essence of envy, hate, lust for power, selfishness, dishonesty, cunning, devastation, destruction, and domination by whatever methods available. Do you recognize this world I have described?'

'Are you suggesting that our world has already been

colonized by this alien intelligence?'

'The greatest invasions happen in secrecy. Remember, the parasites must avoid exposure and rectification of their activities at all costs. They want to steal our inner light; and the best way to keep humans from claiming their own inner light is to give them delusional beliefs about their divinity. Who do you think is the arrogant, vicious, demented impostor deity we come across as the jealous God of our holiest of books?'

Black lost his dazed expression. 'Would you have me believe that God is a fierce, demonic beast?' he cried.

'The measure of your surprise is the extent of their success. It would be so easy to pretend that I am the liar and the fomenter of discontent. But think about the gods that have come to humanity. What do you really think of "gods" who demand blind obedience, urge men on to "holy" wars, mandate that their followers smite each other, favor one race over another, punish children for the sins of their fathers, demand animal and human sacrifices, and promise purgatory and hell to anybody that does not bow down to them?'

Black remained silent, but the thought came... If anything slithers like a snake.

'Tell me the truth, my son, do you really think Earth is a divine place being overseen by an infinitely loving God?'

He was standing at the crossroad and being asked to choose. He thought of the blameless animals in the wild, constantly tormented by flies, fleas, parasites, leeches, intestinal worms, and a multitude of other diseases and troubles. He thought of the starving children in Africa and the food mountains in the West. He thought of the wars, the diseases, the environmental pollution, and the unbridled greed and corruption that fuelled the network. The system was indefensible. He shook his head slowly.

'Only a blind fool or an evil one could not think up some better arrangement than this vile one with its mechanisms of exploitation, misery, suppression, pain, suffering, and ultimately degeneration and decay. These malevolent living machines have infected the human race with their qualities, and taught us to divide ourselves by artificial means, race, color, gender, nationality, religion.'

'But what about Jesus?'

'Remember what he said. "My Kingdom is not of this world." He didn't come to redeem mankind by teaching him that he was born a sinner and his only salvation is by the intervention of God; he came to warn us about the mind parasites. But his story has been exploited through censorship and revision to manipulate humans into believing they are unworthy sinners, needing to grovel, repent, and the constant intercession of the Church. You should also know that the cross is a blot on humanity.'

'How so?'

'The cross is an ancient emblem much older than Christianity. It is a cube unfolded; an icon of domination and control, and a crest of the Lord of the Horde himself. A cross with a man on it is a trophy, the way a hunter mounts a deer he has killed. We are being forced to worship the symbol of our own enslavement.'

Jahanbakh stopped suddenly. 'It would appear your time is up.'

'How do you know that?'

Jahanbakh let his eyes move to the candle flame. 'When you came the flame stopped moving. Time stopped for me. Now the flame is beginning to flutter. Soon it will start dancing again.'

Black noticed what he had not before. How still the air was. It was as if he and Jahanbakh were inside a painting. The frozen flame spurted once and suddenly came alive. Black wasn't even given the time to stand up and walk out of the cave. He was sucked out so fast Jahanbakh became a blur. The last words he heard were, 'Beware the shape-shifters. They can take—'

Where can I find this man named god?
I thought my slave days were over.

—Joshua Udeh

Black found himself on a beautiful white beach, dressed in a pair of Bermuda shorts. The sky was dotted with fluffy clouds, the sun was shining brightly, and the sea was a calm azure. A luminous figure was standing with his back to him at the water's edge. Black went to stand beside him. Silently, they stood looking out to the horizon.

'Why did you bring me here?'

'I thought you might like to walk on water.' Green's voice was neutral.

'Not me; I only ever wanted to stand in it,' Black said sadly.

'Close your eyes and turn your face up to the sky.'

Black did as he was told, and he felt the warmth of the sun on his face and body, and the warm water lapping at his bare feet. He listened to the sucking sound of the silky water in the sand as the waves went back out to sea. It was more delicious than anything he had ever imagined and yet within him yawned a great emptiness. There was so much he did not understand.

'Take any form,' said Green.

Black opened his eyes and looked at Green. 'What?'

'Just giving you back the words you lost. Beware the shape-shifters. They can take any form.'

Black closed his eyes. 'Where are we?'

'A billionaire's private island. His flamboyant house and staff are on the other side.'

Black wriggled his toes and grasped grains of sand between them. A simple pleasure, yet incomparably wonderful. He felt like Cipher in *The Matrix*. He knew it was only an illusion, but so what? All his life he had only ever longed to be reincarnated as a normal person.

'Reincarnation is the goal of those who don't transcend, and human enlightenment is the Archons' greatest disappointment,' Green said softly.

Black took a deep breath. 'Will you tell me how they defeated us?'

'Of course. When man was created the Lord of the Horde was instantly and insanely envious of him. This is the first and most significant trait of the parasite—envy. He desperately wanted to own the rainbow of inner colors man possessed, but despite his unsurpassed imitative skills and his impressive demonic abilities, the Horde's own inability to concentrate, create, or sustain intentionality meant for eons they remained powerless to access the three-dimensional dream world of love, wisdom, and peace that humans wove with their every thought and action.'

Black turned to Green. He had turned away from the horizon and was facing him.

'Their moment to be "the authorities that rule over man" arrived when the dwellers of another dying planet, a ruthless race of self-serving master geneticists, who the Archons had earlier corrupted, fought a great war over Earth. Earth was and still is much prized for its abundant production of raw material and "food". When the master geneticists became the new owners of Earth, the human DNA was rewired and turned into a prison cell. Every multidimensional property was shut down, trapping the new human being into only 2 percent of his conscious mind.'

'If they only came for the resource, and the human being is the best producer of it, anyway, why did they have to do all that?'

'A being that can leave its physical form at will and be in more than one place at the same time cannot be controlled. The original vehicle of experience had to intercepted and damaged beyond use. A smaller brain was fitted into a body that had been purposely reorganized to avoid pain and seek pleasure. Hard-wired with reflexes to serve only the gross needs of the body, their awareness became only the awareness of their bodies. Beyond their skin they did not exist.'

'But I once watched a documentary about the discovery of ancient Sumerian cuneiform tables that claimed that man was hardly more than an ape until benign extraterrestrials contributed their superior genes to form the human being.'

Green smiled. 'They'd like you to think they engineered you from an ape, but nothing could be further from the truth. The real truth is that human DNA is divine, and no matter how hard they tried they could not destroy any part of it without unexpected consequences for the whole. All they could do and did was unplug vast portions of the structure and leave them to lie fallow—what your scientists now call junk DNA. And because they understood that, given enough time, the silenced DNA strands would repair themselves and revert back to their original abundance, the human lifespan was shortened from hundreds of years to what it is now.

'To convince humans of their "ape" beginnings, ape characteristics were added. Their large eyes, the mirrors

127

of their souls, were purposely made smaller, more simian—a brilliant strategy on the predator-controlled conqueror's part. Believing they were not much more than apes they were more easily persuaded to behave like them.'

'But why was all this allowed to happen?'

'Earth is a planet of free will. It encompasses the complete idea that one may have and do whatever one wishes. When all things are allowed many things can be learned.' Green turned away. 'Let's get out of the water.'

They left the water and sat on the white sand. Green lay back, all the fractals stretching and playing, more marine-like than ever.

'There is also another thing they did to the unsuspecting human. One that will be far more difficult for you to accept.'

From his prone position Green fixed his gaze on Black. For the first time since Black had known him, he saw something akin to pity in those beautiful eyes.

Human beings are on a journey of awareness, which has momentarily been interrupted by extraneous forces.

—Carlos Castaneda. *Magical Passes* (1998)

'Well, what is it?' Black prompted.

'Beyond the eyesight spectrum on another level of understanding they hacked into the human mind and placed into it a foreign intelligence. A baroque, envious, cowardly thing. In one fell stroke man became not only their most exquisite source of energy, but also a container for their mind. The human being would be born, live, and die never suspecting that a purely selfish, opportunistic parasite operated inside him, urging him to fashion the world around him to suit its predatory ambitions and insatiable desires.'

Black laughed out loud. 'You're hustling me, aren't you? My mind is not mine? That's crazy.'

Green shook his head gravely. 'I know it's difficult to accept: they attach themselves deep inside the reptilian part of the brain of every newborn as it struggles to take its first breath. It insinuates itself into the dominant position and simulates the real mind. All day long it keeps up an endless dialog, incessantly moving your thoughts from one thing to another.'

'Not in mine it doesn't.'

Green smiled. 'Wonder what's on the National Geographic today? Feeding time, Black. Wish the pigeons would come back. My, what cute chicks! Devious eyes, his. Mmmm... She's nice... There is no escape from its constantly judging, easily offended, self-centered chatter. The best for me; the rest for everybody else. Because the voice is so intensely personal and so familiar that you don't realize it's not yours.'

Black's face mirrored his disbelief. 'No,' he maintained. 'I have full control of my thoughts. I choose what to think.'

'Really? Here's an experiment for you: silence the voice in your head. Keep your mind totally blank. If your mind really belongs to you alone then inner silence should be easy.'

'I am certain I could do that.'

'I think you will find that the parasite's chatter is relentless and quite literally unstoppable for the ordinary human.'

Black was shaking his head when Green's eyes suddenly glowed very bright. 'You don't want to believe me, but you have, as a young child, glimpsed the parasite once or twice in your own bedroom, haven't you? Those frightening dark shadows that you decided you didn't see?'

And Black remembered what he had forced himself to forget. The first time that winter evening when he was not yet five, and again a few weeks later. From the corner of his eyes he had seen fleeting black shadows that looked like big, black oil slicks, but they could fly. They had touched him, a feeling like a cold breeze. He had felt their intense malevolence and been very frightened of them. But they had been quite clearly extraneous to him.

'In fact, the parasite's talking to you now, isn't it? It is surely saying that I am talking nonsense. That it couldn't possibly be true. I must have a nefarious agenda of my own.'

Black was so confused, he just wanted Green to stop. He could just about accept all the other things Green had said—but this? This was too much.

'When you have accepted the monstrous thought that the human mind is the horde's conduit into the physical realm you will begin to understand that every form of suffering on this plane is pre-programmed to steal emotional energy. It is why all the mechanisms that produce, promote, and increase fear, pain, sexual deviance, compulsiveness, violence, hate, guilt, and suffering are ever increasing—they are having a grand feast.'

'Why do they need the red sludge so badly?'

'Because they feed on it. To know what their greatest addiction is you only have to turn on the TV and you will instantly be aware of what emotions are being propagated. They have set the stage for a deeply corrupt and destructive society. The human life has become a banal search for money and sex.'

'I disagree,' Black argued, 'Every day we are progressing. We have better medicines, better education, better architecture; we can circle the world in hours; we have the Internet, which connects us all and gives us immediate access to people and news around the world; and our technological advances are such that we have even landed on Mars.'

Green smiled. 'Is that what your TV has been telling you? All these things you mention man could once do without any machines or gadgets. Now he has to look outside himself, to technology, for them. Do you know *you* were once the Internet? You had your own GPS system and could, at will, travel to any part of the universe—never mind Mars.

'Medicines. You don't have better medicines; you have the illusion of better medicines. Most of your cures are only suppressors of symptoms. Architecture. Your best technology is still unable to recreate the stone-cutting of the pyramids.'

Green shook his head. 'I'm afraid that there is not one genuine step of amelioration of life on this planet.'

'But how is it, then, that no seer or advanced soul from any age has warned us about this parasite race that you claim has controlled and ruled this planet since time immemorial?'

'If a seer truly understood that each and every human being is infected, then he would not be speaking to human beings but to the predator. Do you remember when Jesus said to Judas, "Step away from the others and I shall tell you the mysteries of the Kingdom. It is possible for you to reach it, but it will grieve you a great deal?"'

'Are we totally doomed, then?'

'No. Despite the fact that the entire species has been deliberately bred into psychotic consciousness and trapped inside their own fearful, infested minds they are not technologically animated flesh. At any time they can tap into the vast energies coursing through their bodies at every moment and become gods as is their natural destiny.

'Now with the cosmic retooling the filaments in your double helix are already beginning to evolve and stretch out for their lost encodings. Unimaginable characteristics and super abilities are awaiting the human race.

Black said nothing. He needed time to think.

'Soon you will have to leave; but would you like to swim first?'

Silently Black stood and walked into the water. He felt the cool breeze against his sun-warmed body. The warm water reached his chest quickly. A wave washed into his face making him splutter. He turned back to tell Green that he didn't know how to swim, then he realized. It was like in *The Matrix*. It was not real air he was breathing. Here he knew how to swim. He plunged into the waves and let his arms cleave the water powerfully. With his mind blank he swam out into the open sea. By the time he looked back Green was a tiny green light, and still he swam. Farther and farther away. Until he was suddenly back in his frozen body, brought back by an unfamiliar thud under his window.

A fronte praecipitium, a tergo lupi

(A precipice in front, wolves behind)

Veera laid the ladder he had borrowed from his landlady against the front wall of Bumi's house, and glanced around tensely. Quiet for the moment. If any local busybodies asked, he would say he was being a good neighbor, helping the widow nail back that loose bit of her windowpane. He unhooked his duffle bag from his shoulder and threw it on the ground. Squatting over it, he took out a hammer and looked up. It seemed a long way up. He was apprehensive of heights. His armpits were already dripping with sweat. He stood, determined to climb. Wiping his hands down his trouser front, he placed his hands firmly on the ladder and put a nervous foot on the first rung. It seemed solid enough. Carefully he put his other foot on the second rung. He looked up. The window with the blue light was not too far away, he told himself, and as it turned out he reached it surprisingly fast. He peeped in.

A black boy was lying awake watching television.

He shrank back immediately. His first thought—the little slut. She had secretly taken a black lover, but then it hit him like a bolt. Veera, my boy—you've hit the jackpot with this one. That boy's not hers. She's stolen him and is keeping him a prisoner. Not that it bothered him any. In fact, he liked that. Goodness bored him. The hammer slipped from his sweaty hands and fell into the bushes. He looked through the window again, but the boy must not have heard for he did not move at all. Veera executed his descent with great care and a racing heart.

He returned the ladder and went to sit on the tiled steps of her front door. He lit a cigarette, and tilting his head back, blew the smoke out in wisps. He had tried for ages, but had never managed to blow a smoke ring. It was cold, but he felt as if he was on fire. All his fantasies... She would soon be back.

When he heard her footsteps, he threw his fifth cigarette into the bushes and stood slowly. She came to an abrupt standstill when she saw him. He could smell the fear in her. He smiled. It wasn't a good smile. She stood very still. No return smile.

'What do you want?'

He lit a cigarette and after taking a slow drag blew a perfect smoke ring. He watched it in wonder—well, well, what do you know? His mouth curved into a slow, smug smile. 'Hello, Bumi.'

'I said what do you want?'

He tut-tutted mockingly. 'Didn't your mother teach you any manners?'

'Get out of my way or I'll call the police,' she said, through gritted teeth.

He opened his eyes, which were already large and bulging, to frog-like proportions. 'Police? OK, OK,' he said, his arms raised as if in surrender, as if her threat had frightened him, and moved sideways to allow her to pass. She passed and he sniffed the air like an animal. She wore no perfume other than fear. He waited for her to find her key. When she had the key in the lock he asked, 'But won't the police be wanting to know about the boy?'

She had dreaded and feared this day from the moment she had decided to keep the boy, yet she felt as unprepared for it as if it was the first time the thought that it might happen had occurred to her. She turned around slowly. 'What boy?'

'The one upstairs,' he said, jerking his head in the direction of Black's bedroom window.

Her eyes never left the man. 'That boy is my sister's illegitimate child. He is an invalid and I am taking care of him for her.'

But he had smelled the panic. 'Fine. In that case you won't mind if I call the police and tell them that I suspect you are keeping a boy prisoner. And you see if you can convince them with your cock and bull story.'

'What do you want?'

'You... Tonight.'

She licked her dry lips and saw his eyes go to them. 'I can't tonight.' She forced a smile. She was a bad actress. 'It's that time of the month.'

You little liar, he thought. 'That don't bother me none.'

'It would bother me. Give me a week.'

'You have three days and then I am coming for you,' he said, enjoying the sense of power he felt over her.

She scowled. 'No, no, we can't do it in my house—the boy.'

'No problem. I'll come here and take you to mine. The other men work as waiters and are all back late... So we will be undisturbed.'

She nodded. He leered at her, and leaning forward suddenly, kissed her on the mouth. He needed a wash badly. She felt the sickness rise from deep within. 'See you Thursday,' he threw over his shoulder as he sauntered away.

She turned the key and closed the door, leaning

against it for a few moments. Her knees felt like water. She could not lose the boy this way. Not like this. She wiped her mouth with the back of her shaking hand, and pressed her palm against her mouth to stop the sob that had started in her throat. If her mother knew! She was so far fallen there was no way back.

She looked at her feet. They seemed small; she had always had small feet. He would use her horribly. She knew that. She would be the toilet into which he would flush all his diseased thoughts and urges, but never mind, let it be so. She was not important. There was nothing she would not do for the boy. Nothing. She straightened away from the door. Her hands were still shaking, but her feet were moving quickly up the stairs.

Hurrying toward her boy. So many new improvements had come to visit him. He was changing right before her eyes. This morning she had stroked his face, and the shocked expression in his eyes told her that he had felt something. Some sensations were returning to his face. Perhaps by the grace of God he would be cured, and he would live, after all.

We are the origin of all coming evil.

—Carl Jung, BBC interview (1959)

Across the ocean Shekina opened her eyes from her reconnaissance trip and announced triumphantly, 'I found the rotted fruit.' But in that unguarded moment when she had looked directly into Teddy's eyes, she had registered the unmistakable impression—he wants to have sex with me. She looked away hastily, but he bent over her and warned furiously, 'Don't ever look into my eyes again.'

She nodded obediently and looked down, though not before he caught the beginning of that self-righteous little smile of hers.

Teddy sat angrily across from her. He didn't like this alter. She was too confident. Too bold. She made him uncomfortable. But forget about that now, he told himself. Think, Teddy, think. This is big. The girl was looking straight ahead. Not moving, not speaking. Studiously avoiding his face. He stood up impatiently, and walked around the room. 'Tell me everything you saw, felt, and heard.'

'A man. He has dark thoughts about the target... Who is...' She paused, surprised by the new precept. 'A boy. Yes, I think the target is probably a teenager. Something strange about him, though. He seems very still, too still, but possesses an intense, hidden, warrior-like power—either suppressed or unused because he doesn't know he has it.'

'Is he American?'

'I don't think so.'

'Where is he?'

'Somewhere cold and wet. There seems to be a colorful main street nearby; it could be a street in India, but it's not. There are many brown people living around him.'

'Anything else?'

She shook her head, but stopped when it hurt to do so.

'Fine, you can try again tomorrow.'

Quickly, he brought Dakota to the fore and summoned Miss Monroe. While waiting he paced the room. Although Dakota did not react to his pacing, it made her feel queasy and she longed for her dim bedroom and bed.

It was a relief when Miss Monroe knocked lightly on the door and entered. As usual Dakota was wheeled into her living quarters and gently helped into bed. When the sedative had been administered and the lights turned down, she was left alone. And that was why it was such a surprise when she awoke suddenly after a few hours.

Like most multiple personality disorder (MPD) sufferers she slept with her eyes open so she knew that if she lay very still and kept up her even breathing, the surveillance camera would not notice that she was awake. She had dreamed of the brown woman again. The woman had come to her with her hands clasped one on top of the other as if in them she cupped a butterfly. When she had opened her grasp Dakota had seen that it was not a butterfly, but a handful of brightly colored beads.

'You must take care of them,' she had urged, holding her other hand out to Dakota. When Dakota made no move to take the beads the woman had begun to cry softly.

'Please,' she had begged. 'I have no one else to turn to.'

In her dream Dakota had silently opened her palm and the woman had poured the beads like a waterfall of color into it.

When she had raised her head from the gorgeous waterfall, she had realized they had been standing at the edge of a cliff and the woman was falling off into a dark chasm.

'Who are you?' she had called after her, but she was gone, fallen away without a single sound.

Dakota turned on her side and faced the wall. She wondered who the woman was and why she kept trying to contact her. If there was one thing she knew for sure, it was that she must never again tell anybody else about her. She was a secret.

Without women, men are only a cruel joke

—James Clavell, *King Rat* (1962)

When Black heard the slow rhythmic breathing that signified his mother was asleep, he let his eyes blur on the ceiling and tried to still his mind. He intended to prove Green wrong. There was no alien mind hidden deep within his. But stilling his mind, he was shocked and horrified to discover, was turning out to be quite impossible. Every time he pulled his attention to the imaginary black screen he had created, it strayed away just as quickly, as if with a mind of its own. A hundred different matters intruded: Green, his mother, a program he had watched earlier, a sound on the street below, a stray melody, a trivial worry, a snippet of conversation he had heard, and on and on. He looked at the clock—an hour had passed.

The inane dialog could not be stopped.

But he would not give up. He simply refused to believe his mind was not his and his alone. He would do it if it took him all night. He reasoned that he was merely unused to the strict discipline of guarding his thoughts. Thirty minutes later he realized that he still could not stop the incessant chatter. Frustrated by his inability, but unwilling to give up, he tried again.

This time, he thought, with more success until an image of a girl in a candy-striped bikini intruded, and when he pushed that away impatiently, he heard a sawn-off nursery rhyme in his head—it reminded him of the floating, forlorn voice of Hal, the supercomputer, in that poignant final scene from Stanley Kubrick's *2001*:

A Space Odyssey. When the memory chips that had controlled Hal's artificial brain had been disconnected and it had gone out singing, 'Daisy, Daisy, give me your answer do, I'm half crazy all for the love of you…'

The disjointed, alien nature of the voice in his own head chilled him. He tried to think of another logical explanation why there might be a sourceless voice in his head, but could think of none. As he grappled with the horrendous realization that his mind too, like every other human's on the planet, might be hacked, Green appeared.

'I can't control my own mind, Green,' he confessed.

'Yes, I'm afraid it is part of being human.'

'I don't want to be controlled by a mind parasite. There must be a way to get rid of it.'

'There is, and I will show you how, but the parasite has organized and managed your thoughts for so long that expelling it will leave you with the naked and defenseless newborn that is your mind. It will not be able to cope with what is coming. Let the parasite remain for now. There will be time for its removal later. For now, come with me. We will go to a little bar in Rome. It's rather fun there. People who have partied all night at the Rancho Grande nightclub stop to buy cigarettes, and ease their aching feet in the cool fountains.'

Black Jack looked at the clock; it was 3.30 a.m. A nocturnal escapade. He would like that very much indeed. The predator parasite had just bought itself some more time. He reached out for Green's outstretched hand and his stripped pajamas became a black tuxedo. He looked at his bare feet. Immediately they were shod in a pair of highly polished leather shoes.

They looked very expensive.

'Italian,' said Green.

Black grinned and shot his cuffs the way he had seen James Bond do.

'Very suave,' commented Green. Then they were transported into a network of cobbled alleys. There was something European, but very familiar about the high walls that rose on either side of them. The clothes and hairstyles worn by the men and women who passed them were all from a different era. A time when no one wore jeans. The men were in suits and the women were very elegantly dressed, a few wrapped up in fur coats.

'Where in time are we?'

Green smiled. 'Guess.'

'OK, but give me a clue.'

'We will watch them have their gin and tonic, or...' Green's eyes twinkled. 'We might go in search of a glass of milk.'

In the distance Black heard the sound of a waterfall. *A glass of milk.* For a moment he frowned then his eyes lit up. Of course, for the white kitten. That's why everything had looked sort of familiar. '*La Dolce Vita*,' he cried excitedly. He had watched Federico Fellini's masterpiece late one night on World Cinema, and been enamored by its depiction of a dream world, glittering with beauty and hedonistic pleasure.

They turned a corner and the past burst upon them in an orgy of color, lights, and activity. Fellini was shooting the famous waterfall scene at the Fontana de Trevi. The entire square was filled with curious onlookers and crew. Fellini himself was huddled on his high director's chair, in a hat, a thick, woolen scarf, and his overcoat. In his pudgy hands he loosely clasped an old-fashioned loudspeaker cone.

Like every other man in that square on that wintry January night, Black was drawn to the water where Anita Ekberg, framed by the lights, stood bare-legged and bare-shouldered. The breathtaking goddess of improbable voluptuousness was waiting for her cue to begin cavorting in the fountain. At the edges of the scene a grumbling, fussing Marcello Mastroianni was struggling into a wetsuit of some kind. Black laughed. Funny. All that time he had imagined him to be the epitome of cool.

'Go ahead,' said Green, and Black went forward into the water and stood next to the goddess. She was about his height. Up close she was flawless. There were no more women like her. Beneath the smell of powder and perfume he caught the unexpected reek of alcohol on her breath.

'Cognac,' explained Green. 'To keep warm.'

Cheekily Black reached up and kissed her cheek. She raised a languid hand and brushed her skin as if an insect had landed on it. He turned to Green and grinned. He had never done anything so audacious in his life and he loved it. Strange. Strange, to be actually part of the scenery. All his life the world had paraded in front of him on his TV screen, and him sick with wanting to join in. He got out of the water and his eyes were drawn to a group of youths. They were his age, and despite the bitter cold, they were eating ice cream. Vaguely he remembered the taste of the ice lolly his mother had briefly slipped into his mouth one hot summer day, and conspiratorially whispered, 'Ice cream. It's lovely, isn't it?'

He stared longingly at the carefree gestures and

movements their lithe, adolescent bodies made. Two held hands, lovers obviously. He watched them pensively. Mesmerized by them, he even forgot about the Archons and their dark manipulations of humanity. 'You know how you let me taste the watermelon in the desert. Do you think you could let me feel what it would be like to kiss a girl?'

'Of course, but find a girl you want to kiss first.'

'That won't be too hard.'

Green chuckled and Black pulled his gaze away from the shy lovers. He spotted a blonde girl in the crowd. Her hair was worn in a long, thick plait down her back. She was hurrying away from the crowd. As he watched, a dark alleyway swallowed her. He knew the back of that head!

'Wait one minute,' he called to Green, and ran after her. He saw her pull open a tall, wooden door and slip into its dim interior. He passed through the door. On the other side was a foyer with a lift. She was waiting for the lift with her back to him.

He was walking toward her when Green said from behind him, 'You are only walking through the pages written long ago. This girl lives and will live in the top floor apartment of this building all her life. She died a grandmother three years ago. The girl you are looking for is not here. You will not have to look for her. She has very nearly found you.'

Black turned around. 'Tell me again about that girl. Who is she? What is her name?'

'She is a bright shaman, who has been irretrievably corrupted. Her name will depend on which personality you meet first.'

'What do you mean which personality?'

'She suffered horrific abuse for many months when she was a child, until her tender mind found an escape by splitting off into different parts, of which she has no knowledge. There are numerous people, animals, and creatures inside her.'

'Are you serious?'

'I never joke about such matters.'

'But that's sickening. I had no idea such ghastly things happened, or could even be done. Why did they do that to her?'

'Fear and pain are a good way to introduce knowledge, even higher knowledge. And, of course, to direct her different alters without her knowledge.'

'Do they still treat her badly?'

'She is kept drugged at all times.'

'Wow. Poor kid.'

'Yes, she suffered the unthinkable, but she is not the only one. There are many like her serving the dark ones.'

'Why do they want her to meet me?'

'Like Joan of Arc or Hitler, certain people, places, times, and events have greater impact on the future than others, and that attracts the interest of time travelers from the affected futures who seek to influence the outcome of their timelines. The dark hierarchy know that you are the trigger that could inspire and alter the frequency of the human race and bring back the lost light. It is their intention to either limit your impact or subvert it to their cause. The girl is part of the taint. It will be a big story. You will make headlines across the world.'

'I will?'

'You will,' he confirmed mysteriously.

'Is there no way for me to avoid meeting her?'

'Certain things may not be changed—they are contracts and challenges that you agreed to undertake before you took on this lifetime—but all you have to do when you come face to face with her is to turn your back on her. That is your free-will choice, which she cannot violate. The moment you do that she will become powerless, and be unable to contact you again. But if you don't she will establish a connection that can never be broken.'

'Are you sure there is no catch? What can be easier than simply turning away from her the moment we meet?'

'Well, we will see how successful you are. Your involvement, after all, has been very carefully planned by many. Like I said before, even those which you might think are accidents of fate are not: your abandonment, the woman who found you, the fact that your body rejects animal products which forces you to be a vegetarian.'

'How does me being vegetarian make me suitable?'

'The greatest law of the physical universe is the law of causality. Even gravity may easily be bent and manipulated, but never the law of cause and effect. If you had attempted to battle the dark ones carrying this burden of having extinguished life for enjoyment or survival they would have used it against you. You have to enter pure, with no past actions to reap. Likewise, your skin color is no accident.'

'What's so special about being black, the most persecuted race in the world?'

'You are not black. You are melanin. Melanin is a dark pigment that absorbs and conducts light. Its granules clustered around nuclear DNA act as a Faraday cage that conducts electric fields away from the nucleus, which then acts as a natural barrier to any alien procedures that utilize light and high electromagnetic fields to "tinker" with humanity. It is the reason why most abductees are white. No time travelers may tamper with you.' Green paused. 'For that matter even the impulse that makes *The Matrix* your favorite movie is not by chance.'

'Why?'

'Remember the final fight scene after Neo gets shot by the Agents, and they walk away in the corridor?'

'Of course.'

'He gets up. They turn around, reload, and he speaks just one word, the word of power. He simply says—'

'No.'

'Exactly,' approved Green. 'Everybody is Neo and that moment captures what each and every human should do. That level of courage, willpower and personal responsibility is all that is necessary to change this world. Bullets that stop mid-air and superhuman feats are possible after that. Humans don't have to occupy Wall Street or protest against global warming or picket large corporations. All they have to do is stop doing what they are already doing to fuel the beast. Say no to all that is wrong—that extricates them from this prison. When your time comes, remember that word.' Green stopped suddenly. 'Ah, it would appear that the girl was a meticulous calculation. She has already found you.'

'What, here? How?'

But it was already too late. Green was gone and the kaleidoscope around him was swirling and changing fast.

**And the sons of God looked upon the
daughters of men and found them fair.**
—Genesis 6:2

Black found himself standing in a bright, white room
with no walls, the space simply stretching farther than
the eye could see. There was no source of light that he
could discern either. The girl stood facing him, no more
than his age. Her narrow shoulders were squared with
some inner courage, but she was so thin and bone white,
she looked breakable. Her eyes were deep blue, and
fringed by stubby eyelashes that were the softest brown,
perhaps even caramel. And her long, fair hair had been
neatly trained into a thick plait that curved down the
side of her neck and over the front of her body. She
wore a pink top with a large sequined butterfly on it, tan
slacks and white trainers.

A minute before he would have thought it
impossible, but he was aroused by this waif. Something
about her. Her doll-like perfection exuded a sexual
energy that he found irresistible. Though it pained him
to do so, he began to turn away from what he did not
understand, but recognized as the truth—a strong desire
to remain with her.

'Stay. Please don't run away. I won't hurt you. I've
been looking for you and your friend for such a long
time.' Her accent was softly American.

A voice inside his head whispered, A tiny thing like
that. What danger could she be? The temptation to look
at that seductively red mouth again was incredible, but
he didn't turn back. 'Why have you been looking for

me?'

'I don't know why. I might have been told. There are people looking for you.'

'Who?'

She walked up to him hesitantly. He could feel her energy: warm waves. Friendly. Harmless. He closed his eyes and felt himself powerfully and inexplicably drawn to her. The temptation to turn was so strong he had to force himself to fight it. Those blue, blue eyes. Like the ocean. Unfathomable depths. Calling him. He clenched his fists.

'Just people. I think they expect me to lead them to you, and you to lead them to your friend.'

'How did you find me?'

'I followed you.'

'Do they know where you are now?'

'No. They'd like to, but they can't follow me here.'

'You won't tell them, will you?'

'Of course not. They're not very nice.' He heard her take another step toward him. 'I think they want you dead.'

'Why?'

Without turning around he could feel her frown. 'I don't know. They never tell me. But it is something to do with light.'

'Light?'

'The kind you can't see. Human light. When there is too much light, it is harder for them to carry on with their plans.'

He felt a tickling sensation at the back of his neck. He knew he should leave, but he could not bring himself to break the connection. Not yet. A few minutes more. What harm?

'You know I can't help myself. You're like a magnet pulling me to you.'

He turned around then. She was exactly a head shorter than him and her eyes were bluer than he remembered, and so very close that he could see the intricate patterns inside her irises. She bit her lip and blinked. They were connected at some level he did not understand. He could not turn away from her. He knew that now. He dropped his eyes. To his horror they fell on her chest. He jerked them away hastily. 'What's your name?'

'Winter.'

'Just Winter?'

'Mmmm,' she said, nodding. 'What's yours?'

'Black Jack.'

She laughed. 'For real?'

She had small, even teeth. When she laughed she was unbelievably beautiful. In spite of himself, Black smiled. Shy. His stomach in knots. Wanting her.

'Why are you dressed up?'

Black shot his French cuffs, not like James Bond this time, but self-consciously. 'I was on a movie set with my friend.'

'And what's your friend's name?'

'He doesn't have a name humans can understand, but I call him Green.'

'Do you think I could meet him too?'

'I don't see why not. He said all you need to see him is to purify your heart.'

She said a strange thing then. 'But I have no heart. It was taken away a long time ago by a wizard, and put into a jar.'

'I don't believe it. No one can live without a heart.'

'But I saw him do it with my own eyes.'

'It must have been a trick.'

The girl looked perplexed. 'If I did have a heart, how would I purify it?'

'I don't know; I'll ask Green for you.'

'Yes, I should like you to. Where is he now?'

'I don't know where he goes when he is not with me. Where do you live?'

'In America mostly.'

'Mostly?'

'Well, I kind of come and go. Everybody does, don't they? Don't you?'

'Not me. I'm stuck in one place all the time.'

'Where are you?'

'Perhaps I shouldn't say.'

'I won't tell them.'

'What if they torture it out of you?'

She looked genuinely surprised. 'What a strange thing to say! Nobody will hurt me while Daddy is around.'

Black was pleased to know that this alter at least had never been tortured. 'Where in America are you?'

'In a building called the Black Hole.'

'Will I be able to come and visit you there?'

'No, it's not a nice place. Every day people are given drugs and put to work.'

'Don't you go to school, then?'

'No.'

'What kind of work do you do?'

'Things… For Daddy.'

'Have you never been to school?'

'No.'

'Don't you want to?'

'I'm not allowed to want things.'

Black looked around the odd place they were in. 'Do you know where we are?'

'I think it is some kind of construct built by Green to protect your real whereabouts.'

'How is it you can travel anywhere you want?'

'Anyone can, but no one is taught how to. I have to go now, though. Can we meet here again?'

He paused. A silly pause. As if it was possible to turn his back on her anymore. He could no more turn his back on her than he could on Green.

'I have no other friends,' she said, her voice a forlorn cry.

Black found that he could not bear to disappoint her. 'You know how to find me.'

'I think you look really handsome in that get-up,' she said, so softly he almost didn't hear her; then she was gone.

For their beauty is bitter, and their
delight is depraved.
Their pleasure is in deception.

—Apocryphon of John BG56; 3-7

The Snow Queen was playing on Dakota's TV when the door suddenly opened and Schooner Klaus entered her living room. As she had never had a visitor in all the time she had lived in the Black Hole, she was very surprised to see him, but she stood and greeted him automatically. 'Hello, Dr. Klaus.'

He smiled. It did not reach his eyes. With his right hand he motioned for her to sit.

She obeyed immediately and with her hands clasped under her chin she looked up at him expectantly. He looked around him. She had a fleeting impression—he's wary of me. Why? Shhh... Not your place to ask.

'Nice place you have here,' he commented.

'It's not mine.'

'No, of course not,' he agreed. 'But it is customary to call a place one's own while one is occupying it.'

She tilted her head to one side, considering the idea that she should refer to the place as hers. It had never occurred to her.

'Anyway,' he was saying, 'I've brought you a little something.' He took a lollipop out of his pocket, unwrapped it, and put it into her unresisting mouth. It never crossed her mind to refuse. He stood over her and watched her suck the sweet. Soon she felt floaty. Totally compliant. Good feeling. She smiled warmly at her guest. Nevertheless, the persistent thought—no matter what, don't tell him about the brown woman and the colorful beads she has entrusted into your keeping.

Schooner Klaus leaned forward. When her head started to slip sideways he caught it in his hands and laid her back on the sofa. Then he performed the necessary codes and actions to call forth Winter.

'Daddy?'

'How are you?'

'Very good, but I've missed you very much, Daddy.'

'Of course you have. Now, be a good girl.' He patted her knee. 'And tell me about the boy.'

'The boy?'

'Yes, the boy.'

'I think he is shy and lonely. But he is also very powerful…although I cannot say why because it is only an impression and strange because he is about my age. His name is Black Jack. Which is quite funny because he's black.'

Schooner Klaus stared at her with surprise. 'Black, did you say?'

'Yes, with cornrows on his head that end in colorful beads. They are quite beautiful.'

Schooner Klaus narrowed his eyes dangerously. He had never before heard her offer an opinion on anything. It was another sign that the mind control was breaking down. He must remind her 'do not wish' alters about the grave consequences of wanting.

'Did you do your job?'

'Yes, I think he likes me.'

'Likes you?' Schooner Klaus's tone was scathing. 'Is that the best you can do?'

Tears gathered in Winter's eyes and rolled down her cheeks. She had done wrong. She had disappointed

Daddy. 'I'm sorry, Daddy. I'm so sorry.'

'Sorry? What good is that to me?' He stood up and walked away from her, his back ramrod straight with fury. When he turned back, his eyes were black ice. 'Here is what you will do. You will do whatever is necessary so that you can come back to me and report that he is head over heels in love with you. That there is nothing he will not do for you. He would stand in front of an oncoming train in your place. Do you understand what is expected of you?'

Winter sniffed and nodded miserably.

'And stop that sniveling right now,' he hissed.

'You will do everything in your power to make him fall irretrievably in love with you. First you must bring forth his protective instinct. Make him pity you. And when he has had your flesh then you will teach him to love what shames him. What he cannot find anywhere else but from you. Make him enjoy hurting you so much that he becomes an addict, unable to function without such depths of perversion. Taunt him to go further and further until one day he goes so far that you are irreparably damaged. That is the day you will have succeeded in your task. Do you remember your goddess training?'

Winter nodded. Her face was blank.

'Good. Do not fail.'

'I won't. I'll be good, Daddy. I promise.'

'All right then. Come here.' Instantly she leaped up and ran to him. She sat on his lap and, lifting her tear-stained face up to him, kissed him passionately on the mouth. He opened his mouth and let her kiss him deeply.

'Good girl,' he said, looking at her small, red mouth

coldly. There was already a swelling and a trickle of blood flowing from where he had bitten her hard on the inside of her lip.

'Pain is love,' he told her and watched approvingly when she licked the blood with her tongue. He put her away from him with firm hands, and sent Winter away. When he left, Dakota was fast asleep on the sofa.

We cannot desire that we know not.

—Voltaire, Zaire (1732)

'Hey, remember when you asked me to find a girl I'd like to kiss?'

'Yes.'

'Will it be the same sensations no matter whom I choose?'

'No, the experience will mirror exactly the reaction you would get from a real encounter with your chosen subject.'

'In that case I've found her.'

All the dancing, ever-moving fractals in Green's face disappeared suddenly. Their return was slow, the colors murky. 'Be very careful treading this path. She could be very dangerous to you.'

'I thought it was only a simulation.'

An indecipherable expression crossed Green's face. It made him look almost human. 'Passions open energies.'

'Even if they do, I can never really have her, can I?'

'Not her, no.'

Black looked surprised. 'Is there someone else that I could have?'

'Perhaps. The future is fluid and mutable. Are you ready for your experience now?'

'Yeah.'

'Is it only as far as a kiss, or do you desire to go further?'

Black's eyes smoldered. 'How far can I go?'

'As far as you like; it's a simulation.'

'Do I have to decide now?'

'No, choices can be made during the simulation. Although when you are in the simulation you will be completely unaware that you are in one, and could get carried away by the moment.'

Black thought for a minute. 'It won't harm either of us if I do, will it?'

'Not her, but maybe you.'

'I guess I'll decide during the simulation.'

Green nodded gravely. 'Have fun, Black,' he remarked, but there was no attendant wink or encouragement.

Black found himself in a walled garden on a hot summer's day. He was barefoot, shirtless and lying on a patch of grass under a tree. Winter was sitting beside him in a pair of miniscule red shorts and a white T-shirt. The grass was cool under him. Behind her he could see the house, a large, white bungalow. She smiled at him. He looked at the golden rope that snaked around her neck and hung down to her waist.

'Will you let your hair loose?'

He watched her fingers make pretty little movements to release the thick plait of spun gold. She fluffed it out and swung her head from side to side like a shampoo advert. Where the dappled sunlight caught it, it turned to yellow light. He reached out to touch it. Pure silk, it was. From there his hand gravitated to the warm, silky skin of her face. He caressed it, so new and yet so familiar and dear. He could feel the excitement coursing hot and fast through his veins. But he would not rush. Slowly, his finger slid to her mouth, lingered on her bottom lip. The softness surprised him.

'Kiss me,' he said huskily. His mouth was dry.

She leaned forward, her thin body hovering over his.

He put a hand out and tugged her down so she was lying on top of him, her narrow hip bones, as if made to order, fitting perfectly between his. Suddenly: something he had never experienced; an erection. That part of him that belonged to him, but he had never taken any notice of, took on a throbbing life of its own. Hard, heavy, insistent, and with a mind of its own. He savored the exquisite rush. Strange and yet wonderful. Never had he imagined that it could feel this good.

She brought her lips to his. Gently, a feather. Then her tongue was urging his mouth open. Warm, slippery, seductive, sure. The kiss deepened. He felt her hands entwine themselves around his neck. It felt as if she was melting into him! He could hardly tell where he ended and she began. It shocked him intensely when her little mouth greedily captured his tongue and began to suck it. His mind went blank, and he gave in to the waves of pleasure. One after the other, better and better. There was nothing, but him and her and his erection in the middle of that sunlit ocean.

He thought it would never end.

But she moved, pulling away from him, and lay on her side looking down at him. Her cheeks were flushed and her eyes, dilated and urgent. Her breath was hot against his cheek. He looked down with fascination and something akin to pride at the bulge in his jeans. Her fingers moved to cup it carefully, precious cargo that he had never suspected he carried. He watched her. How expertly she handled him. She had done this many times before.

'It's your first time, isn't it?'

He nodded, embarrassed in the wake of her experience.

'I want to show you something, but you have to come into my world for it. Will you come?'

'Yes.'

She took him by the hand into the house. Through an open door, down a corridor and into a dim bedroom with a high ceiling and many windows. Through the tall windows he gasped at the sight of the Taj Mahal.

'I won't be a minute,' she called, and disappeared somewhere into the house. There was music playing in the background, a haunting Indian melody. He walked to a tall window and stared at the building that seemed to rise majestically out of the ground. No television image he had seen had done it justice. It was an awe-inspiring sight. He guessed it looked so grand and imposing because successive governments had taken care to ensure that no other building around it would ever dwarf it.

He heard a sound and turned around. She was dressed in a skin-tight, leopard print dress and black high-heeled boots. The child-woman was wearing make-up. Her mouth was blood-red. He felt a thrill of excitement run through his body, a growing in his loins. A gentle wind lifted the white curtains.

'He put out the eyes of the architect to ensure that his great monument to his dead wife would never be copied.'

'I know. Sort of spoils the beauty, doesn't it?'

'I disagree. I think it's the most beautiful part of the story. No sense of fake decency or morals stood in the way of his grand obsession. And he was right. There should only ever be one. For whom nothing is taboo and everything is sacred.'

Surprised, he looked into her eyes, made startlingly

beautiful by the paint she had applied.

'I long for a love that has no limits. If I told you that I belong body and soul to you, and that there is nothing you can't do to me, even hurt me, what would you say?'

Black looked shocked. 'I don't want to hurt you.'

'Maybe I want you to. Maybe I want to prove to you that you own me. And the only way to do that is for you to hurt me. If I cry out stop, then I don't really belong to you, do I?'

'That's just plain crazy. I don't need that kind of sick proof. Besides I'd never hurt you.'

'Let's see if you can resist, then,' she challenged.

And she began to strip. Not enough breast and possibly too thin by his reckoning, but he could not take his eyes off her. She was mesmerizing in a way he could not understand. When there was not a stitch left on her she walked to him and led him to the bed. Her eyes were hot and wild. She lay on the bed and slowly opened her legs, so his entranced eyes would latch upon her exposed sex, juicy and glistening. Then she rolled to her front and rose to her elbows and knees. Turning her head to him she whispered fiercely, 'Fuck me. Fuck me hard. I like it to hurt.'

When he pulled his eyes to hers he saw that they were changed beyond all recognition. It was as if she was under some sort of demonic possession. From those incredible eyes evil thoughts and instructions were flowing into him, summoning dark forces of sexual desire buried deep inside him. He felt almost electrocuted by the intensity and vibrancy of her call. Instinctively, he knew that her occult lust would create an irresistible thirst that would urge him to more and more depravity and perversion until it would be near impossible to stop after a while. Heart and mind he would be its slave.

He had come to her on a romantic impulse, but now his entire being had become a throbbing, clawing need to grab those snake-narrow hips and ram into her, so hard she screamed.

'Don't tease yourself with doing it, do it,' she taunted, a devilish glint in her eyes.

The voice urging him to submit to her corruption was alien and hurrying away from his sight, but finally, he saw that it was living inside him, in the vast and mostly undiscovered world that was his mind, at a depth where his consciousness had never thought to penetrate. Yet, at that moment there seemed to be nothing more important than the aching, undeniable craving in his loins and the secret pleasure of the addict; abandoning himself to the worst excesses of the parasite, just this once. Just this once he would be like everybody else; he would take.

He unzipped his jeans.

But when he put his hand on her body he was suddenly confronted by her past. He saw *all* the men who had used her. Oh, the shame of it! Grown men who should have known better, forcing themselves upon the poor innocent, her mouth, her tiny openings. Such unspeakably cruel and vile things they did. And the child confused, bound, frightened, suffering, screaming, crying, bruised, bleeding, battered, and finally, one day—liking it. Her only savior—to be a better sex slave. He saw a dirty wall scratched with the words: Winter was here.

'No,' he shouted.

And suddenly the world exploded around and all was

gone. The girl, the kiss, the erection, the mounting excitement, the depraved thoughts, the shocking images of her abuse. Black felt shaken to the core. It had all been so astonishingly authentic that he had been totally fooled into believing it was real. For the first time he appreciated how easily the human mind could be manipulated, but, more worryingly, how very nearly he had succumbed to wickedness and evil.

'Well done,' Green congratulated, his eyes dancing. 'You passed your first test.'

'I want to help her. How can I help her?' Black responded unhappily.

'She is not who you think she is.'

'I don't care. I want to help her all the same.'

Green faced him with a look of resignation. 'Of course you do. I am in the timeline where you reach out and help. Very well, let's see where this takes us. After all there are timelines in which she is victorious; perhaps we are in one of them. An ordinary therapist will kill her before they help her as she has more than one suicide alter. And all are programmed to self-destruct if it appears that the core personality is beginning to remember. The only way to help her is to find the core personality, get her to come out of hiding (difficult in itself), reclaim all the other personalities, and own all the horrors and atrocities. I must warn you the re-gathering process is a long, painful one. She will not like what she finds.'

'Her core personality is not Winter?'

'No.'

'Will you help me find her core personality?'

'I'm sorry, Black, but if I am not very careful then without understanding exactly how, for such is the power of the illusion, I will become entangled in this world, and become trapped like a bird in a cage. I cannot even fight for what is right. What you fight you become. See the trap?'

'Can you at least tell me how I can find her?'

'Use your imagination and creativity. It is the most powerful tool at every human's disposal.'

'My imagination and creativity. How?'

'You can create and destroy universes with the kind of power you have inside you.'

'That's great, but where and how do I start?'

'You already have the means in you. You just have to recognize it.'

'And if I find her, what do I do?'

'Not if, when. Give her crayons.'

'Crayons?'

'Yes, what human children use to express themselves on paper and their parents' walls.'

'Why crayons?'

'Slaves are always under hypnotic suggestions to forget what they have experienced. The brain only appears to comply, but secretly records the event. The crayons will help bring the memories back. One by one they will come pouring out onto the paper.'

'That's it?'

'That's it. The rest she will do herself. I told you before she is a very powerful shaman squeezed into a small girl's body.'

Those who danced were thought to be quite insane by those who could not hear the music.

—John Milton, *Paradise Lost* (1967)

'You'll never believe what happened to me today.'

Black gazed up at his mother expectantly. She used merry chatter as an armor, but he could see that she was secretly worried about something, something other than his impending death. Not only did he see it in her eyes when she forgot to be happy; he had heard her having nightmares. Last night she had sobbed and shouted, 'Get out, you ugly, little man.'

'I was at this new shop buying a hairdryer for Lady Carrington, and the girl at the till suddenly congratulated me. Apparently, I was their one thousandth customer and I'd won a water filter.' Bumi lifted up the bag she had brought into Black's room and showed him the water filter. 'Looks good, doesn't it? The manager, such a sweet man, explained that it filters out even fluoride, which he said is put into the water, but shouldn't be. He told me it's the main ingredient in rat poison. Imagine that! I wonder why they put it in the water system. Anyway, Lady Carrington didn't want it and she said I could keep it. So now it's ours.' She beamed.

Black looked into Bumi's eyes and formed the question, What's the matter, mother?

And the thought must have reached her—for a split second it stopped her in her tracks, but then she flashed another bogus smile, and soldiered on with her monologue.

When she left to install the water filter, Black made a mental note to ask Green what was distressing his mother. Then he returned to trying to figure out what Green could have meant when he had said, 'Use your imagination.' Meticulously he went through every conversation he had had with Green and suddenly it occurred to him.

Of course. Green had taught him how to do it in the desert. Lucid dreaming. He would find her in his dreams. With his mother gone to sleep he followed Green's instructions, and awakened in what looked like a deserted three-dimensional mural.

He had entered the internal world of the core personality.

Under a dull gray sky, a black and white checkered floor served as the base for a confusing jumble of staircases, all of which seemed to lead nowhere, either simply stopping in mid-air, going off in horizontal directions, or ending in mirrors. At a glance it was impossible to know whether one was coming or going. Something squeaked under his foot. A headless doll. He saw that the floor was strewn with broken toys, some so gruesomely mutilated that they made him feel quite uneasy.

A gust of wind blew an abandoned metal bed onto the tiled floor. It had steel manacles, and a shelf underneath that was full of dangerous-looking, blood-caked instruments. Its wheels creaked eerily. He shivered at the sight, and was nearly startled out of his skin when he heard a strange cry coming from behind him. He looked back and a screaming monkey, its long teeth bared, was running toward him. Without thinking he ran as fast as he could in the opposite direction. He slipped into an odd enclosure, which turned out to be a graveyard. He looked back to check how near the monkey was and stepped into air.

He had fallen into a freshly dug grave with an open coffin inside. And landed on a bed of writhing snakes. He was so petrified he froze. The coffin's lid closed with a loud thud and the darkness became alive with movement and sound. Snakes in search of warmth slipped and slithered onto his bare skin. From outside the coffin came first the scary sound of hammers nailing down the lid, then soil being shoveled onto it. He was being buried alive. Overcome by a primordial terror of certain death, he began to gasp for breath, until Green's voice said in his head, 'This is her world. These things happened to her. But it is only a dream. Physical laws need not apply.'

Physical laws need not apply.

Quickly, he grabbed hold of a thick snake in his hand. 'Poof,' he said and the snake disappeared. He touched the lid of the coffin. 'Poof,' he said and it disappeared. You can fly. *You can do anything*. He sprang lightly out of the six-foot hole. He looked at the gnarled dead trees around him. 'Become a meadow full of life,' he said and suddenly the empty boughs were covered with green leaves. The graves became full of tall grasses and wild flowers. He could smell the flowers and hear the lazy buzzing of the bees.

He looked to the gray sky. 'Sunshine, please,' he said, and the sun drenched his landscape golden. He built swings and benches. He changed the black and white floor to a myriad happy colors. The hospital bed became a gazebo with climbing roses. Pleased with his creation

171

he decided to look for her.

'Find her,' he said, and in the distance he saw a black, shiny cube sitting on a briar. He went to it. There was no entrance. She was a prisoner. He thought up a pathway and a door to the cube, and entered it. She was on the floor hunched over something.

'What are you doing?' he asked.

She did not look up. 'I have to watch that the sand in the hourglass does not run out. If it does I will die, and I'm afraid to die.'

Black moved closer. The hourglass was so small that it was barely a minute before she had to turn it. She couldn't take her eyes off it. If she ever did, or was accidentally distracted, it would surely run out. It was the most pitiful thing he had seen. He knelt down beside her and yet she did not dare turn her face away from the hourglass.

'Become much bigger,' he said and the hourglass grew right before their eyes. 'There, it will now be an hour before you have to turn it again.'

She fell back and looked at the enlarged hourglass suspiciously as though it was a trick of some sort. She seemed almost afraid of it. Then she turned to him with huge eyes. She looked the same as Winter, but he did not recognize her, or she him. Her eyes narrowed. She came forward slowly, her hand outstretched, and touched a bead in his hair.

'I dreamed of these.' She looked into his eyes. 'Do you know an Indian woman with long, black hair?'

'That sounds like my mother.'

'Where does she live?'

'With me in England.'

She nodded thoughtfully, her hand dropping to her

side.

'What's your name?'

'Dakota.'

'Do you live here?'

'No, I come here when the others take over.'

'I see. What is this room?'

'I don't know.' She frowned. 'But I have always been alone here. It's not a good place.' She turned her eyes away from him and back to the hourglass. 'Thanks. Turning the hourglass was very difficult work.'

'No problem. In fact I'm going to make an even bigger one and put it into a self-turning machine.' And the hourglass was immediately part of a rotating machine. 'This way you never have to worry about it again.'

Dakota stood and backed away from him. Kindness always came with a price. 'Who are you and what do you want?'

'My name is Black and I came to give you something. Now that you don't have to watch the hourglass all the time you probably could use these,' he said, and reaching into his pocket took out a handful of crayons. He held them out to her.

She reached for them, biting her lip uncertainly. 'I have no paper.'

He reached into his back pocket and fished out a large art pad. He gave it to her. She took it with both hands.

'Well, I have to go now, but before I go I want to show you something. Come,' he invited, his hand outstretched.

She shrank back in fear. 'I can't go outside. It's too horrible.'

'I've changed it,' he said. 'Please, just peep out of the door.'

He led her to the door and stood aside so she could see the flowers, the balloons, the ice cream cart and the sunshine that he had dreamed into existence.

For a while she said nothing. 'You did all this?'

He nodded.

'What about the graveyard?'

'Gone.'

'And the boy ghost?'

And suddenly Black knew. The graves were the people she had had a hand in killing.

'He's gone too.'

She nodded slowly.

'What about the monkey?'

Black put his fingers in his mouth and whistled. It was loud and clear, the way he had always dreamed of doing. And the monkey came running, but it had a bow around its neck and looked tame.

'I have to go now, but I will come back to visit you soon.'

'Please do. I get so lonely here.'

'I promise to. Be sure to use the crayons now.'

'Thank you, Black.'

'My pleasure,' he replied. He waved to her and walked down the colorful checkered floor. A song in his heart.

'I want to go to Green,' he said, and just like that he was back in the white room without walls.

'Very impressive,' Green complimented. 'I knew you could do it, but never so proficiently. It becomes more and more obvious why you were chosen above all others.'

'What is the significance of the hourglass?'

'Her thinking is buried in fairy tales. She has been programmed to see herself inside them. Even her handlers will pretend they are fairy tale characters. She has been led to believe that if she is good and obedient the sand will not all fall out. If at all she is disobedient, the sand begins running out, and her life is on the line. There is no room for mistakes. If she is careless death will come.'

'She seems very pitiful.'

Green eyed him thoughtfully. 'That is not all you feel about her. You have to be very cautious with her. She has many angry and cold-blooded alters who have killed before and will again. Her alters do not have a chance to understand what they are doing and she does not have any control over them. Any moment, another hostile aspect, and they are mostly that, can take over. Some of her alters have been victimized so much that given half the chance they will immediately take on the addictive power of victimizing someone else.'

'One last thing: what's worrying my mother?'

'I'm sorry, Black. Telling you would be infringing upon her free will. She doesn't want you to know.'

> Hold out baits to entice the enemy.
> Feign disorder, and crush him.

—Sun Tzu, *The Art of War*,
6th century BC

Sitting across from the girl, Teddy realized that something was amiss. 'Were the coordinates for the boy's address correct?' he asked, his eyes watchful.

'Yes,' she answered, her expression bland.

'He was there?'

'Yes.'

'And you saw him in his physical form?'

'I did.'

Teddy frowned. The brief, barely informative replies were out of character. Just then, he knew. It was not Winter who sat across from him, but Shekina. Shekina had disobeyed her orders. He had never come across such a situation. Looking intently into her bold face, he said, 'Shekina?'

'It is I.'

'Your instructions were very clear—only Winter was to interact with the boy. Why did you not leave and let her handle him?'

'I kept the body when I realized that the boy is totally paralyzed. He is unable to even blink! There was nothing Winter could have done with him.'

Teddy couldn't hide his surprise. 'Totally paralyzed?' That was a game changer. Still she had disobeyed—and that was a ruinous game changer too. 'I suppose you did the right thing. I will see you tomorrow as usual.'

'Teddy.'

'What?' he asked, never suspecting what she would

do next.

She smiled at him, coldly, deliberately, and did the unthinkable. She looked into his eyes and remote viewed him, her controller, her handler. She felt the malice in him and smiled that cold smile. His eyebrows shot up.

'Return to sender,' she said, and heard his howls of rage in her head.

'Bitch,' he cried, his voice shocked, strangled, strange. No longer the cool, cold, military man. The mental intrusion was intolerable. He had been designed to retaliate, he wanted to reach for the gun on his person, but he could not.

She looked at him from under her lashes. It was a gesture that did not sit well with her innocent child's face. 'I take full responsibility for myself,' she said, and curiously watched a vein in his forehead bulge. He appeared to be fighting for control of himself.

He stood, in great pain. Cold sweat was pouring off him. As he lurched from the room he saw her calmly depress the button that summoned Miss Monroe and reach for a pen. Unable to bear the horror in his brain any longer he clutched his head and hurried down the corridor, which seemed to stretch for miles. He glanced back every few pain-filled steps, the feeling of being pursued was so strong. What had she done to him? He rushed into his office and fell into the chair behind his desk. From a drawer he pulled out a syringe and pushed it into his vein. Then he lay back in his chair with closed eyes and waited.

When the black menace had passed he picked up his phone. Strangely he felt no animosity toward her. She had proven herself able to elevate the information up the channels to a higher level of responsibility than him. But at his level of responsibility he had to let Owl know. A threat. Beyond anything he had known before. His hand was shaking as his fingers moved over the telephone keypad.

'Yes,' answered Schooner Klaus.

'There is a problem. The Sparrow has turned.'

'Has she been returned to her cage?'

'I think so. I haven't contacted Miss Monroe yet. Shall I?'

The silence on the other side stretched. 'Don't do anything. I'll handle it from here. Just send me the latest video of your session with her.'

'Of course. One more thing—'

But the phone was already dead in Teddy's hand. 'The boy is paralyzed,' Teddy finished slowly. He put his hand to his forehead. He knew the drugs he had taken would not keep down the nightmares that night. He felt oddly frightened.

Miss Monroe wheeled the girl into her quarters. She helped her into her pajamas then into her bed. The girl turned to lie on her side and face the wall. Miss Monroe pulled the girl's pajama trousers down to administer her sedative and was surprised to see writing on the girl's flesh. As if in a trance, unable to stop herself, she went closer to read the ink.

You too are a slave.

She jerked back in shock and began to back away, but the girl turned over and looked directly into her eyes. She froze, unable to do anything but stare helplessly into the girl's eyes, her mind blank. Then she calmly recapped the syringe and put it back into her pocket. She nodded at the girl as if the girl had given her instructions, and left the girl's quarters silently. She walked down the corridor calmly—nobody could have suspected anything out of the ordinary—but once in her quarters she dashed to her desk and sat at it holding her head. It hurt.

She opened a drawer, extracted a piece of paper, and from another found some pens of different colors and began scratching them on the paper. She drew so fast it was as if she was possessed, as if the images were all trapped inside her and clawing to come out. When the paper was full she extracted another, and another, until there were no more. Then she began to grab at anything in her reach. Quickly, the memories are bleeding.

When there were no more surfaces to color she began to scratch the table. When the table was covered she rose and walked to the walls. Her arms ached. The pens were empty, but she couldn't stop scratching. A pen rolled under her foot and she slipped and lay sprawled on the floor. She pulled herself up and sat on top of her drawings. She lifted one from underneath her and studied it curiously. Then another. All different and yet all similar.

Dark pictures of a little girl being hurt by adults. Look at that child. Poor thing. Howling for help; and that wisp of smoke coming out her body, that's her leaving when the horror and the agony became impossible to bear. But who is that ageless adult male who consumes human blood, the keeper who holds all the knowledge? Were those slit pupils real, or contact lenses meant to terrify a child?

All her parts were still pulsing and trying to get out, and she must let them out soon or they will tear their way out. She stood tiredly and went to the mirror. For most of her life she had felt held by a sort of black cloud. She had no life, a lot of missing time, and she couldn't figure out her emotions. She couldn't figure out anything. Now she knew why the butterflies were all around her. She touched the face in the mirror. Who was that poor, disheveled creature?

'Don't cry,' she consoled. 'Please don't cry, Alice.'

She screamed in a shrill voice [...] but nobody, not one of the immortals, not one of mortal men, heard her voice.

——The Homeric Hymns, 'To Demeter'

Bumi opened her front door and came to an abrupt halt. A strange man was sitting at her small dining table calmly pouring himself a cup of tea. She frowned at the key in the palm of her hand—the door had been locked—and looked up slowly at the man. He was watching her with eyes devoid of any emotion but disconnected neutrality—a scientist who mutilates a thousand animals in the search of a better face cream. The room seemed oddly still. He was oddly still, but there was the instant and unwavering sense of something predatory about his cold stare, as though he was homing in on prey. Even the extraordinary impression that he was not human! Her first thought was to flee as quickly as possible. But what of Black? The thought was like an electric bolt. It made her start. It made her bold. She took a step toward her fear.

'Who are you? What are you doing in my home?' she demanded.

He put the teapot down. 'More to the point what are you doing in this country?' His voice was strange. Indescribable.

An immigration officer. So many years had passed that she had begun to relax. She had never really imagined finding one of them in her house. Perhaps in a sweep in one of those dodgy Indian restaurants or

183

Laundromats, but never in this small space she called home. She took an involuntary step back. 'Oh.'

'Oh,' he mimicked.

She looked toward the boy's room. The door hung open—the bed was empty. She felt the odd sight drop into the pit of her belly. A stone it was.

'Where is my son? What have you done with him?'

The man indicated the chair opposite him. 'Join me,' he invited and began to pour tea into a second cup that he must have put out earlier for her. His nails were clean and beautifully manicured. A silver watch glinted at the edge of his immaculate white sleeve. He gazed at her thoughtfully. 'How is it there are no official records of Black's existence?'

He was not here for her. Suddenly she began to feel really frightened. What had he done with Black? She must be careful. Mechanically, like one of those battery-operated toys, she walked toward the indicated chair and perched awkwardly on the end of it. He pushed the milk jug and sugar bowl toward her. She picked up the cup and saucer. The cup rattled. She looked at him nervously.

He had a cold, handsome face. Square-jawed, the way Americans were. Tanned. Not English, for sure. The wintry blue eyes seemed to have narrow flints in them. They regarded her without expression. She returned the rattling cup and saucer to the table.

'Would you like some biscuits with your tea?' he asked, and stood as if to get them. He was imposingly tall and muscular. The flat felt small and cramped. He was dressed in a black suit, black shoes, a black coat. His stomach was flat.

She shook her head distractedly. The deliberate

charm, it masked something heartless. A cold piercing intelligence.

He resumed his seat.

'Where is Black?'

'I would have thought a better strategy for you to employ would be to concentrate on answering my questions. At the moment you are looking at some serious trouble.' He took a sip of his tea. His tone was friendly, almost chatty. 'Where did you get the boy?'

She looked at him challengingly. 'I've done nothing wrong.'

An enquiring eyebrow arched. 'No birth certificate, no national insurance number? The boy doesn't exist outside this room, does he? How did you come by him?'

'Look, I didn't steal him if that is what you are implying. I found him in a rubbish dump when he was a baby. His mother had abandoned him. And when I found him he was totally helpless. I knew no one could give him a better home than me, so I kept him. If you think that is so wrong, call the police.'

'Call the police? Are you sure? Don't you think that might be a dangerous move for you? Seeing that you are an illegal immigrant.'

She stared at him defiantly. 'What's this all about? You don't really want me.'

'You have guessed correctly. I am not interested in you. I only want to know about the boy. The sooner you tell me what I want to know the sooner I will leave.'

'Why are you so concerned about my son?'

'I have seen the…er…family album. Not much of a life for him from what I can see.'

'He is happy here with me.'

'Can he read?'

'Of course not. He's a human vegetable.'

'What language do you use when you speak to him?'

'English.'

'Does he have any special dietary requirements?'

'He is a vegetarian. He vomits if given fish or meat. He likes milk.'

'The tubes in the kitchen are for feeding?'

She nodded. He had searched her flat. Who was this man? 'If you think a crime has been committed, call the police. In fact, I insist that you call the police.'

'I'm afraid that it is much too late for that now. I suggest you don't entertain such ideas. You might never see the boy again,' he warned pleasantly. But such hate and malice emanated from those handsome eyes that she was shocked. What had she done so bad that anyone would hate her so much?

There was a knock on the door and he went to open it. And that was when she noticed the black cables that seemed to come out of the ends of his trouser legs. How utterly strange, her mind registered.

'I am finished here,' he said to whoever was outside the door and walked out.

Two men came in, both well dressed, both burly, and started advancing. She was a rag doll in their powerful hold. She thought she had screamed, but the darkness came so suddenly it was impossible to tell if she had or not.

When she awakened it was seven o'clock and dark.

She was lying on the sofa bed, cramped and cold. Her neck felt stiff. She looked around the tiny flat with all its cast-offs from the great manor. The old Aubusson carpet with the large stain over which she had placed the coffee table, the heavy brocade that she had cut into perfectly wonderful curtains and the little birthday presents—a crystal rabbit, a clock from Harrods, the Venetian glassware. They had moved nothing, taken nothing, except her heart.

She felt a raging thirst and pulling together her weary limbs stumbled toward the kitchen. She leaned against the sink and drank two glasses of water. She shed no tears—none would come. The horror was frozen inside her. She went back to the sofa bed and sat there for hours with only the light from the street lamp. Who were those people? What did they want with Black? Why?

She jumped when the doorbell rang. Oh, of course. She switched on the light and went downstairs. She opened the door without looking at him and went back up the stairs. She heard him close the door and come up behind her. She turned around to face him. Veera stood in her living room. As unwashed as when she had first found him.

'Are you ready to go?'

She waved a hand toward the boy's empty room. 'The boy is gone. Never approach me again,' she said frostily, and walked away toward the kitchen.

His sly eyes immediately suspected a trick. What had she done with the boy? Hidden him? She was not getting away that easy. He followed her into the kitchen. He would have her, if necessary, by force. He reached the kitchen door and stopped.

She was standing by the kitchen sink, but she was swaying like a drunk and wielding a knife. When his eyes found hers he knew then that he would never have her. She looked insane. The intensity of her hatred made his skin crawl with fear. She would stick that knife into him with a song in her heart. He turned around and hurried out of her empty home without looking back. She had not hidden the boy. Something bad had happened to that child and she blamed him.

"Will you walk into my parlor?" said the Spider to the Fly.

—The Spider and the Fly (1829)

Black woke up in a white, windowless room that he recognized instantly as the place the unicorn had shown him. So it had begun. There was no fear in his heart. Only terrible pain. She had betrayed him as Green had said she would. The betrayal was bitter, but he couldn't hate her. How could he? He was more than half in love with her, and all he knew was an unquenchable loneliness and a yearning to reunite with her. He told himself that she had no control over herself and managed to convince himself that she could be saved still. And that he was the one to do it.

How he did not know yet.

The door swung open without Black having heard any footsteps outside. Either there was a deep carpet outside or the walls and door were soundproofed. He noticed the door was very thick, like those used for vaults, and he wondered about it.

A young, slim man walked into the room. He had bland features. His straight brown hair had been cut into a shining bob around his head. 'Hello, I am Carter Page,' he announced in an American accent. 'I believe you are unable even to blink.' He sounded almost as though he was in awe of the thought. 'So if you can hear and understand me simply look at the boxes on the screen. Green is for yes and red is for no.

Black looked at the lighted green box with YES written inside.

'Good.'

'Shame you can't read. It would make my life so much easier.'

Yes.

Carter looked at Black curiously. 'What do you mean yes? I was told you can't read. Can you?'

Yes.

He clapped his hands like a delighted child. 'That's fantastic. Did your extraterrestrial friend teach you?'

Black looked at the red box.

Carter raised his eyebrows. 'The TV?'

Yes.

'*Sesame Street* like everyone else?' He tittered at his own wit. His hand pointed to a screen built into the wall that came alive when he touched it. 'You are hooked up to a state-of-the-art computer. I think you will find it very user-friendly. To charge it I will go through the alphabets with you and the computer will register which part of your brain you are using. Then when next you think of that alphabet it will show it up on the screen. In that way you will make your sentences. Are you ready to start?'

Black's eyes darted to the green box.

Carter produced a remote control from his pocket. The letter A came on the screen. 'Look at it and think of it.' His remote pinged. 'Good.' He tapped on his screen and the next letter appeared. When all the letters were done, he said, 'Feel up to some numbers?' Zero to nine were quickly commenced with. 'OK, we're ready to roll. Let's practice speaking. Spell your name.'

To Black's amazement, one by one, the words 'Black Jack' appeared on the screen.

'Very good. Now tell me how you feel.'

A bit faster this time. Fine.

'Now don't spell it, just simply think the word "fine".'

Instantly the word 'fine' appeared on the screen.

Wow, Black spelled out.

Carter laughed. His laugh was infectious. 'You are good at this. What's your name again?'

Black Jack.

'Excellent.' Now let's do longer sentences, like; I'm hungry and I want to eat.'

Why am I here?

'Not for me to know, kid. But rest assured there are people who do and they will be around to see you shortly. I just do what I've been paid to do, nothing more.' He paused. 'Let's see, where was I? Ah, you'll probably not notice it, but your food won't be going down your throat anymore. Quite barbaric, that. There are tubes that go directly into your stomach. Also, I have to say, you have the most remarkable eyes. They don't dry out even though you never blink. A medical marvel you are. Don't let anybody tell you otherwise.'

Black liked Carter. His chatter was lively and interesting. He helped Black imprint a list of a thousand words into the computer. After he had left, Black looked at the TV screen that had been set to a non-stop cartoon channel. He wanted to turn it off so he could think, but he did not dare because he did not want his captors to know he could.

The heavy door opened and a man in an electric wheelchair rolled in. Black stared at him. His body was grotesquely twisted, stooped and heavy; and his legs shriveled, useless things. He had a large forehead, plump cheeks, a narrow nose, thin lips that turned down at the corners, and small, mean eyes. They reminded Black of black holes that swallowed everything and gave nothing back. The emptiness was so profound, it seemed impossible that there was a real person behind them. He was also astoundingly pale.

'I sit out in the sun for two hours every day, but it never seems to color me.'

Black stared at him. Did this man read minds? Then he realized, and his eyes darted to the screen. The computer was picking up his every thought. All his thoughts were no longer his own. He had been tricked.

'Don't regard it as a trick. You might find it a great help in communicating.'

For some seconds Black tried to keep his mind blank.

'You might as well speak to me. Otherwise you will get very bored. You could be in here for years.'

Who are you?

He seemed to smile, that is, his lips tried to rise at the corners, but failed. Their downturn was so severe that he ended up with a grimace. His real intent and feeling were in his eyes, which remained black holes of nothing. 'In our situation, Black, names are meaningless. Although, I must say, I do quite like yours, Master Jack. Being a gambling man, I am unable to resist a good game of Black Jack. The only game to better it is Russian Roulette.'

How should I address you?

'You may call me Kite.' He tried again to smile, but it was useless. It was like watching a snake smile.

Why have you brought me here, Kite?

'Well, it appears that you have made friends with someone that I am rather curious about.'

Green?

192

'Yes, Green. Where is he now?'

I don't know.

'How do you meet?'

He comes to me.

'Can you contact him?'

No.

'What is he like? Is his a fearsome splendor?'

Fearsome? He is gentle and radiant with dancing fractals.

'Gentle!'

And kind.

'Are you sure?'

Yes. Very kind and gentle.

'Tell me everything you know.' He leaned forward eagerly in his wheelchair and Black Jack felt a chill go through him. The overhead light shone on his skin making it appear so diaphanous that the veins underneath showed through. His hands appeared almost blue.

Why do you want to know?

'For the sake of humanity you must tell me.'

Humanity? You don't care about humanity.

The dead eyes stared hard at him. 'Yes, in fact, you are quite right. I don't share your sentimental view of humans. They are…a cancer on the face of Earth.'

Aren't you human?

'In a manner of speaking. Some are superior to others.'

You think you are superior to other humans because you have sold out to our oppressors in exchange for wealth and power? But humans are light beings who are waking up despite all your efforts to keep them asleep.

Kite laughed. A musical sound at odds with his

repulsive appearance. 'Waking up? Would you be prepared to put that New Age nonsense to a test?'

We are waking up.

'In that case, you wouldn't mind being part of a little experiment. A game to see if this waking race of wonder and light will come to your rescue.'

Why have you brought me here?

'I just told you. You and I are about to embark on a most interesting gamble. To know whose belief is true—yours or mine.'

I have nothing to gamble with.

'There is always your sad, miserable life.'

My life?

'It's quite simple, really. The masses will be shown what they think is a live feed of you on a hospital bed and they will be given the opportunity to vote. If they vote no they will add to the vote that preserves your life; but if they vote yes, they will be asked for their name, passport number and address so that a hundred US dollars can be sent to them. And at the end of our game we will know if human beings are the simply wonderful creatures of light and love that you think they are, or if they are the stupid, lazy, selfish, spineless trash that I think they are.'

Black noted that there was no emotion other than disdain on Kite's face. He spoke as if he was better than all of humanity, as if he wasn't human at all, but of some higher race, and the elitism of his higher position made the murder of another human being acceptable. It was also obvious that his opinion of human beings was irredeemable. Black remembered his mother telling him, 'Coldness rots the soul in the end.'

'Well?' Kite watched him closely.

So what if humans are all you say? Why is it so important for you to prove it?

The small eyes flickered. 'It is not important at all. It's simply an...amusement, that's all. Do you agree to play or not?'

Black Jack knew he was lying. Sometimes he could read his mother's mind. He tried then to read the man's thoughts, but he came up against an opaque veil. What lay on the other side was thick and evil. Still Black thought he knew the real reason why he was in that white room.

He was the bait for Green.

Kite followed the boy's thoughts on the screen. The artificial obstruction was the effect of an occult rite and was there for a very good reason. What was behind the wall would terrify him. The game would not be played and his goal would be so much harder to achieve.

What if I don't play your game?

Kite's eyes gleamed with malice. 'There is no real consequence to not playing. You will die, of course, in time, in this room. Naturally your mother will be deported.

And the...er...girl will be used in a blood ritual. There is much demand for her *type.*'

Black felt fear clutch his heart. What happens to them if I lose?

'Your mother will be left to carry on with her...little life. The girl's mind will be wiped clean. It will be as if she had never met you. And her life, too, will carry on as before.'

What happens to me?

'You will simply be injected with a dose of something lethal.' His startlingly white hands came up vaguely. It

195

was clear that the matter did not interest him.

And if I win?

The man couldn't even pretend neutrality. Silent laughter shook his lips. The child was a simpleton. He never lost. But then he looked into the boy's eyes and suddenly felt a frisson of fear run up his spine. The room seemed to become colder.

'It's freezing in here. Raise the temperature,' he growled.

Vents appeared in the sides of the room and warm air poured in. He turned slightly away from the boy. Of course the boy could never win. The game was rigged. Yet, he had unconsciously been moving away from him. He was almost at the door. He wanted to push himself back to the center of the room, but as if there was a force field around the boy that was repelling him, he found himself, unwilling, no, unable to get closer. Kite pulled himself together. Humans, he told himself, were dirty, lowly, cowardly creatures, and this one was no exception. He turned to face Black.

'Forgive me, it is hard for me to get warm. If you win...' He paused and looked expressionlessly at the boy. The words left his lips smoothly. 'Then everything goes back to the day before we found you.'

And the girl?

'She will be set free.'

You promise this?

The man's eyebrows shot up. Clearly, his rotted soul had not expected such innocence. 'Of course.'

How many dollars are you prepared to lose?

'Billions.'

Black was so shocked by the reply that his mind simply repeated Kite's answer. Billions.

Kite looked disdainful. 'Money is not real. It is created out of nothing as electronic entries in bank accounts around the world. Before we carry on, let me clearly state your rights. This is a most dangerous game and you have the right to your own self-determination, the right to choose to play this game or not, and even the right to leave the game at any time. You now have the right to do whatever you want. What do you want to do?'

I want to play.

The total absence of any kind of fear in the boy annoyed him, but he did his best not to show it. 'I'll watch every move you make. As long as you play the game by my rules, you and your loved ones will live. The cards are stacked in my favor because, well, it is my game.'

A screen lighted up on the white wall. It showed Black lying on a narrow bed with a shaven head and electrodes attached to his skull. There was no image of Kite in the room, but the clock at the top left of the screen counted time as if the images were from a live feed. At the bottom of the screen there were two blank rectangles—one counted the yes votes and the other the noes.

As Black watched the screen the number '1' appeared soundlessly in the blank slot underneath the yes vote.

Kite smiled his cold grimace. 'That's my vote.'

It is beautiful to be alone. To be alone does not mean to be lonely. It means the mind is not influenced and contaminated by society.

—Jiddu Krishnamurti

Miss Monroe entered the girl's quarters carrying a breakfast tray. She had not gone in the morning to awaken her in the usual manner, for she had watched the girl on the closed-circuit camera all night and seen that she had slept not at all. Hour after hour she had sat in the living room, still as a statue, staring at the blank TV screen.

'What *are* you doing?' she had whispered, but by the time morning came she was no wiser.

When she entered, the girl turned to look at her. There was no expression on her face. Miss Monroe went forward purposefully and put the tray on the low table in front of the girl, but she ignored it.

Miss Monroe straightened and crossed her arms in front of her. 'I thought you couldn't read or write.'

'Dakota can't. I can.'

'Who are you?'

'Shekina.'

'Why have you taken over the body, Shekina?'

'There is something I have to do.'

'You do know that they are watching you, don't you?'

'Yes.'

'And that you can't win. They *will* get you.'

'I know that too.'

'Aren't you afraid?'

'No. They still need the body.'

'Can I help?'

'Thank you, but I don't think so, Miss Monroe.'

'You might as well call me Marilyn from now on.'

'Marilyn? Do you think that's really your name?'

For a telling moment Miss Monroe looked confused. What a fool she had been. She had never questioned anything. Her whole life must be one sick joke to them. 'Probably not.' She hesitated. 'I think it might be Alice, though.'

'Alice in Wonderland.'

'Alice in a gray place.'

Shekina nodded.

'I suppose you won't be wanting your drugs today.'

'As it happens I do want them.'

'Why? No afternoon session has been scheduled for you.'

'I'd like to keep the routine.'

'All right then. I'll be back for the tray later, as usual.'

'Alice, when you come back can you bring me a bar of chocolate?'

'Chocolate?'

'Mmmm.'

'Any particular type?'

'Nope.'

When Alice was gone, Shekina lifted the tray cover and looked curiously at the steaming food. She unwrapped the cutlery and proceeded to eat, chewing slowly, tasting every bite. When all the food was gone she took her medicines. She chewed them, even though they were terribly bitter. There was orange juice in the cup. She sipped it and, lifting the cup over her mouth, let the last few drops fall on her tongue. Then she sat back to wait for the chocolate.

Alice walked in with a Hershey bar. She handed it to Shekina. 'It was all I could find in the kitchen,' she explained apologetically.

'Thank you, Alice.'

'See you at lunchtime,' she said and left.

Shekina unwrapped the bar slowly. Then she leaned back into the sofa and bit into it. She closed her eyes and let it melt on her tongue. When she opened her eyes to take another bite she noticed some writing on the inside of the chocolate wrapper. Casually she picked it up and pretended to study the ingredients. Then she turned the wrapper around. Alice had written:

I'm going into town to get help for us.

She crushed the wrapper in her hand, went into the bathroom and flushed it down the toilet. Then she went back to the sofa and, staring at the empty TV screen, returned to the task of trying to contact the boy by following the electromagnetic signature she had followed before. Blank. Nothing. She sat forward. She knew he was not dead, but being kept in a place that concealed his signature, like one of those storage vaults where top clearance secrets are kept. Those places are so sensitive that even the slightest change in the air caused by a remote viewer would trigger the alarms.

It meant they would sense her presence as soon as she found him.

But she was not afraid of them. What she needed was a bridge or a moment when the door to this facility would be open. They had to feed him, monitor him. She would wait. She lay without moving for hours. Time had no meaning for her. She had only one objective: to find that boy.

Suddenly she sat straighter. Someone, a young man, was holding the door open and she saw through it. The boy, the bed, the equipment. Then the man and the boy were lost. The door had been closed. She memorized the location. The door would open again to let the young man out, but she did not want to enter the room just yet. Instead she projected her mind around the room. Twelve by twelve by twelve. Of course, he was being held in a cube.

She took a deep breath. She needed Teddy.

They promise you heaven, so they can
steal this world.

—Shahir Zag

Black found himself in a white landscape. Everything
was white—the trees, the sky, the ground. A figure
materialized against the white backdrop. It was Green,
and yet he was no longer green! From head to toe he was
varying hues of blue.

'What happened to you?' cried Black.

'Next phase has started.'

'What do you mean?'

'Your season of learning and childlike innocence has
passed. We have crossed over into dangerous times, of
bows and arrows and hunting; and adulthood.'

'Where are we?'

'I brought you here because the room you are being
held in contains rather advanced hardware not only able
to detect the minute fluctuations in the air caused by
any enemy remote viewers entering it, but also designed
to disable and trap them with electromagnetic waves. By
entering I will harm their machinery, which will
constitute as meddling in the ways of men.'

Black nodded distractedly. 'Have I done the right
thing in agreeing to the game?'

'You had only the illusion of choice. Under black
magic rules, the subject of malicious intent *must*
acquiesce first. The victim must seal his own fate or be
in agreement on some level for the power to work. It is
the same reason why the vampire has to be willingly
invited into your home to drain off your blood. After

being warned, the victim is deemed to be going on by their own free will, even if he has been thoroughly manipulated to do so, as you were.'

'Is the real point of this game to get to you?'

Green shook his blue head.

'Kite seemed *very* interested in you, though.'

'Of course he is, but this is really a battle for your energy. Not just yours but all of humanity's. Come, I want to show you something.'

Black reached out for the offered hand and they were immediately back to somewhere between Earth and the moon.

'Look carefully at Earth and this time call on intent—it is a force that exists in the universe and is available to all—to see what you did not see before.'

Black concentrated on the blue marble floating in space, but what he saw altered not one iota. 'What am I looking to see?'

'It is easier not to see, and it is the unconscious choice the vast majority of humans make. Close your eyes and take the lid off the possibilities that you are open to, then will your perception to expand.'

Black closed his eyes and determined that this time he would see the truth, no matter what it was. When he opened his eyes it was like watching a series of *CSI* when a black light is shone into a spotless bathroom and suddenly it becomes a ghostly killing ground. Earth was suspended inside a glowing green net, like a fishnet, only the holes were perfectly hexagonal with not a single tear or imperfection anywhere. 'What is that?'

'That's the counterfeit matrix. As with all high technology, it is built with mathematics and sound. It is the fence that regulates what frequencies enter Earth's biosphere. It is also, as you rightly deduced, a net. For catching and holding humans.'

'Until we die?'

'Not even then is escape possible. You are recycled into the system. Endlessly. Drug addicts will speak degradingly of their chosen poison, but they will never give it up. Humans are a drug.'

Black couldn't take his eyes off the glowing net that was suspended around Earth. 'What does the net have to do with this sick game I am being forced to play?'

'That is their signature—hide everything in plain sight. This is not a game. This is ritual sacrifice on a global scale that is calculated to alter the course of humanity. It is an attempt to use a twilight code to subliminally communicate with and imprint the subconscious of the millions, perhaps even billions, who will read about it, hear about it, or watch it on their television screens.

'If enough people are poor enough, greedy enough, desperate enough, or foolhardy enough to believe that their contribution is hardly significant, and decide that a hundred dollars is worth more to them than you, the corresponding lowering of their energy will mean they will be powering their own prison. The dark hierarchy must saturate the collective vibration with as much fear, chaos, war, austerity, suffering and moral degradation of the human spirit as possible during this time of awakening. The lower the frequency, the harder it will be for the mass awakening to occur.

'This is a battle to decide who transcends and leaves the net and who stays to face the coming degenerated world of the self-appointed overlords and the micro-chipped, enslaved, more machine than human population. Naturally, it is their intention to drag as many souls as they are able into a future where everyone is jacked directly into the matrix.'

'And me, what is my contribution?'

'Their intention is to turn you from a warm-hearted, compassionate person to a loathsome, hateful, sexually perverted psychopath whom they can take over, mind and body. Your intention must be to remain innocent at all times. Remember, their job is to change the hologram to change you. Your job is to change you to change the hologram.

'Oh, one more thing. If you are still planning to see Dakota using the same method as before, I should warn you that they are monitoring your sleep. The moment the computer detects rapid eye movement it will jerk you awake with an electric shock.'

'Am I not out of my body now?'

'Yes, but shielded by me. You have another ten minutes to see Dakota. You might want to tell her the story of Milarepa.'

'Why?'

'It might help her.'

'I don't think I remember it anymore.'

'Here, let me refresh the memory for you.' Instantly Black remembered the story with the same clarity he had when his mother had first told it to him five years ago.

'By the way, if you do see your mother say to her: conspiracy theorists.'

'Conspiracy theorists?

'Mmmm.'

'Just that?'

'Just that.'

'She'll never understand.'

'Don't worry, she will be guided.'

'Will you come to see me again?'

'Yes, tomorrow at this time.'

'Thank you, Green, although you're so blue now the name seems incongruous.'

Green laughed, the fractals on his face and hands shining bright. 'Goodbye, my friend,' he said, and disappeared.

And Black found himself whirling away to an unknown destination inside a long tunnel.

Oh, cross over shame like the wise Dove
Who cares not for fame, just for shy love.

——Ian Hunter/Mott the Hoople,
'Hymn for the Dudes' (1973)

Standing on the colorful tiles of Dakota's inner world, Black stopped at a mirror to look at his reflection: white T-shirt that screamed BAD in bold, black lettering, slim-fitting, black leather pants, and black boots. Astonishing, how changed he was! His shoulders were straight and broad, his mouth was beautifully closed, his eyes bright and his body lean and strong. He was wearing a silver digital watch. He glanced at it, noted the time, and quickly made his way to the cube. She was standing at the doorway he had built for her, looking out anxiously. At the sight of him she started down the pathway, and stopped a foot away from him.

'I was worried about you,' she said.

'Why?'

She shrugged and looked down at her red shoes. He recognized them as Dorothy's from *The Wizard of Oz*, and felt a great rush of emotion for her. How cunningly they had spun her into a world of fairy tales where she would be trapped forever. Never growing up, never living. Like him.

'How are you?' he enquired.

She looked up into his gentle eyes. She had missed him. But she never missed anybody. She smiled shyly. 'I'm OK, I guess, but I'm really glad you've come. I wanted to thank you properly for the hourglass device. It works very well. And thank you for my crayons. I've used them so much they are all nearly stubs now. Do you want to see my drawings?'

'OK.'

He followed her into the cube. It was very neat in there. All the drawings were in one corner. She brought them to him.

'It seems impossible, even to me, but when I start drawing it is as if these things actually happened, but somehow I forgot them. And when they are there, on paper, I still can't remember them, but it feels as if a little piece of me that was lost has been found.'

Black could hardly believe what he was seeing. Page after page, he was assaulted by unbearable images. Worse tortures than he had seen happen to Winter were depicted. Little girls crouched in fear, strapped spread-eagled on narrow cots; booted men with whips; what seemed to be some kind of abortion with blood squirting everywhere, and watched by a group of screaming, blood-splattered children; rapes; orgies; mutilations; killings; and, oddly, the ubiquitous snake in the background—perhaps they were phallic symbols. The only words he ever saw on the drawings were the words, 'no' and 'help', repeated over and over. Her art crushed and defeated him.

But when he looked at her, she seemed peculiarly calm and unaffected by the shocking brutality of her drawings. Yet, how could anyone survive such ordeals and not be totally damaged?

'Do you know, they drowned one little girl who looked exactly like me in ice-water until she shot out of her body.'

'Why?'

'Because she was supposed to go into the next room

and look at a certain page of a closed book.'

'And did she?'

She frowned. 'I don't remember. Perhaps if I draw it.' She touched his arm suddenly. 'I'm worried, Black.'

'About what?'

'I don't know, but I seem to have been here for a long time. I don't think I've ever been sent down this long. Something must be wrong.'

'I believe things might be changing. I'm playing a game, and if I win they will set you free.' Black looked into her lovely eyes and felt an aching in his heart. He thought he would burst with the ache. He didn't tell her that once the game was over she would never see him again, or he her.

'Who told you that?'

'A very powerful man.'

'Then he was lying. Don't play his game, Black. They will never set me free,' she said sadly.

'Why can't you fight them? I was told that you have great powers, which they are afraid of.'

Dakota looked at Black curiously. 'What kind of powers?'

Black looked at his watch. 'Perhaps you will remember them later. I have very little time left, but I must tell you a story before I go. Have you ever heard of Milarepa?'

'I don't think so.'

'In that case, come with me.' He took her by the hand and led her to the gazebo. They sat amongst the perfume of the roses and Black began.

'There once lived a very famous saint called Milarepa. One day he returned from collecting firewood to find the cave he lived in had been invaded by ferocious demons. Anyone else would have run away, but not him. He believed that every obstacle in life was simply a challenge requiring an appropriate response. Very politely he asked them to leave, but the demons replied by growling and advancing menacingly upon him. Immediately, Milarepa began to utter the most powerful exorcism recitations he knew, but these attempts brought forth only jeers and laughter.

'Next, he tried to pacify them with Buddhist teachings—the merits of compassion and mercy—but the lessons seem to send them into a great rage. At that point the saint decided to test the teaching that all phenomena are projections of one's own mind. The demons were nothing more than the unwanted parts of himself. Instead of viewing them as external demons he would see them as they really were, radiant helpers in his spiritual path.

'He began to sing to them. Charming, sweet melodies, resonant with caring for the ways these beasts had suffered, what they needed to heal their pain, and what he could do for them. With unshakeable fearlessness he welcomed them to stay the night with him. "Do not hasten to leave," he said, "for it would be my greatest pleasure if you stayed. We will discourse and play together, pit black against white. See who wins."

'All but the most terrifying and largest of them began to tremble violently. Shrieking and swirling together they rushed out of the cave in an awful gust. The last remaining one rose onto his hind legs and opened his huge jaws. His fangs dripped with foul-smelling saliva. Milapera realized further surrender was necessary, so he stepped closer to the huge demon and with pure love and compassion put his head in the gaping black mouth of the beast. Instantly the demon melted into nothing and Milapera's home was his again.'

Black looked at his watch. Just over a minute left. 'I have to go, Dakota, but I will be back soon. Goodbye.'

'Goodbye,' she said, but he could see from her faraway expression that she was still in Milarepa's cave, and that the story had meant more to her than it ever had to him.

He walked away, but he could not leave without looking back. She was standing amongst the roses, watching him leave, a sad, lonely figure.

'The next time you come, will you bring me a small wolf?' she shouted.

'A what?'

'A small, gray wolf with a silver and black face and yellow eyes.'

'OK,' he said, turning away, knowing the wolf of her desires was already bounding from the fields toward her. But it was such a strange request that he turned to watch. He was surprised to see not the small wolf that she had asked for, but a large, silver-gray wolf loping fast toward her. It stopped about five or six feet away from her, sat, and began to howl.

She raised her arms out to it and said, 'I'm sorry, Shadow. I'm so sorry.'

The wolf leaped on her chest, almost knocking her over. Then it set about licking her face and showing such uncontrollable happiness that Black knew he was not witnessing a meeting, but a reunion. He looked at the silver clock face. He had spent longer than he had intended.

'Mother,' he said, and suddenly he was in a barren landscape with a stormy blue and black sky. He could hear the thud of feet behind him. He was being chased by an invisible enemy. He was in his mother's nightmare. He saw her in the distance. She was running barefoot in the opposite direction and calling his name. He called to her and she stopped and turned around. When she saw him she did not run toward him but simply stared at him in an uncomprehending daze. He took one step and he was beside her.

'I'm alive. Don't worry about me. It's hard to explain but I'm playing a game. And when the game is over I will be home. Remember this when you wake up, it's very important—conspiracy theorists.'

And suddenly he was zapped awake. Searing pain in his brain. His first taste of pain.

Carter was standing over him with a sunny smile. 'Sorry,' he said, 'but REM sleep is not allowed. And in case you didn't know, REM stands for rapid eye movement.'

And Black knew that Carter was not such a friendly guy, after all.

> The highest form of ignorance is when you reject something you don't know anything about.
>
> —Wayne Dyer

Bumi woke up with a start in the darkness of the boy's bedroom. She had dreamed of him, but it had felt so incredibly real. Her heart was still thudding hard. She touched her hand—he had held it. It was four in the morning. The street outside was quiet. The loss of him engulfed her. She pushed her face into his pillow and breathed in the lingering smell of him. She had never stopped using baby shampoo on his hair. To her he was still her baby.

In the dark her head reared up suddenly, her eyes staring. He had said, *conspiracy theorists.* Whatever could that mean? He had said it was important. She turned on her side to face the window and heard the letter flap of the downstairs door lift and fall. At four a.m.! She slipped out of bed and ran to the window. A man in a long, dark coat was walking away. She hurried downstairs in her bare feet. The wooden floor was so cold she was covered in goose bumps.

There was a white envelope on the mat. With shaking hands she opened it. An A4 paper held an indecipherable string of letters. However, she knew www meant it was something to do with computers. Something she knew nothing about. She sprinted up the stairs, changed; then did a strange thing, one that she had never done before. She plugged in the microwave, put her coat into it, closed the door, and turned it on at

215

full blast. Puzzled by her own actions, but unable to stop herself, she watched her coat turning through the glass door. Then she unplugged the oven, took the coat out of it, and pulling it on, ran out through the front door. She took the night bus into Shepherds Bush where the son of a Pakistani woman she knew ran an all-night Internet café.

Ashan looked up from his computer screen when she opened the door. 'Oh, hello, Aunty,' he greeted, clearly surprised to see her in his shop.

She was too wound up to smile. 'Can you help me, please?'

'If I can, I will.'

'Can you tell me what this is?' she asked, coming forward and holding out the A4 paper.

Ashan glanced at it. 'That's just an address for a website.'

'Can I see it, please?'

'Of course.'

She watched carefully as he keyed in the letters and punctuation marks. The screen became black. PLAY GOD appeared in bold flashing letters. An invitation to access the language of your choice appeared next. Ashan clicked on the box that said English, and up popped a computerized image of a man with platinum blond hair and blue eyes. He was dressed in a doctor's overcoat. A folded stethoscope showed in his pocket. He was standing in a virtual doctor's consulting room.

'Wonderful. You found us.' He smiled. 'You better come with me, then,' he said and walked into what looked like a hospital corridor. Blue doors led off from it. 'Behind these doors are terminally ill people. All of them will die in the next few months. Today we are

216

going to visit a youth paralyzed since birth. In the next few weeks he will be dead. By means of a computer he has communicated his desire to let you choose if he should live or die. You have exactly one minute to decide.'

Ashan's face swung toward Bumi. Her hands were cupped over her mouth and her horrified eyes were transfixed by the screen.

'But this is a very special decision,' the virtual character explained. 'If you decide he shouldn't die, the boy will remain as a useless vegetable until he expires in the next few weeks, but if you decide to help by terminating his suffering, you will be prompted for your passport number and address, and one hundred US dollars will be posted to you. Nothing will be asked in return. The game allows one vote per person. Watch a live feed of the subject now.'

An oblong button began flashing.

'Do you want to watch?' Ashan asked her.

She could not speak, only nod.

The screen opened up to a boy. A real boy. Black lying in a white room, surrounded by sophisticated machinery. He appeared to be hooked up to some of it.

'Whoa! What the fuck?' swore Ashan.

'That's a lie,' Bumi shouted, her face contorted with fury. 'He doesn't need those machines.'

'You have one minute to decide,' a computerized female voice chimed in, and the clock began a countdown. Fifty-nine, fifty-eight, fifty-seven, fifty-six, fifty-five…

'Quick, quick, press the no button,' Bumi cried in a panic. Unbelievably, there were already more than two hundred yes votes.

'Please enter your country of origin and your passport number now,' the voice instructed.

Ashan looked enquiringly up at Bumi. She covered her face with both hands and tried to remember. 'One. No, no, six. No, wait.' And suddenly the numbers that she had not looked at for years, in a passport that had long expired, arrived in an unexpected rush in her head. She snatched her hands away from her face and said them clearly.

With lightning-quick strokes—Bumi did not think human fingers were capable of moving that fast—Ashan typed the numbers in and pressed the enter key on the keypad. The number '1' appeared inside the no box. The first no.

'Thank you and have a nice day,' said the voice. The screen became a purple wall with a rotating black cube in the middle of it.

Bumi's heart was beating so loudly she could hear it. She felt her knees give way and her hand grasped Ashan's shoulder. His reaction was fast. He shot out of his chair, grabbed her by the waist, and gently guided her to the chair he had vacated.

'Sit, Aunty,' he advised.

She sank slowly into the chair.

'Shall I get you some water?'

Bumi shook her head slowly.

'What's going on, Aunty? And who's the boy?'

'I don't know what is going on, but that boy is my son,' she said slowly. The words were strange and bitter in her mouth. She shouldn't have had to hide the fact before, when she had had him.

'Oh! I didn't know you had a son. My mother never mentioned it.'

'He is adopted. The issue never came up in conversation with your mother.'

'Look, shouldn't you go to the police? This is well illegal.'

'I can't. If I do they will kill him instantly.'

'But you can't let them play with his life like that. There are a lot of sick people on the net. Hardly has the game started and already there are two hundred yes votes. At this rate they'll end up killing him.'

'Will you vote no for me?'

'Of course,' he said.

She looked at him. 'Now. Please.'

'Err…can't remember my passport number off the top of my head. But I'll do it as soon as I get home, OK?'

'Thank you, Ashan. You are a good boy. God will be kind to you.'

'Glad to help, Aunty.'

'Will you ask your mother to vote too?'

'Yeah, sure.'

'Listen, if I say conspiracy theorists to you, what comes to your mind?'

'Kook, nut, lunatic, tinfoil hat, a bit strange…' He stopped when he saw Bumi frowning worriedly and realized it was something important, possibly connected to the boy. 'You want me to Google it for you?'

'Google it?'

'Er… You want me to type it into the search engine and see what comes up?'

Bumi was lost even with 'search engine'. She had no idea, but she quickly agreed with this suggestion. 'Yes, yes, do that.'

He typed the words in and reams of stuff appeared

on the screen. At that moment the door opened and a lanky youth with a backpack entered.

'Wait one moment, Aunty,' Ashan said, and went to serve his customer.

Bumi cast her eyes down the page and a name jumped out at her. She pulled the cursor the way she had seen Ashan do, clicked on it, and found herself on a green and black page. They seemed to her magical colors, why, she couldn't say. There was a photograph of a blond man; attractive, possibly in his late fifties. There was something wrong with one of his hands. Bumi had seen that type of deformity in the first Lady Carrington—arthritis. She peered closer. Courage. He had courageous eyes.

Ashan came back.

She pointed to the picture of the man. 'Will you help me write to him?'

'David Icke?'

Bumi nodded.

Ashan shook his head. 'I don't think that's a very good idea, Aunty. This man is like a broken record, banging on about pedophiles in high places.'

Immediately Bumi recalled the sly references she had overheard Lady Carrington make about their important friends with their odd nicknames and their preference for 'little people'. Unbidden, the memory of that one time many years back when she was still employed at Lord Carrington's stately manor came back. She had opened the door of a guest bedroom that should have been empty and seen a naked boy lying on the rumpled bed. He had turned his small, white face in her direction and looked at her blankly, the way children sometimes do. He could not have been more than ten years old.

His mouth was red and swollen. She had stood there staring, startled by the sight, when a man deeper in the room had drawled in a bored voice, 'Shut that door. You're letting the draft in.'

Shocked to her Indian core, but indoctrinated into her servile position by the fear of losing even that lowly position, she had immediately obeyed. Not my place, she had told herself, scuttling away as fast as she could. She had never told a soul. Even now the hot shame of having done nothing that morning was raw. She looked into Ashan's dismissive eyes. 'If that is what he does, then I admire him greatly. It takes a great deal of courage to stand up for what is right with no thought for one's own safety.'

'Well, that's not the worst part,' Ashan maintained, his eyebrows rising. 'This is a guy who believes the world is run by reptilians!'

One week ago that would have caused her to think David Icke was more than a little mad, but she could not forget the eyes of the man who had offered her tea in her own house. It had been like talking to a snake or a crocodile—there was nothing but the emotionless calculation of a cold-blooded predator. Or the strange cables that appeared to come out of his trouser legs. 'How do you know it isn't?' she asked.

Ashan looked at her as if she had lost it, but saying nothing, he politely helped her write the letter and send it using his email address.

'One last thing, Ashan.'

'Yes, Aunty?'

'Can you think of any reason why anyone would put their coat into a microwave oven and turn it on full blast?'

'Well, if one was a spy, it would destroy any RFID chips hidden in it.'

'RFID?'

'They are tracking devices that can be so small they would fit into the dot on the top of the letter "i". Often they are placed onto the labels of clothes.'

The explanation didn't make any sense to her, but she put it at the back of her mind, thanked him profusely, and took the bus to work.

The milk and morning papers were sitting neatly by the side of the front door. She picked them up and quietly let herself into the darkened apartment. Both Lord and Lady Carrington were still asleep. During the time of the first Lady Carrington she had had to iron the newspapers, but the new Lady Carrington had declared such gestures exercises in ridiculous affectations. She put the papers and the milk on the table and sat in her coat on a chair. Soon she would make the one slice of nearly burnt toast with a scrape of butter and marmalade for Lady Carrington, and a couple of soft boiled eggs and soldiers for the Lord, but for now she stared at a spotless tile on the floor and thought of the unreal turn her life had taken.

If a man smite thee on one cheek, smash him on the other!

—Motto of the Satanic Order

Shekina cleared a space in her mind and called them, first Teddy, then the biotech. Ten minutes later, Teddy opened the door to her quarters and came into the room, his face vacant.

She stood up. 'Take me to an ops room. I need to do a session.'

Wordlessly, he turned around and led the way.

They met no one in the corridors, but if they had it would not have mattered. The biotech was already waiting inside the ops room. His state was such that he appeared to be in a trance. As if they were all parts of a well-oiled machine, unspeaking they strapped her securely into the chair, attached the EEG headband and the heart monitor wires, and administered the first dose of psychoactive drugs into the IV line. The lights were turned down and brainwave tones were sent through her headphones. Shekina focused her mind on the vector coordinates she had memorized. The image of the cabalistic tree of life was projected onto the screen. When the flower on the screen started to spin she concentrated on it until the vortex of its spinning absorbed her.

At precisely that moment Teddy launched the electric shock that coursed from the trip seat into her body, and she flew at incredible speed toward her vector intention. In seconds, she was very deep in the ground inside a DUMB (deep underground military base) corridor. She stood in front of a thick door. Experimentally, she put one leg through the door. Her foot disappeared through it, but did not land anywhere. She tried the wall and got the same reaction. She put an arm through and felt a sucking sensation. The room was a trap.

She looked behind her into the empty corridor. Then she took two steps back and jumped into the room, calm, cool, and fearless. To land on the floor like a cat. Alert, precise and aware that the only way she would leave that room was badly. She straightened quickly and scanned her surroundings. There was no danger inside the room. Her eyes met Black's. He was watching her with dismay.

You should not have come, he said in her head. This room is a trap.

She moved forward and stopped about four feet away from the bed. 'I know.' The incomprehensibly marvelous eggs had said, 'When the time comes give her to him.' That time was now. The eggs were waiting to hatch.

Why are you here?

'I have very little time. Let's not waste it with chit-chat. I am giving her to you now.'

What are you talking about?

'It is my duty to protect her, but the eggs are more important than any of us. I have disobeyed my masters and will sacrifice myself for the eggs.' She looked fierce and fearless. She seemed not to be a young girl but a woman of great magical powers.

He saw her become very still and a change came over her features. The boldness fled from her eyes, and softness fell about the contours of her mouth. A drop in her shoulders made her appear almost smaller. Suddenly it was his Dakota—not the pale thing he had found crouched over the hourglass but a brighter, more vivid version. He felt a flutter in his chest. A shame that she should see him in his helpless form. He had been a hero in her world and now he was nothing.

'Oh!' she gasped. 'Your beautiful hair. It's all gone,' and with childlike innocence ran to comfort him. But when she tried to put her hand on his shoulder, it went right through. 'Ugh,' she cried in shock. 'What's happening to me?' She was so unschooled in the ways of her other alters that she did not even realize that she was an astral projection. His eyes moved to the computer screen and her eyes automatically followed. He made the words.

You are traveling in spirit. It's OK, don't worry. I do it all the time. But it is dangerous for you here. You must leave now.

'I don't know how I got here. How can I leave?' she whispered fearfully.

It's all right, don't worry. One of the others will come back soon and all will be well again. How are you?

'I'm fine, but what's happened to you? Are you ill?'

I'm not ill. This is what I am like in the real world.

'Oh!' she exclaimed, greatly surprised. She hugged her arms around her thin body, and looked around the room. 'But why are you imprisoned in this windowless room?'

It is supposed to be a game. The world will decide whether I live or die.

She turned to him quickly. 'That's a horrid game. I don't want you to die.' She stopped, puzzled. But she never wanted anything. She looked into his eyes. The

225

thought of his death actually caused her hurt.

'Is there anything I can do for you?'

There is nothing you can do. This is something I agreed to do. Never mind that now. The story of Milarepa, did it have any significance for you?

At first, she looked as if she was about to say something else, but then she allowed him to distract her. 'Our demons are our fears. To defeat them we must invite them to stay, and integrate ourselves with them,' she said woodenly.

He wrote on the screen. What do you fear, Dakota?

'The others.'

So you know what to do.

She began to shake her head at the prospect. 'No, I can't do that.' She was still shaking her head, when her face began to change and Shekina fought her way through. Her eyes were stormy with some great effort. 'Sorry,' she whispered hoarsely, 'but I can't hold on anymore.'

Then her beautiful face contorted and she was sucked out of the room as if she was no more than a thin rag in the path of a powerful vacuum cleaner. It was as Green had shown him: the world was not as the TV had led him to believe. The powers that should not be had the technology not only to net, but to store the electromagnetic part of humans.

Shekina was flung violently back into the trip chair. There were new electrodes placed on different points on her body to record her nerve impulses. The theme song of Dakota's favorite movie came through her earphones, *Somewhere over the rainbow...and the dreams that you dare to dream really do come true.*" But it was through a device on her head, through the mastoid bone inside her head, that she heard Schooner Klaus's voice.

'Hello, kitty, it's your programmer here. Click your heels, it's time to go over the rainbow and look into the white light.'

Shekina fought hard not to look, sweat poured from her chilled skin, but she was no match for the tritone—two specific notes that when played together could alter her brainwave activity to cause her severe pain or put her in ecstasy. This time it was ecstasy and, against her will, her eyes, unnaturally blue with drugs and intense emotions, opened wide to the excruciatingly bright light.

They were getting rid of her and bringing Dakota back. Poor Dakota. The pain was always for her. Then it all went black.

'Who's been a naughty little kitty, then?'

With a heavy load and a long journey

—Confucius, *Lunyu* (475BC - AD220)

Bumi knocked briefly, pushed open her neighbor's back door, and entered it. Renuka, the lady of the house, was standing by her stove. Something was bubbling in a pot.

'What's the matter?' she asked, concerned. She had known Bumi for many years now and she had never seen her so disheveled and distracted.

'Have you got a computer?' Bumi asked.

'Yes, Anand has one upstairs. But I don't know how it works.'

'Please, you must help me. This one favor is all I ask. If I open it for you, could you please vote on it for me?'

'Vote for what?'

'You see, a little boy's life is on the line. He is very dear to me. I know it sounds odd and it is the most unbelievable thing, but there is a barbarous plan to kill him according to how many people vote to save him on the net.'

'A barbarous plan to kill someone?' Renuka said, perplexed. 'This makes no sense, Bumi.'

'Please, you have to believe me.'

Renuka looked worried. She didn't want to get involved in anything that could endanger her own family. They were quiet people who kept themselves to themselves. Her husband would be very annoyed with her if she brought trouble upon their family. She wondered if it was even safe to allow Bumi to use Anand's computer.

'I promise you it won't get you or your family in

trouble and it won't cost you anything. I've voted too. Come on, I will show you.'

Against her better judgment Renuka agreed and the two hurried up the stairs and into Anand's untidy room. Immediately, she began to apologize but Bumi shook her head impatiently. 'He is a teenager. It would be unhealthy if his room were clean.

'We need your passport number.'

'Why?' Renuka asked, already regretting her decision to allow her friend to use her computer.

'Because each person is only allowed to vote once.'

Renuka went to her bedroom, opened a locked cupboard, and from a rubber-banded bundle of all her family's passports extracted hers.

They switched on the computer, got connected to the Internet the way Ashan had shown her, and went to the Play God site. She was shocked to see that the yes figure had already risen to 390 and the no figure was only 3. Silently, she thanked Ashan; he must have voted for him and his mother.

When prompted at the right time, she hit the no button. Renuka read out her passport number and Bumi carefully keyed the numbers in. The screen flashed the 'Thank you for voting' message and filled once more with the live feed of Black. Bumi's shoulders slumped. Seeing three hundred and ninety yes votes had frightened her. She had only a few friends left so there was no way she could even hope to reach that figure. She thought of David Icke and prayed that he could help.

She would have liked to stay and utilize the other passports in Renuka's hand but Renuka's husband, Ashok, had come in from work and was calling out to his wife.

Immediately Bumi sprang up. She pressed her friend's hand. 'I'd better go, but thank you so much, Renuka. I'll never forget this.'

Renuka accompanied her friend only to the top of the stairs, then went back to sit at the computer and watch the live feed. When her husband called out to her again she shouted him upstairs. 'Come and look at this,' she said. 'Can you believe they are asking the public to vote whether this boy lives or not?'

Ashok shook his head at his wife's naivety. 'What utter nonsense,' he dismissed, and sat on the chair his wife had vacated. He clicked out of the website, went back in afresh, and he stared at the screen in disbelief. Then he looked up at his wife. 'They are offering a hundred US dollars if we vote yes.'

'Really? Bumi didn't tell me that. Anyway, it's one vote per person and I have already voted, no.'

'You have, but I haven't. And if I vote yes we will have a hundred dollars, and we will not have affected the outcome. We have to take care of our situation. We are not responsible for this boy. Who knows what karma he has come with to end up in this situation? We have nothing to feel guilty for. And anyway, *who is* this boy?'

'I don't know. Apparently someone that Bumi knows.'

'Go get all our passports.'

Renuka picked up the bundle of passports that were lying on the table. 'Why?'

'We are going to use Anand's and Meera's passports too. Anand will vote yes and Meera will vote no. Which means we will not be changing the outcome for this boy, but our family will still be better off by two hundred dollars.'

'I don't know: Bumi did come to me for help. This is not helping, is it?'

'Hey, if we wanted to be selfish, we could make four hundred dollars.'

Renuka folded her arms across her ample chest.

'If it makes you feel better I will tell everyone at my office to vote, no.'

'What if they vote, yes?'

'How would that be our fault? Besides, I don't understand why you're making such a fuss. Look at that boy, for God's sake. He looks more dead than alive. We are probably doing him a favor. What kind of life is that, hooked up to all those machines? And I think it was rather sly of your friend not to tell you that voting yes was worth a hundred dollars. Surely that was your decision to make. I should be annoyed with her if I were you.'

'Yes, I suppose that was not very trusting of her. I will phone my sister in Pondicherry and tell her to do the same as us.'

'Good, and while you are at it, call all my relatives too.'

His wife made a face. She didn't like Ashok's people.

Renuka sat beside him and together they did the deed. Nevertheless, Ashok went up to bed peeved that Bumi had taken advantage of his wife and there was no way to change one's vote. As he brushed his teeth vigorously he decided he would tell all his relatives in India to vote in the morning. A hundred dollars in India was big money. There was no doubt in his mind that the powers that be would shut down this facility very quickly.

The Investigation
Portland Cybercrime Unit, FBI

Dan Wells, head of the FBI's Cybercrime Unit in Portland, Oregon was a tall, spare man with thinking hazel eyes and a cautious mouth. A man who took extraordinary pride in his work. Forty successful prosecutions in less than seven years. The rest of his life could be characterized as a failure of monumental proportions: messy divorce, kids who wouldn't speak to him, a cold apartment, a bare fridge, and a lonely, unmade bed. He knocked briefly on his superior's office door and walked in.

'Sir?'

Robert Kilton sat behind his desk; thinning hair, cotton shirt, unbuttoned camel waistcoat, and a belligerent look that Dan knew well. He grunted, and nodded toward the chair in front of his desk. Dan sat. Kilton turned his computer screen to face Dan. 'Seen this yet?' he asked glumly.

Dan's eyes narrowed. 'What the hell?'

'Kinda creepy, huh?'

'It came online eight hours ago. Some sick fuck is streaming it live from somewhere on planet Earth. But by a strange coincidence, and you know how I feel about coincidences, our offices had two phone booth tips minutes apart about six hours after it came online. So it's either local or someone wants us to think it is.'

'Jesus, what is wrong with people? Eight hours ago and already two thousand people want this kid dead.'

Kilton leaned back into the comfort of his ergonomic

leather chair and said nothing.

'Obviously, we can't shut it down?'

'Yep. The site is being hosted by thousands of servers around the world.'

Dan looked at Kilton, his eyes narrowed. 'Who's the kid?'

'No idea.'

Dan frowned. 'A kid that sick must have a medical history. Where are his relatives? He didn't get to be that age without carers, relatives, friends, doctors, nurses, social workers. Someone must know or miss him.'

'None of the two thousand have come forward,' Robert said dryly. 'Get your team on it. See what you can do.'

Dan left the office frowning. Something very strange about the whole thing. Nobody ever in his experience would pay out hundreds of thousands to complete strangers for nothing. He stopped by the vending machine and returned to his department with coffee and a chocolate bar.

Mary Manning, a charmingly freckled, young thing looked up from her screen. She scowled at him playfully. 'What did *he* want?'

Dan stopped by her desk. Silently he went around to where she was sitting and, leaning forward, typed in the website's address. The others crowded around to watch.

Their eyes widened. '*Untraceable*,' Mary declared.

'Yep, it's right out of it,' agreed Kim Meers, easily the best mind in his team.

Dan turned toward them with a frown. 'Catch me up. What are you two on about?'

'It's a Hollywood movie,' explained Mary.

'Diane Lane,' said Kim, flicking her raven black hair

away from her neck.

Dan's eyes followed the movement. There was something about her large dark eyes over high cheekbones, and the ponytail that ended in a tangle of glossy locks on her shoulders and back that reminded him of a gypsy. A wide-mouthed, barefoot tawny-gold witch. He knew the sexual tension was bad business, but there was nothing he could do about it. It often made him unnecessarily short and angry with her. He let his glance flick back to Mary. 'There was a movie about this?'

Mary tapped some keys. 'It's in your inbox. Go watch it.'

Dan grimaced. 'Right, as ever we're going to follow the money. Meers, you vote yes. Let's see if the money is real to start with. And arrange to call on some of these bleeding hearts that voted yes too.'

'I'm on it,' said Kim and began to walk toward her desk.

'We're not doing any press releases just yet. Let's keep it under wraps. Lots of people out there that could do with a hundred bucks.'

Anne, black and secretive, spoke up from her computer terminal. 'Your plan just got foiled. A British website is running the story.'

'What?' He went over to her screen and read the story, aware that all the others were logged into their terminals and were just as quickly devouring the words. 'Who the hell is this guy?'

'A crackpot who says reptilians rule this planet,' replied Mary.

Dan's mouth dropped open. 'You'd better be kidding.'

'Nope.'

'Relax, that's the bad news.' Steve Tanner, a bespectacled loner, chipped in. 'Here's the good news. He has a huge following and an excellent Alexa ranking both in Britain and here.' He tapped at his keyboard. 'Look, thirty thousand hits just for today. And they are all trying to... er..."do the right thing". So there won't be too many trying to cash in on the boy's predicament.'

'No,' Kim disagreed quietly. 'That's not the good news, Steve; that's the bad news. If he is running with the story then Fox and CBS will be at it too and it won't be "good" people trying to save a dying boy anymore.'

Dan looked worried. 'Steve, contact this Icke guy. Find out how he came by the story?'

'On it, Boss.'

'Somebody give me the figures again.'

Mary spoke up. 'Since the reptilian guy's involvement, the numbers are 3,500 against, and 2,010 for.'

Supreme excellence [in warfare] lies in destroying your enemy's will to resist without fighting.

——Sun Tzu, *The Art of War*
(6th Century BC)

Miss Monroe set the girl's tray on the low table. There was a note hidden in another chocolate bar. But when she raised her eyes to meet the girl's, a gasp of shock escaped her lips. Immediately remembering the cameras, she modified it into a cough.

There was nothing behind the girl's eyes, not even the vaguest recognition. Her brain had been damaged so badly that all of her memory and most of her intelligence was gone. To all intents and purposes they had lobotomized her. There would be no more sessions, no more Shekina. All her powers were lost forever. In fact, there wasn't even a Dakota. Just this drooling sub-human that they would soon terminate, and who was staring stupidly at her.

'I brought your lunch,' she stated unnecessarily.

Slowly Dakota moved her eyes away from Miss Monroe and back to the TV screen. Miss Monroe turned away from the intolerable sight and hurried out of the room. Outside the parked motorized cart carrying lunch for all the others was waiting for her, but she ignored it and walked down the long corridor. Fuck the cameras, she thought, and began to run. In her room she closed the door and stood against it, breathing heavily. What they had done to the girl was unpardonable. There would be no exoneration for her if she remained in that godforsaken place. She went to the phone on her desk and dialed his number.

'We need to meet,' she said, when the connection was made.

'I am very close to you. Meet me in the park in an hour's time. You know which bench is mine.'

The empty line purred in Miss Monroe's ear. In the bathroom a calm and collected woman looked back. She smoothed her hair and, taking no personal belongings that would create suspicion, left her quarters. If she returned it would only be for the girl. She'd had enough.

Miss Monroe stood at the edge of the green. In the distance she could see him. He was sitting on a park bench with his back to her. But there was no mistaking that shaven head or those hulking shoulders upon which sat the glinting metals of his uniform. She stepped onto the grass square, walked diagonally across it and gained the path that led to the man. Now she could see that he was not alone; there was a little girl no more than five or six sitting on the bench with him. She could have been his daughter, but she was not. There was something unnatural about her. They were both eating ice cream, but her left hand was clenched into a fist in her lap, and there was a glazed expression in her eyes. She paid no attention to her surroundings or to the woman who had stopped right in front of them.

'Commandant,' Miss Monroe greeted in a voice she had intended to be firm and strong, but that came out shrill and frightened. You must hold your ground, she cautioned herself firmly. You must look evil in the face and not turn away, if you desire your freedom.

'Hello, Alice,' he said, not looking at her, but gravely

contemplating the pale yellow appearance of his ice cream.

The ground shifted under her, as he had meant it to. 'So that *is* my name.'

'Is he any good, that psychiatrist you found?'

'You've had me followed?'

'It would be silly to allow your secrets to run around unchaperoned. You'd be surprised to know how many of them work for us.'

Alice began to shake. 'You are lying. He doesn't work for you. He's helped me a lot.

'Are you now... er...cured?' he sneered.

'Not totally.'

'Is that why you are shaking like a leaf in high wind?'

'I know now what you did to me.'

'What did I do to you, Alice?'

'You tortured me, and raped me when I was,' she pointed a shaking finger at the girl sitting beside him, 'her age.'

He looked at her for the first time. His eyes were very light in the brightness of day. They were silver. She realized that she had never seen him in daylight. 'As a matter of fact, I do remember you. You had a very beautiful body and a voracious, quite insatiable appetite for sweet drops. You would do *anything* for one. Indeed, you were quite the minx. I believe you liked it. Every bit of it. Don't you remember when you begged for more?'

Alice felt herself begin to fall apart. 'That's a damn lie,' she screeched. 'I hated it. I hate you. I was a child.'

'Control yourself, my dear. That's all in the past now. You have nothing to fear from me. Flesh has a very strict sell-by date as far as I'm concerned. Anyway, you didn't come here to reminisce. What do you want?'

'I've come to right a wrong.'

'Well, go on then,' he prompted.

'I want my freedom and Dakota's—she is of no use to you anymore.'

'And if I don't agree?'

'I will reveal all to the media. I have recorded everything I know about you and the killings that go on in the Black Hole, and I have given copies to two solicitors. If you have me killed they will flood every newspaper in the country.'

He took a deep breath. 'Hmm…' he said, and stood. She wanted to turn around and run as if the Devil himself was at her heels, but if she did, she would be running for the rest of her life. And how long would it be before they caught up with her, anyway? Schooner Klaus towered over her. He said nothing, simply raised his free hand and slapped her hard—not so hard that she fell backwards, but hard enough that she stumbled.

It had a strange effect, that slap from him. She straightened. Her cheek was flaming red, but she felt strangely calm and free of him. She turned and walked away from him. She walked without looking back. When she made it to the edge of the park she seemed to find a new sense of purpose and began to look around her as if searching for something. There was a hot dog vendor at the entrance. She began walking toward him. As she passed him by, he said, 'Hey, sexy, buy a dog?'

She turned her face toward him and smiled, a brilliant smile. When she reached the road she waited at the curb. There were cars passing. The wind blew and dislodged a few strands of hair. She reached up, pulled the band that held her hair and flung it away. To the man waiting to cross the road on the opposite side, it was a glorious sight. He would remember that moment forever. As he watched her, full of life and beauty, she ran into the road, right into the path of an oncoming bus.

Schooner Klaus heard the screeching tires, the bang, and the shouts. Foolish girl. After all this time, she still didn't understand that *he* held the keys to everybody's suicide alters. As for those solicitors, they should have known better. Both would be dealt with. In his experience no more than a threat was needed when men with families misbehaved. He glanced down at the girl. She had finished her ice cream. Both her hands were tightly clenched in her lap, and her big green eyes were intently watching some children playing in the distance.

> The American people won't believe anything until they see it on TV.
>
> —Richard Nixon

'Wow! 5,442 say die and 35,292 say don't,' Carter commented, flashing a salesman's smirk.

'You don't get it, Carter. I'll die in a few weeks, no matter what the results. But it's good to have proof of what I've always known. That humans are basically good.'

'Whatever. Don't break out the champagne just yet, though,' Carter advised, his voice and face impartial. Obviously it did not matter to him either way. With a smile he moved to the computer screen that kept a record of Black's brain activity, and began to scroll back. As he read the thoughts that had gone through Black's head, he chuckled softly and, glancing over in Black's direction, said, 'You sure worry a lot about that girl, don't you?'

Black felt heat rush up his neck to his face. He felt embarrassed and humiliated that his most private thoughts were not only being trampled over by an unfeeling brute, but mocked.

'What's going to happen to her?'

'Don't know.'

And, Black thought, don't care.

Carter left after taking some notes and adjusting the equipment in the room. The lights were dimmed right down so that only the light from the computer, game screen and television glowed bright. Black began to concentrate on the computer cursor. To his great surprise the cursor began to move almost immediately. It was even easier than changing the channels on his TV at home. He scrolled upward and began to read his own thoughts. They surprised him.

At every turn there was the voice urging fear, worry, anger. Each thought agitated: negative, self-pitying, ungrateful. And always underlying every thought was that great obsession—himself. As Green had put it, the best for me and the rest for the rest.

Here, thanks to the bad guys, was the parasite exposed in all its glory.

He brought the visual back to its original screen then he practiced deleting one letter from the end of the last sentence. Surprisingly easy. He deleted his thoughts for the last ten minutes. He must not let them know that he knew about the parasite.

Black let his eyes blur on the ceiling, and thinking of Green he willed himself to sleep. He woke up in a blue corridor. The glowing blue figure of Green was standing motionless in it.

'Where are we?'

'Just a mind construct. Blue corridors are easy to erect and almost impossible to detect. Let's walk down it.'

They began to walk. Black turned to look at Green.

'I know you want to go to the girl,' said Green. 'But I have to warn you that you won't like what you see. De-programming is a euphemism for frying the human brain. She will not recognize you.'

Black looked at him in horror. 'How bad is she?'

'Very bad, though she will recover somewhat in time.'

Black felt as if his heart was breaking. 'I want to see

her, anyway. Will she be able to see me?'

'Yes. As much as they would like to, they cannot separate her from her psychic powers—she is…special.'

'Will you help me?'

'Of course. I will guide you there.'

'Can I go now?'

Wordlessly, he held his hand out.

Black did not take his hand. 'I need to talk to you; will you come to see me again tomorrow?'

'Yes.'

'Thank you. I owe you so much.'

Green smiled sadly. 'You have four minutes and twenty-three seconds.'

'What happens after?'

'Carter will wake you up with some "news". Hurry. You now have four minutes and thirteen seconds.'

Black took Green's hand and for a moment the blue corridor swayed and twisted like a snake. Then he was standing in Dakota's living quarters. She was sitting in front of the TV, but her body was leaning forward unnaturally. Without changing position she turned her neck slowly and looked at him, without curiosity, stupidly. The action reminded him of that of a small animal. Then for no reason her eyeballs rolled in their sockets, making her look weird and vacant. It was obvious that she was heavily drugged. Without any sign that she had registered his presence she turned away and stared at the TV screen. Despite Green's warning, Black was crushed by her appearance. He went closer.

'What are you watching?' he asked. *The Wizard of Oz* was playing.

Her eyelids drooped and her eyes shifted oddly. Then she hunched her shoulders and brought her neck in, almost as a turkey would, until her chin was sitting on her chest. She didn't know what she was watching.

She seemed so foreign and lost that Black felt a sick despair creep into his soul.

Perhaps he should start with something easier. 'What's the time now?'

Dakota did not respond.

'Are there no clocks in this place?'

She shook her head slowly. She was communicating with him.

'If we find a news channel it will show the time.'

'No news.' The words were slow and thick, but he had her speaking.

No news channels? 'How many channels have you got?'

She held both her hands up and carefully counted out four fingers and showed them to him.

'I see.' He looked around him and noticed her food tray. He touched the base of a dish. It was cold.

'Hungry,' she said.

And Black felt fury, white hot, at her destruction, at the men who had done it. He had to turn his face away from her so she would not see it and misconstrue it as directed at her.

'Dakota lonely,' she muttered suddenly.

He turned back, full of compassion. She was trying to stand up. Clumsily, unsteadily. There was something wrong with her feet. They would not obey her. He could not risk going closer. If her hand went through him she would be frightened. She gave up, fell back, and looked confused.

He looked at his watch. His time was very nearly up. 'I've got to go now, Dakota, but I will be back.'

248

'Promise.'

He smiled at her. 'You will wait for me, won't you?'

She nodded.

'You won't tell anybody about me, will you?'

She shook her head vigorously. A three-year-old child.

Then he was back in his body. Carter was clicking his fingers smartly. 'Well, well, look who's made it simultaneously on CBS, ABC, and NBC?'

Seek not the kingdom of shadows,
For evil will surely appear.
For only the master of brightness
Shall conquer the shadow of fear.

—The Emerald Tablets of Thoth

'I want to help her.'

'Not a good idea, Black.'

'Why?'

'The only way you can help her is if you went back in time. And that would be very unwise.'

'Unwise?'

'Remember when you watched Superman turn back time by turning planet Earth at dizzying speed in the opposite direction?'

'Mmmm.'

'Well, it won't be as simple as that. Going back in time is fraught with great danger. There is a very high probability that you could get stuck in it.'

'Stuck?' Black felt fear slice through him—a premonition? He brushed it away before it could take root.

'Any manipulation of time usually causes it to solidify. First, it will appear to be racing through you, while moving at normal speed for everything else around you. That will be your only warning and your last chance to get out. If you are unable to at that moment, then the very air around you will change. It will take on a soup-like thickness and turn greenish. The sensation will be similar to being in a storm shelter while a tornado is raging directly on top.

'Movements will then be restricted only to those you can make in quicksand. For a few seconds the green will fade out and the objects around you will start to shimmer and lose their solidity. Physical objects will become clear liquid—not because they have lost their physicality, they are still there, but because solidity is a function of time. They will appear to you with waves running through them. Then the thickness will set around you like jelly around a fly, trapping you so thoroughly you cannot move a single muscle. But you will be able to feel everything, though.'

Black gave a nervous laugh. 'Not much difference to what I live through every day, then.'

'No, it is indescribably worse. The realm between life and death is like being in a deep freeze, but most humans will experience that mixed state badly. It is an environment that is so incomprehensible and so frightening to humans that almost all who have ventured there have spontaneously combusted. And because their perception will be so distorted by their surroundings, it will become impossible for them to tell whether a minute or a century has passed. As such they will experience themselves burning for what appears to be years, even if only minutes have passed before they are pulled out. And the one or two who have escaped and come back have gone mad owing to their inability to comprehend what happened to them.'

There was a short pause. Black thought about Dakota—poor, dribbling Dakota— speaking in the third person: 'Dakota lonely.'

'I will take the risk,' he said.

'You are very courageous.'

'No, I'm not. I'm actually afraid, but I care about her. And I must do this.'

'Love. What a beautiful thing it is when it touches the human heart.'

'Show me what I should do.'

'All right. The easiest way for you to get to her is to meet her in the past just before her de-programming and do something that will change the course of her actions. Choose your entry into the past carefully and plan your moves even more carefully. There is no going back. If you snag your clothes on a twig or a nail don't look back. The artificial matrix is designed with tricks and traps to snare you. Never look back, no matter what happens. Do what you have to do and get out.'

'OK.'

'I see that you already have a plan.'

'Is it a good plan?'

'Yes, very imaginative, a trait much admired by my kind.'

'Will it work?'

'If we are in the timeline where it does.'

'And if we aren't?'

'Then what can go wrong will go wrong.'

'No matter what happens, thank you for all your help.'

'Be as quick as you can.'

'I am ready whenever you are.'

'Remember, any intervention at all from me will cause me to get stuck in this dimension, so expect no help. Good luck and do not tarry for a second longer than necessary and never repeat any action.'

'Even if I get stuck, I will have changed the future for her, right?'

'Yes.'

'I'm ready.'

A blindingly bright light shone from Green's forehead and something resembling a tunnel opened up. It was like a three-dimensional fractal, a dancing five-pointed star full of light. Black stepped into it and felt it pull at the soles of his feet and the palms of his hands. Locked into the tunnel he could not decide if he was spinning or if the world outside the tunnel was spinning.

When the spinning stopped the tunnel opened out to a corridor. She was in front of him. She was pulling her hand out of a thick door, the door to the room where he was held. At that moment she turned to look back at the corridor. He had arrived seconds before the jump. Instead of seeing an empty corridor she saw him. She turned around to face him.

'Don't go in there,' he warned. 'It's a trap. I've come from the future and I've seen what happens if you do. You will be sucked out like a rag to a place where you will become nothing, and Dakota will be de-programmed. Her brain will be so badly damaged that she will barely be able to function.'

'But I am supposed to give her to you.'

'You already have. Now go back and quickly. Pretend you have never been here. Do nothing to call attention to yourself. There are things afoot—big changes are about to happen.'

'There is a video record of everything I have done, and this trip.'

Black did not hesitate. 'I think I can erase it for you. Quickly, we must hurry. Go the way you came and I will follow you.'

She made her jump back into the session room and he followed. The tunnel stayed next to him. Teddy and the biotech were waiting for her return, but they could not see him. Black immediately set about erasing the video records.

When Shekina came out of the trip seat she said, 'Don't worry about their memory banks. I'll take care of that. But there are also the images from the corridors and those from my room. They are held in the central unit.'

'OK,' he said, and did to the central computer digital image records what he had done to the computer records in his room. Seconds later the job was done and Black knew it was time to go. He turned toward the tunnel that was waiting beside him, but his eyes caught a flying cockroach. It landed on Teddy's cheek. How strange that such an insect should live in such a clinical place. What did it eat to survive?, he wondered, and automatically looked back at it. It was only for a split second, but that was all that was necessary. The artificial matrix had set him a trap and he had fallen into it.

Almost immediately he felt that first and last warning to 'get out' that Green had told him about. Time rushing inside him while all around him everything was normal.

Shekina, her face contorted, shouted out, 'Run, Black, run.'

But even then it was already too late. The air was turning green around him.

Before he could react, jump into the tunnel, the green faded out and Teddy and the cockroach began to shimmer and undulate. The effect was similar to what heatwaves do to things in the distance. Teddy became as

255

liquid as a glass before it shatters under the influence of a soprano's high note.

Black turned and tried to make for the tunnel, but it was as if he was running in wet cement. Without warning it hardened and he was unable to move a single muscle. Not even his eyes. He started to become disorientated. A sickly yellowish light shrouded him. It smelled of rot and decay. And fear. Terrible fear. Suddenly, true to Green's word, he began to burn from the inside out, the horror of which was beyond anything he had ever encountered or could ever have imagined.

Eshu throws a stone today and it kills a bird yesterday.

—Yoruba poem

Miss Monroe walked into the girl's quarters carrying her lunch. The girl was sitting in front of the TV, but it was turned off. At Miss Monroe's appearance, she turned and smiled at her.

'What are you doing?' asked Miss Monroe, straightening up and looking her in the eyes.

'Thinking,' replied the girl, her eyes bright and full of life. 'Did you bring me chocolate?'

Miss Monroe put her hand into her pocket and brought out a bar.

'Oh, good,' she said and, as she took the bar, slid a piece of paper into Miss Monroe's hand.

'Well, I'll be back later to pick up the tray.'

'Thank you.'

Miss Monroe did not get a chance to look at the paper until she entered her own quarters and sat at her desk as normally as she could. The girl had neat small writing.

I remote viewed your psychiatrist – he's one of them. Do nothing out of the ordinary (not even chocolates for me). Stay down for now and don't try to get any kind of help for me. Things are afoot. There is a way out for us.

Miss Monroe felt strong gratitude fill her heart for the girl. She did not know that her real savior was a boy lying in a bed deep underground who had gone back into the past and changed the future. In this future she did not have to see a brain-damaged child and in a rush of emotion confront Dr. Klaus. In this future she did not have to die.

Back in her quarters Shekina ignored the food on the table and returned to doing what Miss Monroe had interrupted. Helping Black. She vowed that she would not stop until she had won them all over. She began with Africa and stopped just before she reached China.

> ## Learn how to see. Realize that everything connects to everything else.
> —Leonardo da Vinci

Schooner Klaus came awake gently in his darkened bedroom. For some delicious minutes he relished the luxurious softness of the goose down pillow under his head and neck, and the lovely warmth of his deep bed. He stretched slowly, enjoying the languorous movement inside his muscles. Quietly, avoiding the sight of the woman beside him and without waking her up, he slid out. He did not enjoy the sight of his wife's overly bronzed, sagging arms, which were inevitably exposed at this time of the morning.

Last night was fuzzy in his memory. He remembered going to a club, a special place where they played kings and queens in the back rooms. He didn't know why he still felt the need to frequent such seedy places, but it was only there amongst the most degenerate of humans that he felt he could be himself. In places like that there was no need to pretend and hide. All was filth, and so was he.

He walked silently into their bathroom. When they had been on their honeymoon his wife had seen this design in a ladies' toilet in Richmond, England. And she had never forgotten it. Ten years ago when they had moved into this house she had recreated it. An English design. Blue patterns on white, like china. Pretty. He switched on the lights and stepped up to the mirror and blinked, his eyes still unused to the sudden brightness. Someone had written on his bathroom mirror with pink

259

lipstick.

His jaw dropped as he read the message that was scrawled across the mirror in bold handwriting. His first reaction was one of fear. That someone had entered his bedroom while he had slept and written on his mirror. Then the expression in his eyes changed to one of disbelief. Below the mirror, lying without its lid, was the lipstick used. He picked it up slowly and looked at the blunted edge. And tried to remember. How? When? He looked again at the words.

*FOR HEAVEN'S SAKE CATCH
ME BEFORE I KILL
AGAIN. I AM PURE
EVIL*

No doubt about it. The handwriting was his. He sat on the broad, wooden toilet seat—an English antique specially flown in. He turned toward the mirror and looked at his own shocked face behind the writing. He had no memory of writing the words. He closed his eyes and thought hard about the night before. But it remained illusive. Shadows. And it occurred to him that this was not the first time there were gaps in his memory.

There was only one explanation and that one was totally unacceptable. Alters inside him! That he was not the puppet master he had thought, but a puppet with others higher up pulling at his strings was too horrible to contemplate. He refused to consider it. For now, damage control.

He went to the door and looked in on his wife. Her

sagging arms were lying above the bedclothes, and her breathing was even. She never awakened early—the pills always kept her dead to the world until her alarm went off in a couple of hours' time. He went back into the bathroom and locked the door.

Meticulously, using toilet paper, he cleaned the lipstick marks. They came off easily. He peed on top of the soiled toilet paper and flushed it. Then he brushed his teeth, shaved, and went into his dressing room. He opened his wardrobe door and looked at the row of faultlessly tailored identical uniforms. He selected one and carefully dressed in it. When he was ready he stood in front of the mirror. There had been no writing on the mirror. Of course not. He had been overly imaginative even as a boy. He was no puppet, he was the puppet master.

I work all night, I work all day, to pay the bills I have to pay. Ain't it sad?

—ABBA, 'Money, Money, Money' (1976)

It was a Saturday.

Kim was sitting at her kitchen table in her pajamas and dressing gown having breakfast. She put her slice of toast down when she heard the post hit the floor. After donning a pair of white gloves she picked up the bundle and sifted through it quickly. One envelope caught her attention. Plain white and marked PRIVATE. It had no return address on the back. Discarding the rest on a side table in the hallway, she took it to the living room. It crackled enticingly. Carefully, she sliced open the top and looked in.

Tinfoil.

She pulled the tinfoil out by tugging it at one end with pincers, and unraveled it. Five twenties. One hundred dollars. She sat back and looked at it, then put the notes back into the tinfoil and the tinfoil back into the envelope. It would have to be sent off to the lab, but already she was sure they would not find a single fingerprint anywhere. She sat on the couch and Sheba jumped into her lap. She stroked her soft, white fur absently. So the money was real. Until she had seen it, she hadn't been able to believe that there existed a group of people—and she was certain that it was a group—who would pay out for a game of this nature. It made no sense.

Then she opened her computer and went to the Play God website. The ones who had resisted, stayed warm,

263

and said no, were only in their thousands, but the ones who had been seduced by the snake and found an excuse for murder had made the yes figure fascinating to watch. In the beginning it had climbed quickly, but then its rise had become more and more rapid, and now it was changing so fast that the numbers were blurring. Kim sighed.

The sun was setting on all their collective souls.

Leaving her computer open, she went to retrieve her toast. It was already cold. She ran her finger on the buttered side and offered her finger to the cat to lick. The cat diligently went to work. Kim ate and watched the boy and thought of the sad, desperate woman who had gone to David Icke for help. The thought made her feel quite tearful and she was about to look away from the sight of the boy when suddenly she thought she saw something. She stopped chewing, hurriedly swallowed the bit of bread, and, leaning very close to the screen, squinted at it. She remained in that position for thirty-one minutes, and then it happened again. Now she knew.

It was Saturday, but she picked up her phone and called Dan.

"Who'll carry the coffin?"
"I," said the Kite,
"If it's not through the night,
I'll carry the coffin."

—'Who killed Cock Robin?',
Tommy Thumb's Pretty Song Book (1744)

'Except for his brain activity, which is abnormally high, all his bodily functions including breathing and heartbeat have reduced to almost hibernation levels,' explained Carter.

Kite looked at the screen that charted Black's brain output. It appeared jagged and fast. 'Under what circumstances would you normally see such a brain pattern?'

'Normally one wouldn't, and certainly not for this long. This is the signature of someone who is in a state of extreme panic and fear and perhaps even terrible pain. A normal human would pass out, go into parasympathetic shock, and even dissociate, but his brain has been in this state for the last four hours.'

'You may leave now.'

Carter went out and the door shut behind him.

For a moment Kite remained where he was, close to the door. Then he inched his wheelchair forward. Little by little he conquered a foot of ground. He could feel himself begin to sweat, but he continued to push forward. Another foot was won. But then he stopped, unable to go an inch closer. He shivered with some unknown dread. Uneasily, he retreated to his original position and gazed at the boy's staring eyes and face.

Even that was difficult to do. There was something about this boy that unnerved him, and made it impossible for him to be in the same room as him. Nobody had ever had this effect on him, and he hated the power the boy had to intimidate him with nothing more than his presence.

It was obvious that he was suffering greatly, but in his suffering he seemed to have gained even more of this natural force field. His power was increasing, which was worrying. Before, Kite remembered, he could go halfway into the room. Now, next to the door was the best he could do.

He rubbed his forearms and glanced at the screen. 3,472,223 stood with him, and a mere 267,907 bleeding hearts had done themselves out of a hundred bucks. There was no way the boy could win. He maneuvered his wheelchair carefully in a tight circle, never turning his back on the still figure on the bed, and left the room with a great sense of relief. Outside in the corridor his assistant was waiting for him. He dropped his mobile into the inside pocket of his jacket and straightened.

'Get me out of here,' Kite said, whirling past him. His wheelchair was speeding so fast his assistant had to run to keep up.

'There has been some development with the investigation. One of the officers, a young woman, has noticed that the film of the boy is not a live feed.'

'How did she do that?'

'She observed the boy's eye movement repeated every half hour and figured out that the film was on a loop.'

Kite nodded, impressed. 'Bright girl. Can we use her?'

'No, she has "opinions".'

'Shame. Throw something her way.'

'Of course. When would you like us to do so?'

'As soon as can be arranged. Make sure there is full worldwide media coverage of the event.'

'Yes, sir.'

'Anything else?'

'Fish has been in touch. The brotherhood requests an audience tomorrow at noon.'

Kite nodded absently. The more distance he put between him and the boy, the better he felt. But only when the boy was dead would he be at ease. They finished the rest of their journey in uninterrupted silence.

Blessed are the weird people, misfits, writers, mystics, painters, troubadours, for they teach us to see the world through different eyes.

—Jacob Nordby

Kim put her first mug of coffee for the day down on her table and asked, 'What's going on?' The other team members were excitedly crowded around Dan's workstation.

Mary looked back and chuckled. The sound came from deep within her throat. 'Our players have made a mistake while trying to contact you.'

'Contact me?' Kim walked quickly toward her colleagues.

'Yep, while you were sleeping. We've got a location.'

Kim's forehead furrowed. 'We do? How?'

'We caught their email on the exit node.'

'What? We intercepted them on the last hop of their tracks. The technology that has confounded our best minds so far didn't expect us to be monitoring exit traffic! With all their savvy sophistication they didn't install SSH tunnels or a VPN or a private bridge into their communication system. Not even a Whonix? I don't buy it. And I'm surprised that you guys do. Anyway, what did he contact me for.'

'Just wanted to crow.'

'Looks to be an abandoned warehouse downtown,' Steve said.

Kim's frown deepened. She looked at her colleagues

in frustration. 'An abandoned warehouse, downtown? No way!'

'Why not?' asked Dan, but he already knew; he just wished it was otherwise.

'Doesn't fit the rest of the MO.'

'You hanging around to drink your coffee, Meers, or coming to find out what's in this warehouse?'

Kim put on her black jacket with FBI written in yellow on the back over her green sweater and followed him. Outside they got into his Chevy Impala and Dan floored the pedal. The SWAT team were already mobilized and waiting for orders to storm the warehouse. An ambulance was on the ready. As they rounded the corner, they saw that the press were also there.

'Who told them?' Dan shouted.

'Whoever wants us all here,' Kim said.

Dan gave her an irritated look.

They pulled up a little distance from the padlocked gates. One of the SWAT team came forward.

'The surveillance robot we sent in shows the place is empty.'

Dan gave the go-ahead and the man said, 'Go,' into his mouthpiece. Instantly his team poured into the building through the front, back and roof. Through her earpiece Kim could hear their distinctive 'Go, go, go' orders. She put her fingers on her mouth and waited. A few minutes later the team leader radioed back, 'Clear.'

The SWAT team leader came out of the building. He looked around, found Dan's eyes, and shrugged.

Dan walked toward the open door with Kim following close behind. At the doorway he stopped abruptly. That it was a set-up to bring them there was obvious instantly. Kim's mobile took an incoming message. She looked at it. Unknown number. She opened the message.

Good detective work, Ms. Karajah.
Better luck next time?

She stared at the words for a bit longer, before showing them wordlessly to Dan.

'Who the hell is Ms. Karajah?'

'Many years before I was born my father changed his name, *before* he left Palestine for the land of the brave and the free. There is no record of his old name in this country and probably not even in Palestine anymore.'

'Jesus, who *are* these people?'

Kim looked around them. The interior was vast, dim and completely empty but for a chair with an open laptop on it. It had strategically been placed under a skylight. Light full of dancing dust motes streamed onto it. A photographer's dream. They walked toward the arrangement, their footsteps echoing in the silence. The screen showed the boy in his white room. Kim reached a hand toward the screen.

'Don't touch anything,' Dan warned. 'For fuck sake…'

Kim's voice was calm. 'Why? I'll bet a year's salary that this entire place is cleaner than an obsessive compulsive's hands after he's washed them. We're not going to find a single fingerprint or a speck of DNA.'

'Even experts make mistakes.'

Kim unzipped her jacket. 'Do you ever get the feeling, Dan, that we are chasing ghosts? That we are purposely being led on a wild goose chase? Have you

271

ever wondered why you were given this case?'

Dan looked at her suspiciously. She was the best in his team, but he didn't like the way this conversation was going. 'What are you getting at?'

'Think about it. Why isn't NSA's Utah Data Center helping us? With their super computers we might stand a chance.'

'Ever heard of Executive Order 12333?' Dan queried sarcastically. 'NSA has no mandate outside of collecting information that constitutes foreign intelligence and counterintelligence.'

'Yeah, sure. Ever heard of the Patriot Act? They're not helping because somebody don't want them to. Because we're not meant to get anywhere. Whoever is playing this game is too rich and powerful.' She pointed to the screen. 'That's two hundred million right there. In cash! Who's got that kind of money and is able to mobilize it worldwide without leaving a trace? Who wants to? And admit it, possessing technology that's higher than the FBI's?'

Dan's eyes were withering. 'Can we just do our jobs?'

'Is that what our oaths say? Look the other way when our government engages in wrongdoing and outright corruption—'

'Have you come across something that suggests our government is involved?'

'No, but—'

'Good. I've got to go sort out the media,' he said, beginning to turn away.

'Did you vote?'

He looked at her strangely. 'Of course not.'

'Not even to vote no?'

'Not even to vote no,' he said, but his mind was

already outside with the gathered media.

Kim ran her finger along the bridge of her nose. Dan looked at her mouth. That mouth was meant for different things. 'But at some point,' the mouth said, 'one has to stop wondering about who and think of the why. Why do they want us to vote?'

'Oh fuck. You're not going to start your conspiracy theories again, are you?'

'OK, you tell me. What's the agenda here?' Kim waved her hand to encompass the whole space. 'What's the purpose of all this? When you don't know the why, you can never hope to defeat anything.'

'Right, let's hear what you think is the "why" of all this, then.'

'In a strange way this actually reminds me of 9/11.'

Dan's jaw dropped open but Kim ignored him and carried on.

'An intricately choreographed ritual performed on a grand scale, amplified incalculably by the electronic media. Would we be closer to the truth if we viewed this spectacular, highly symbolic theatre of cruelty being broadcast to millions of people as a transformative Satanic black mass? Where the "pews" are filled by entire nations? Could it be we are all being alchemically paganized and brutalized? That, by the very act of voting, we are becoming active participants in their ceremony of human sacrifice.'

Dan looked at Kim in disbelief. 'You're crazy, you know?'

Kim shrugged. 'Or we could put it down to cognitive dissonance?'

'What? Just because I don't subscribe to your Satanic black mass theory I'm suffering from cognitive dissonance?

'OK, let's hear *your* theory, then.'

'I've got no time for this,' he dismissed, and turned away from her.

But Kim called out, 'You do know that you're never going to find him, don't you? They're going to kill him, Dan.'

Dan didn't turn back. 'Don't touch anything,' he cautioned, his voice harder than he had intended. His footsteps echoed in the empty space. The door slammed. She walked to the screen and stared at it. The yes figure was climbing with dizzying speed. 'Where are you, kid?' she asked the small, motionless face.

> The price of anything is the amount of life you exchange for it.

——Henry David Thoreau

Mummified inside the icy shadows between the living and the dead, Black's brain had been pulsing and racing so frantically for escape from that never-ending torment that he almost missed the faint sound. When the burning had stopped, the frost had come. Slowly, inch by inch, he had become entombed inside ice. The intense pain of the ice was worse than the searing. Don't panic, he had told himself and tried to keep some air in his lungs. But he was not breathing air. How could there be pain without the body? he thought, but there was pain, piercing pain. He became immensely confused. Was he already dead?

Like a sightless, crouching creature that must scent its prey, he did not try to raise his immobilized eyes toward the pale light that filtered into that terrible place, but tried desperately to sniff out the faint sound.

'Look through my eyes.'

That voice—barely audible, but he thought he recognized it—brought the first crack of movement into his congealed, terrorized body. He turned his grateful face toward the heavens, but the immediate effect of his release from the complete lockdown was the flowering of a new agony, white hot, inescapable. His skin hurt so much that it was as if he was being flayed. His throat unlocked and he moaned soundlessly.

'Are you there? Oh, God, are you there?'

Every small movement was followed by immense pain, but it was better than his hellish frozen state, and his stiff fingers grasped and pawed painfully in that eternity of bleakness for something that he could latch onto. Anything with some color or movement. There was nothing.

He fell upon himself, destroyed and defeated. It was hopeless. He must have conjured up the sound. No one traveled this damned road. The freezing gray of the place had swallowed him whole and sucked everything out of him. He could no longer think like a human being. He cowered with blind fear, his mouth as dry as ashes. The cold was getting colder.

'Look through my eyes.'

There: that sound again.

Black's mouth moved silently. 'Green.'

Despite the intolerable agony, he raised his eyes, the needles in them plunging deeper, and tried to peer into the half-opaque nothingness that enshrouded him. But it remained impenetrable. He began to cry hopelessly. His tears burned a path down his cheeks. He was damned eternally. It was only his mind playing tricks with him.

Then he felt it, the first miraculous rush of warmth inside him. The warmth grew. He was not alone. Green was inside him. Suddenly he was no longer looking through his eyes but Green's. And how the maze changed. He began to make out shapes. As he looked he saw the black pits of nothingness and...escape. A narrow, blackened path lit up as his eyes fell upon it. His limbs were warm once more, his skin amazingly painless. He moved his legs toward the path. His gait was confident, tall.

'Thank you, Green,' he tried to whisper, but his voice was like sandpaper that rasped his throat and made it burn. As soon as his foot touched the path, Green was gone. His limbs were so weak that he could not do more than drag his body slowly along the path. On either side miles of icy twilight. Not daring to look left or right, he kept his eyes fixed on the path ahead. The path he traveled came to an abrupt end. A steep drop into a yawning black void. It was so vast that Black knew if he fell he would be falling forever. He was but an ant in that dead landscape.

'Jump,' he heard in his head.

Black didn't hesitate. The blackness of the void was infinitely preferable to the desolation and madness he would leave behind. The air rushed against his ears and grasped at his body like long, freezing cold fingers. He screamed and the screech reverberated eerily in his own ears. He could vanish without a trace in this blackness. But he didn't vanish and he didn't crash.

He was caught.

The fractal tunnel had appeared out of nowhere and connected itself to the soles of his feet and the palms of his hands. His euphoria was unimaginable. The tunnel released him as suddenly as it had taken hold of him. He dropped out of it and landed on his hands and knees. In his vision were the ends of Green's watery robes. He sat back on his haunches and slowly raised his head and looked into those beautiful eyes, so dear and yet so unfamiliar.

He could no longer hide behind the truth that he had ignored because it was more fun to pretend otherwise. Green was not a human boy with skin that lit up and glowed. He was a being who was infinitely, indescribably, and incomprehensibly more advanced and intelligent than any human. Those few seconds of seeing through his eyes had changed everything. It was not just the vividly saturated colors or the incredible celestial sounds.

In Green's world, time did not flow as humans perceived it, but was simultaneous, which was why he could access any time or place on Earth and come and go as he pleased. And since every thought and action is recorded and all real communication in the cosmos is telepathic, nothing appeared to be hidden from him and others like him.

In those few moments Black had understood the entire universe and accessed with breathtaking clarity and detail its workings, but those moments were slipping out of his fingers. His own mind could not stretch to those heights of perception. Soon even those would be gone forever. The life humans experienced using their five senses was but a pale, artificial dream by comparison.

'You interfered?' he whispered. He owed Green a debt that he could never repay.

'I did.'

'Why did you risk getting stuck in the lying matrix? I'm losing the game, anyway.'

'Take my hand and I'll show you why.'

There will be, in the next generation or so, a pharmacological method of making people love their servitude, and producing dictatorship without tears, so to speak, producing a kind of painless concentration camp for entire societies, so that people will in fact have their liberties taken away from them, but will rather enjoy it.

—Aldous Huxley

'Where are we?' Black asked, throwing his head back to look at the tree trunks soaring up, straight and tall toward the skies all around him. The ground was thick with undergrowth and there was only a dying light left to the day, but the air was still hot and humid, and filled with the clamor of insects and birds. He heard the sound of running water nearby.

'In a Malaysian rainforest.'

'What are we doing here?'

'We came to see him,' said Green, pointing to a flying mosquito. The mosquito froze in mid flight.

Black went closer. There was a bubble around the mosquito. Up close, the insect was intricately built with compound eyes, a feathery antenna, a diamond-shaped thorax, and beautiful white markings on his slender legs. 'What's so special about him?'

Green came to stand next to Black. '*He* is a transgenic mosquito, released to combat dengue fever.

279

The farthest he will fly is two hundred yards, and being male he will never attempt to consume the blood of a single living creature, but he is created in the hope that during his lifetime, which can be measured in days, he will mate with a wild female mosquito and cause her to produce defective offspring, which they believe will, if not eradicate the disease eventually, then at least contain it. Millions like him are being released in other parts of the world with the same intention. The next planned project will tackle malaria.'

Fascinated by the mosquito's stillness, Black gazed at it in wonder. He wished he could see the world through Green's eyes again. What would this little creature look like? Breathtaking slices of condensed light and stunning color? But he had only his own limited five senses and feeble mind. 'A good thing, surely. Malaria kills millions, mostly children,' he said, repeating what he had gleaned from the TV.

'Remember this, Black—bacterial DNA always becomes part of the host's DNA, but don't draw any conclusions just yet. We are playing connect the dots.' He extended a long, slender finger and touched the bubble. It broke and the mosquito sailed away. He turned to Black with his hand outstretched. 'Next dot awaits.'

Suddenly they were standing in a remote, snow-covered tundra. An icy wind blew across the desolate wilderness.

'We are in polar bear country, thirteen hundred kilometers from the North Pole, on the island of Spitsbergen.'

There was no sign of life that Black could see, and the only sign of civilization was an imposing concrete structure that jutted out of the mountainside. They were, in fact, standing on a road that led up to it. A pair of solid steel doors formed its entrance.

'That,' Green continued, pointing to the tall doors, 'is the sole entrance to what some call the doomsday vault. Built deep into the mountain it has been designed to withstand the melting of the ice caps, earthquakes, and even nuclear strikes. It is unstaffed but monitored around the clock and formidably protected by blast doors at the entrance, a second door approximately a hundred and fifteen meters down, then finally two keyed, air-locked doors.'

'What are they so fiercely protecting?'

'Seeds. The Svalbard Global Seed Vault stores samples of three-quarters of the world's seeds.'

'Why? Are they expecting a doomsday scenario?'

'Not that I know of, but here's a little coincidence for you to consider. Building started in 1984, a year after the first genetically modified seeds were created.'

'There's that word again—genetically modified.'

'Good. Let's go,' Green said and held out his hand.

Black found himself seated next to Green inside an airplane.

'First class view of the American skies,' said Green.

And indeed the seats were wide and plush. There was only one other passenger and he seemed to be fast asleep in his tracksuit. From behind a curtained cubicle, Black could hear ice clinking.

'Air hostess preparing drinks,' explained Green.

Black looked out of the window.

'See that whitish line.'

Black noticed that the sky above the line was bluer than the sky underneath it. 'Yes; I see it. What is it?'

'That is the geo-engineering spray line. The official stated reason for the chemical releases is to ameliorate global warming. The truth is a different matter. Aerosol gases cause global dimming, which translates to twenty percent less sunlight getting through to the planet. However, the white haze is a highly advanced smart dust composed of metallic oxides, synthetic fibers and engineered biologicals. These nanoparticles bloom and spread out over great areas and shred the ozone layer, which allows more of the sun's thermal energy to penetrate, which in actuality causes global warming. CFCs and carbon emissions are negligible factors.'

'Why are they doing this, then?'

'The answer is in the smart dust. The engineered biologicals are mostly desiccated human red blood cells that have been engineered in such a way that they exactly mirror the life form, but resist destruction and can self-replicate outside the human body. The other biologicals are pathogens that have been altered and cloaked so that the human immune system will not recognize them as foreign. The bacteria and viruses go to work altering the cellular DNA of a living organism slowly. If the host gets ill, the virus or bacteria will be wiped out by the body's immune system, but after the illness is eliminated, the altered cells remain and continue to reproduce. The changes can be so subtle that the body continues to operate as previously, or so the victim thinks.

'The other enemy lurking in the dust are the nanofibers designed to endure almost anything—extreme temperatures, chemicals, acid, bleach. They integrate themselves into the very cells of the living organism and create new processes that will override its natural system, then artificially and exactly mirror the ones they have overtaken.

'The last piece to this jigsaw puzzle are the metallic oxides. They are there for many reasons but the two most important are these. They contain aluminum and barium. The aluminum when it is washed down to the Earth causes a slow, silent death to plants and trees that will require more genetically modified plants and trees.'

'But I watched a program on the National Geographic channel about the minerals. Doesn't aluminum occur naturally in the Earth's crust, anyway?'

'It does, but never as a bio-available particle blowing in the wind. It is always bonded to other elements and thus unable to leech into other living organisms and damage their DNA. These metallic oxides have also made both the air and the human body more conductive. The vastly increased electrical biofield provides the DC current to activate these synthetic organisms to self-assemble. And electromagnetic frequencies emitted by cellphone towers, HARP, and Gwen greatly increase the vitality with which these forms grow in the human body.'

Black suddenly remembered a documentary he had watched about a mysterious disease called Morgellons. Sufferers had colorful fibers, plaques, crystals and gel-like objects that looked eerily like worms and insects coming out of lesions on their bodies.

'Morgellons is not a disease, but an unintended effect. The people with Morgellons are those that have bodies whose genetic make-up rejects the technology. Regardless of whether the Morgellons condition is present or not, every living thing on the planet is currently being colonized by these artificial life forms.'

'Why are they doing this?'

'Genetically modified food, tainted inoculations, poisoned air, and mosquitoes that introduce unwanted viral genetic information into the recipient host are all multi-pronged steps toward singularity.'

'Singularity?'

'Singularity is a point in space time where the rules of physics no longer apply. One interpretation is the arrival of the human plus. Or the rise of the artificial man and the hive.'

'My God. If every human being is already infected, how far are they toward their goal?'

'Not so far. Not by any means. This is their middle phase, but there is another first phase taking place. Let me show you.'

He held out his hand and Black put his into it.

They stood not far from a poor dwelling by a forest. It was cold, and the ground was thick with snow. A little boy, dressed in thick country clothes, was playing at the edge of the forest. Black could tell instantly that there was something not quite right about him. He almost had the face of a Down's syndrome child, but not quite. Black immediately wondered whether this was what they wanted the human race to be. A dumbed-down herd of unquestioning worker bees.

'No, no,' said Green. 'This is Yuri. He will remain in his forest home until his early death. He will never lead anyone or build anything of repute, but he is very special.'

'Why?'

'He has previously unseen DNA. Earth science has known only one other almost like him. A blind, severely handicapped boy with three strands of DNA. The scientists do their tests but they can't understand how or why his junk DNA is switched on. Yuri has four strands. You see, despite all their efforts, the powers that shouldn't be have woefully underestimated the human spirit. It is alive. There are already children born with livers that can process all the chemicals in junk food; children who are immune even after repeated infections with AIDS. Others can pass solid objects through other solid objects using their minds, see through various parts of their bodies, or fill glasses with water by simply looking at them.

'As the super-psychic children in China have demonstrated, the human DNA is a biological Internet—it communicates. Progress is infectious, unstoppable. Just watching a child perform a psychic feat can cause another child to manifest the same phenomena. First one child, then another and another. Until a whole new united human race with godlike powers is born. And the illusion will crumble. The dark hierarchy's only hope is to capture as many lost souls as possible to drag into their brave new world where there will be no rebellions, no chaos, no waste, no overpopulation; only a mutated transhuman who will serve a master class.'

'What can a boy who has four strands of DNA do?'

'Why don't you go forward and find out?'

'Will he be able to see me?'

'Of course.'

Black went closer and the boy spotted him amongst the bushes. His small, round face lit up and he began to laugh with great delight. When Black was very close he suddenly reached out a hand and grasped his arm, but instead of his hand going through Black, Black felt his forearm firmly held by his pudgy little hand. Black gasped. The boy was multidimensional!

He could operate beyond the third dimension.

From the dark interior of the house a woman's voice called out, 'Yuri, come in. You are making so much noise you will frighten the bears.'

Yuri seemed to find that idea funny beyond belief. His laughter rang out in uproarious peals. 'Ha ha,' he laughed, clutching his stomach. 'Mama is so funny!' he communicated, but using hand signals. It was a language, ancient and strange, but Black understood him perfectly.

The boy's laughter was catching and Black could not help joining him. The laughter came from deep inside him. He had never laughed like that in all his life. It was a wonderful feeling. The more he laughed, the better he felt. He laughed even while he felt 'things' beginning to shift inside him. Then the boy's mother, a large peasant woman, came out of the small house. She stood at the door with her hands on her hips and scolded, 'Come in here, you little brat.' Her voice was stern but her eyes were gentle and filled with love.

The boy ran in clumsily.

Black looked back at Green. 'How many strands are activated in me?'

'Six. There are many more things you can do, but the most important thing you are doing is simply lying in your bed. Remember when I said that the focus of all those millions will transfer strength to you. Well, every person who watches you, regardless of how they vote, will be internally and invisibly changed by you.'

'Is Dakota one of us?'

'Yes.'

One can never consent to creep when one feels the impulse to soar.

—Helen Keller

The sun was shining and everything looked peaceful, but Dakota knew something was very wrong. She had been over the rainbow for too long. One of the others had taken the body. Perhaps for good. She thought about Black and if he would ever come to see her again. He had promised and yet so long had passed since he had come. She had promised him something too. She moved the sleeping wolf's head off her stomach onto the ground and sat up amongst the long grasses in the meadow. Shadow raised his head and looked at her enquiringly.

'Sleep,' she said softly, and he lay on his chin, and watched her with alert eyes. She stood. Immediately the wolf sat up and made to follow her.

'Stay,' she commanded softly, and he lay back down obediently. 'Good boy,' she praised and rubbed his stomach.

Leaving the meadow she walked slowly toward the mirrors. She was frightened of them, had always been. Mirrors were special things, enchanted things. Another world lived behind them, as Alice in Wonderland had found out when she had gazed into the looking glass. When she reached the place where all the staircases ended in mirrors, she stood for a moment in the sun. For the sun ended where the tiled floor began.

A little voice in her head warned, *Don't open locked doors. There may be demons behind that will eat you.*

But she squared her shoulders and walked onto the tiles. It was decidedly colder; her hands began to shake. Determined to move forward, she crossed the floor and put her feet on the first step of the staircase.

Go back, go back, said the voice. *Back into the sunshine where it is warm and safe.*

What am I scared of?

Nothing.

Well then.

But the next step made her feel almost dizzy with unexplainable fear. Like a frightened animal she ran back to the sunshine. Trembling with fear she stood looking at the imposing jumble of staircases and the gleaming mirrors that stood at the top of each one.

She thought of Milarepa. *Invite your fears, they are your creations. Befriend them; offer them your head.*

'I must do this,' she told herself, jamming her fists into the pockets of her jeans. This time she didn't try to walk up the stairs, she ran up, her feet moving so fast they were almost flying. There was no time to think or fear. Before she knew it she was standing in front of a mirror. At first it reflected her image like an ordinary mirror, then, as she had known it would, it changed. It became a doorway into another world.

You never grow old in mirrors, the little voice said.

A little blonde girl was squatting on a floor. She was too exhausted even to cry. She simply hung her head low. There was a bowl in front of her and inside it Dakota knew was the girl's own excrement. A stern-lipped woman with black hair slicked back in a bun was standing over her. She was gently tapping a whip against the side of her leg.

'Eat,' she ordered.

As if she was a trained circus animal, the girl immediately got to her hands and knees and moved her head toward the bowl.

'Don't!' Dakota screamed.

Both the woman and the child turned to stare at her. The child was visibly horrified, but the woman appeared mildly surprised, as if she had been told that such an interruption was unlikely, but it could happen. Her expression turned scornful. 'There is nothing you can do,' she mocked. 'If you come in here you will *all* die.' She turned back to the girl. 'Eat,' she commanded, and raised the whip.

The petrified girl moved her head toward the bowl.

'No!' Dakota shouted and put her hand through the doorway. The woman's face changed to one of fear. Alters screamed. One came to the front and shrieked at her. 'You fool. Look what you have done.' Dakota screwed her eyes tightly and put her hands to her ears in terror. Even then she heard the terrible sounds. This was death. But then nothing happened. She opened her eyes and stood looking around her. The mirror lay in useless fragments, but nothing else had happened. False. They had been false, again.

She must destroy them all. All the images of pain and degradation and suffering. One by one she ran up the stairs and shattered the mirrors. All the horrors slipped away to nothingness. Where it was born, there it went to end. All the pain went with it.

She went back to the meadow.

Shadow was waiting loyally at the edge for her. When he saw her, he came flying toward her. She knelt down and opened her arms.

'Oh, Shadow,' she said over and over again full of

guilt. She had seen him in the mirror. She had seen what he had done for her. How his big, strong body had lain down inside the fighting cage and willingly let her take his life. Shadow put his great paw in her hand and forgave her. She held him close.

'Come,' she said to him and they walked until they came upon a stone. It was just the right size. She picked it up with both hands. It was time to enter the black cube. She made Shadow wait outside. It could be her end, but she'd be damned if she didn't do it. She went in and smashed to pieces the self-turning contraption that Black had built for her. She let the stone fall from her hands and stood next to the hourglass watching the sand run out. When it did she waited.

Nothing. Nothing happened. Another lie.

She walked out into the sunshine toward Shadow, her triumph tinged with a dim dread. Soon it would be time to face her biggest fear. The others. And all the terrible things they had done in her name.

And the multitudes asked him, "What then must we do?"

—Luke 3:10

The sun had not even appeared on the horizon when the old man set off. He glanced at it, high and bright in the African sky. Another two hours remained of his journey. He had to get to the voting station before two o'clock or he would lose his chance to vote. His clothes were worn and torn, and his bare feet were as hardened and gnarled as tree roots on the dusty path. He had never learned to wear shoes. Shoes and vaccines were white man's curses. This way he was always connected to the Earth. He knew what she was thinking. She was his mother. He carried a staff and around his thin, lined neck he wore the bones that his ancestors had worn since before time began. He was a witch doctor, but he hardly practiced his profession anymore. Nowadays everyone went to the clinics. There was almost no business left; a spell or two, and even those were stretched out in the month.

He squinted against the sun. His belly rumbled loudly. It was yesterday that someone had given him some plantain to eat. In a small leather pouch where he carried his holy stones he had put his birth certificate. Though he had never used it and had never imagined he would need it before this, it was frayed and badly stained. Still the information it carried was discernible and that was all that mattered. There was a beetle on his path and he carefully avoided stepping on it. She was a daughter of the Earth.

When he got to the voting station he saw that many had already gathered outside the wooden shelter. The ones in front were squatting and the ones at the back were standing. They were half-chatting and half-listening to the speeches made by the headmen of the different villages. There was a man videotaping the event. They seemed to be mostly men, but there were a few women and children too. They were seated on the ground lazily swatting away the flies. He didn't know who had organized the event but someone from the city had come to collect their votes and names.

He stood for some minutes listening to the men speak. Each had come forward on behalf of their villages to collect the money that the Americans were giving. They spoke of how the money would help them in their moment of need. Some even thanked God for this act of kindness and charity.

Finally he stepped forward.

'Which village do you represent?' the man in charge of organizing the event asked.

Odingo looked around the gathered faces—even though he was more than eighty years old his eyesight was so good that he could discern even the whites of the eyes of the men who stood at the back. He felt their hunger and inexhaustible poverty in his own empty belly.

'I speak for no one but myself,' he declared. His voice was strong and rang out like a bell in the dusty afternoon.

'Speak then, old man, and be quick about it,' called a youth impatiently.

'One hundred American dollars,' Odingo cried out suddenly, and cast his unblinking eyes around the crowd. The whites of his eyes were red, making him look fierce and frightening. 'That is what the Devil has offered to buy your soul.' A murmur of unease spread through the gathering. 'So we agree to kill this innocent child to fill our bellies and our children's bellies for one month or two, or even three, but then what?' He paused. A great hush fell upon the crowd. Only the insects dared speak.

'I'll tell you what.' He jabbed a horribly yellowed and curving fingernail toward the crowd. 'You will be hungry once more, but then you will be a hungry murderer. What use to prolong your life if you have to steal the life of another to do it? Are we vampires? They came for our grandfathers, made them slaves; our fathers they made poor: now will they have us as vicious as them? When we kill this boy, we kill ourselves. Awaken to your actions.' He thumped his bony chest with his fisted hand. 'I will die before I take one drop of blood from this boy simply to keep this rotting carcass alive. Never.'

'He is dying anyway.' It was the youth again, but his voice was different, hesitant. He did not know how to stand alone. He needed to be in the midst of a crowd to feel safe, to be brave. 'Have you seen the way the votes are? Our votes will not make a difference. The boy has no chance.'

'The boy has a chance.' Odingo's sunken eyes shone with a strange light. 'He is protected by divine forces. I have seen it in a dream. But that is not of concern. We do what is right, our responsibility. We must cast our friendly eyes in his direction. Beyond that nothing is expected of us.' He banged his staff on the podium he stood upon. The crowd jumped. 'I vote no.'

A young girl standing in the middle of the crowd called out, 'I will vote no too, Grandpa.'

Her father looked down at his daughter in shock; she had been ever the quiet little thing since her mother had died. He had come here to feed her. She looked up at him. 'Don't worry, Father, I'm not hungry,' she said. He looked into those familiar dark eyes and, blinking back the tears in his eyes, he raised his head and in a loud voice said, 'I vote no too, Grandpa.'

It began with the women, like a murmur that grew louder and louder until it was a great roar. One by one and then in groups they rose from their squatting positions and joined the chorus. 'I will vote no too, Grandpa.'

The old man nodded. He felt proud of his people. The white man had come to enslave, rape, plunder, and steal their land and its riches. As if that was not enough he had brought his manufactured diseases and his ungodly vaccines, all while carrying a book that preached love and forgiveness. But his people were people of spirit. They survived and they would survive again without this blood money.

'Bah one hundred dollars!' he said, and spat on the ground.

From the shade of a tree a teenager, a visiting American student, was using his phone to record the entire event. That night he did some minor editing to his tape and uploaded it to his YouTube channel.

The next morning Jennifer went to Kim's table. 'We have a video going viral.'

'Yeah, I saw that, but look here. There is something weird going on around the world. In India, hundreds of

294

gurus, some of whom have been meditating in the jungles and the Himalayan mountains for years, have come out to urge the Indians to vote no. And in Russia, an old, blind, eighty-year-old psychic has come out of her self-imposed exile to encourage all Russians to vote no. But here's the bizarre thing. She has had exactly the same vision as many American psychics. She claimed to be have been visited by a blue-eyed, blonde girl who told her that the fate of humanity rests on our collective decision. From the Balinese to the Inuit, the indigenous psychics the world over are all telling their flock to vote no. The no votes are pouring in so thick and fast we are nearly reaching the five hundred million mark and the yes vote has almost frozen by comparison.'

Kim laughed. 'What do you know? The boy is winning.'

'I voted yesterday,' Dan confessed almost shyly, and Kim launched herself at him.

Stunned by the swelling curves of the body under her blue sweater Dan held his hands around her awkwardly.

'Thank you, Wells,' she said, tilting her face up to him and laughing exuberantly. She had never called him Wells before. He grinned and hugged her back. Her hair smelt lemony. Kim had odd ideas, but this thing he had for barefoot gypsies was getting simply too great to resist. Maybe he would pluck up the courage and ask her out to the Red Dragon.

Steve and Mary exchanged surprised glances. 'I'm off to do some voting too,' Steve said and scuttled off to his table.

'Well, since everybody else is,' said Mary with a wink.

'Hey, you know what's weird?' said Kim

disentangling herself from Dan.

'What?'

'China's the only country that hasn't changed its voting pattern. I wonder why?'

Black cat or white cat: if it can catch mice, it is a good cat.

—Deng Xiaoping

Chu Lai walked into his supervisor's room with his laptop securely tucked under his left arm. It was a large room with a massive portrait of Chairman Mao hanging on one wall. He shivered slightly. The air-conditioning unit was always turned up to maximum.

'What is it?' Sun Li said without looking up. He was a fat man with a wife, four mistresses, and five children. His hair was thick and straight with a side parting and his small, suspicious eyes broadly scanned the page of the newspaper he was reading.

'Our agents have detected that many of our citizens are playing the American death game. In total 675,000 people have voted yes.

'The American death game?' the leader asked, turning the page of his newspaper.

Chu Lai opened his laptop and carefully placed it next to the newspaper. Sun Li eyed the screen emotionlessly. When the screen went back to the image of the boy he turned his attention back to his newspaper. 'And how many no votes?'

'Three hundred. But to be honest this is a good opportunity for some of our citizens to make some money. After all, if the Americans are crazy enough to throw away their dollars our people should go for it.'

Sun Li turned another page. 'Did I ask for your opinion?'

Chu Lai's face turned red. 'No, sir. Of course not. I

apologize profusely, sir. It won't happen again.'

'Who is running the game?'

'It looks like it has the protection of the black section of the American government.'

'What are our figures compared to the other countries?'

'Unfortunately, sir, as it stands we are the only country that has more yeses than noes.'

His black eyes left the newspaper. 'What? What about Nigeria with all its crooks and thieves?' he demanded.

'No, sir.' Chu Lai turned the laptop toward himself. He tapped a few keys and turned the screen to face his superior again. 'Here are the exact figures.'

But his boss waved his effort away. 'India?' he queried with the same unemotional voice. 'Surely with so many beggars their people are poorer than ours.'

Chu Lai shifted uncomfortably. 'No, sir. In fact, they have many millions more voting no than yes. Something in the region of a hundred million.'

'Mmmm.' Sun Li laced his fat fingers on his princely belly. 'Do you see now how we look when we debase ourselves for a currency that has been so debased it is almost worthless? If they were giving an ounce of gold or silver it would be worth it.'

It might have been a joke, but Chu Lai did not dare smile. 'Yes, sir.'

'Send out a decree that anybody who votes yes from now on will be fined the equivalent two hundred American dollars in yuan. And anybody who votes no will get a letter of commendation from the leader. Let's see which country beats us for the kindness of our hearts.'

Acta est fabula, plaudite!

(The play is over, applaud!)

— Said to be Emperor Augustus's
last words

It was Carter who first showed Black that human beings kept colors around them. This must be what they call the aura, he thought. Carter's was murky and splintered into many jagged bits. Ever since Black had touched Yuri, unusual things had been happening to him. Yesterday, while being cleaned he had felt the scrape of the washcloth on the soles of his feet. Ticklish. And last night, even more incredibly, it had taken him a whole minute, but he had actually blinked!

'I thought you might want to see this,' Carter said, coming into the room and changing the channel on the TV. 'The President of the United States of America is giving an address about you. The message is being beamed all over the world: billions of people worldwide will be watching this.'

Black looked at the screen and there he was, the President of the United States of America. Tall, black and statesman-like. He managed to sound at once caring and forceful. 'My heart goes out to this poor child,' he began. 'How frightened and alone he must be. If you can hear us, we warn you that we, as a nation, will not allow this heinous travesty on our soil. We are looking for you and we will not rest until we find you.

'To those who have perpetrated this crime, I say, "This is your last warning. Give up this sick game and free this innocent child, or you will feel the might of this great nation upon you. You can run but you cannot hide. We will hunt you down. You will not be safe no matter where you go." He paused. Was that a tear that he was wiping away? 'But this is also one of those moments that makes me proud to be human, to know that people from all over the world are coming together to rescue this innocent child with their votes. On behalf of him I thank you all.'

'Does he know the truth about me?'

'Not the details obviously, but he is an obedient worker to his masters; he understands that it is not the dastardly terrorist plot he is pretending it is. Politics is a dirty game.' He checked his watch. 'Now I have to set up your TV. In ten minutes Kite will be calling to speak to you.'

'Why has he not come himself?'

Carter shrugged. 'Who's gonna know?' he said and began the process of setting up the video camera so it faced the screen; Black assumed so it would enable Kite to read his thoughts and responses.

A man Black did not recognize came on the screen. 'Ready?' he asked.

'Yup,' replied Carter.

'OK, I'll put him through.'

Kite's pale face came on. 'Well, it appears you won.'

Instantly Black felt a cold claw within him. It was not fear, it was like a warning. A premonition of danger ahead. Instinctively, he knew where he would find the cause of his uneasiness. He glanced at the screen and to his astonishment the yes figure had suddenly picked up enormous speed and was racing upwards so quickly it was almost a blur. He could not understand it. He was winning, and so far ahead, and now the game was going

300

the other way. Then he understood. Foul play. His eyes swung back to Kite. 'What are you doing to the results?'

'Ah, that. The computer is now running on its default algorithm.' He chuckled at Black's naivety. 'What do you think the stock market, the precious metals markets, and all the voting systems run on? We decide everything. Nothing is real. It's all one big illusion. Didn't your *friend* tell you that?'

'Does the rule of free will still apply when one is playing with a cheater?'

'I'm afraid it does. One should know better than to play with a...er...cheat. But in this case at least, there is no cheating involved. There was nothing in our agreement about what results the world would be given.' His eyes were cold. 'You won this one and you will get everything you were promised.'

Black remembered. *To win they must first destroy your heart.* 'So that is what this game is really about. Tricking the masses into believing the lie that the human heart is such a cold and calculating thing that it would send an innocent boy to his death for a mere one hundred dollars.'

'Through strange angles are the gates through which my ancient Lord may come. The killing of the god is a universal custom in my world. It is called Agarthi. God was created in man's image so as to represent him and the sacrifice of one brings untold despair. The horror that comes of the killing of the god feeds the formless ones.'

Black glanced at the screen. The yes figure was already close to overtaking the no figure.

'Won't it look suspicious, all these yes votes coming in so fast?'

'Mass media is the link between power and the masses. Without it to shape and mold ideas there would be uproar and resistance at every step of the agenda. They will do their job. And the sheep will believe everything they see and hear.'

After the euphoria of thinking he had won, Black felt sick with despair. He thought he had done something good for humanity. Instead he had evoked their participation in their own oppression.

'Did you imagine that you would *save* everyone?' Kite mocked. 'Most of them are beyond hope. They don't care about anything except the selfish thoughts and desires created in their tiny brains and what happens in their meaningless nine to five existences. They wake up in the morning, jump onto their technological leashes, punch some buttons, and actually believe that they are experiencing something valuable. Their pointless lives are not worth saving. They are fatted cattle that must be culled. Let the rider of the pale horse pass among them. Let them be the last of their kind.'

'I thought that is what you wanted, obedient worker bees for your hive.'

'This lot!' Kite spat contemptuously. 'Of course not. They are nothing, but a fornicating, lazy, stupid herd imbued with ideas of individuality and freedom. No, no, what we are aiming for is a scientifically created race that will be intelligent, hard-working, and free of sexual urges. They will be connected to a world brain. Control of all living beings will be from outside by us. And that day is coming.'

'You sneer at them for their stupidity and laziness when it was you who made them like that.'

Kite's horribly pale hand came up to wave away something. A fly that was trying to land on his face. Black noticed that he wore a black ring. In his head he heard the phrase:

And God had a ring. With his name on it. Until his ringed hand swept upon the air of heaven, fruit could not fall and die, because nothing could die.

Black looked at Kite in shock. The words formed on the computer screen without his control.

Your god is a demon.

Instead of being upset, Kite looked as if he was thoroughly enjoying himself. 'Look around you. Does it look like your god is in charge or mine? My god created all of yours. We are the illuminated. We will inherit everything.'

'Demons lie. You appear to be a big man, controlling so many and yet you are only a pawn of the real controllers, aren't you? They tempt you with Earthly pleasures and power, but what of your soul? Will it burn in hell?'

Kite appeared genuinely amused. 'Is that what your god taught you? I will not burn in hell. When I perform the rituals to leave this body, I will become one with my master, and be as powerful as him.'

'So why did you want to meet Green?'

Kite's eyes glittered. He must have been in a place where the temperature was quite high, because the pesky fly was back. He waved it away impatiently. 'I suppose it can hardly matter now. He has the codes. I wanted them. I still do. '

'Codes?'

'The codes to the matrix. They give one the ability to manipulate reality in the physical realms or what you and I understand as unlimited power. It will mean one suddenly has 360° vision. Distance becomes void. You think of someone or someplace and they are there or you are instantly there. Time will be accurately viewed as an intentional fabrication. And, of course, the beauty of cyclical time is that it holds the secret of immortality.'

'What makes you think Green has the codes?'

'Both demons and gods jealously guard them.' Kite smiled suddenly. 'Goodbye, Black. If you see Green again give him my warmest regards.'

Carter stepped forward. 'This won't hurt,' he said.

But it did. For the first time in his life Black felt the prick of a needle in his flesh. Then a kind darkness gathered him in her arms.

> Aye, when the blood was offered, Forth came they to dwell among men.

——The Emerald Tablets of Thoth

The first thing Black saw when he came to—was it really all over?—was his mother's tear-stained, worried face. Bent over him in his own bed. When she noticed his eye movement she gave an odd cry of joy. Yee-yah. He stared at her in amazement, not for the odd sound, or how much she had aged in a few days, but for the beautiful, glowing colors that surrounded her. Flashes of gold, white, blue, and a purple so royal and rich he did not think it existed. With no inkling of the astonishing colors she walked inside, she hugged him and cried and laughed and thanked a whole pantheon of Hindu gods for returning him to her. Her joy knew no bounds. Hours they remained together, she talking and he listening, as it had always been. What a joy. How much he had missed her. Tears flowed from his eyes.

When she saw them she dashed her own away roughly with the backs of her hands. 'I know I shouldn't cry, but I can't help it. I thought you were dead, but out of nowhere they came tonight, drugged me, and while I was unconscious, installed you in your bed. I really thought I'd never see you again when you lost the game. It was the most unbelievable thing: more than a billion people signed on during the last couple of hours and voted yes. I didn't want to watch that man in the white mask and coat come into that room where you were to be injected with what they said was a lethal dose of poison, but I had to. I had to watch or I would never have believed that it was done.

'Oh! It was terrible. I followed your heartbeat on the monitor and watched it become weaker and weaker and finally become a flat green line. Until that moment I had never suspected that human beings could be so cruel, so indifferent. I mean, I know we let millions of children die of starvation, but that's only because none us really has the ability to do anything about it. But that they would decide in cold blood to murder a sweet child right before their eyes. We are a terrible species.' She closed her eyes tiredly. 'I never thought I'd say this, but I am actually ashamed to be human. Perhaps Lord Carrington's friends, the eugenicists, are right, after all: humans are a cancer on this Earth and we deserve to be wiped off its face.'

It was dark outside and the clock showed it was 3 a.m. She refused to go to bed and for hours Black heard of all that had happened while he had been away. It was nearly five when she fell asleep in a chair she had pulled up to his bed. He watched her sleeping and felt a great welling of love for her. She did not know it, but he had felt her hug, her rough palms on his body, and her lips on his face. Slowly, triumphantly, he closed his eyes, and thought of Dakota.

So long since he had seen her last. Kite had kept his part of the bargain by rejoining him with his mother, but was he the kind of man who waits for your guard to be down before he smashes you with his clenched fist? He remembered Dakota's forlorn voice, 'They will never set me free.' Black longed for sleep so he could meet her in his dreams, but sleep was a sea far away. The harder he tried, the farther the tide went out. He opened his eyes. He was fortified with a drug that kept sleep in a knapsack.

Morning arrived. His mother fed him and bathed him. As she had done all his life, but it was dishwater strained through a rag. He was Eve without a fig leaf. Shame, what shame. When her hands moved over his most intimate parts he cringed and worried. What if he became a rock? But he didn't. The moment was quick, and passed without emotion or incident. She kissed him on his face and left. Happy. None the wiser. All was well in her world.

The next eight hours were torture. He could not sleep and neither could he distract himself from the vultures that circled Dakota.

It was exactly three o'clock when Green appeared. He was blazing yellow.

'Yellow?'

'It is the color of fall, when things are withering and falling to the ground. Our time is nearly over.'

'Oh, Green,' he whispered. 'How will I do without you?'

'Don't lose heart.'

'How can I not?'

'I have a gift for you.'

'Gift?'

'Yes.'

'But first tell me about Dakota? Is she well?'

'Be patient, she is well but I will tell you everything before I leave.'

'Kite said you have the codes.'

'I do.'

'You never said.'

'You never asked.'

'Has any human ever received them?'

'Yes, in the distant past when men still retained a measure of their awareness.'

'Can I get them?'

Green looked at him strangely. 'Your controllers want the codes so they can live forever in the artificial matrix as the rulers and the owners of unimaginable wealth and unlimited power. That is what all the bowing and scraping to accommodate entities that require blood and sacrifice by all their secret societies is for. But even the deceiver demons they venerate as gods know how dangerous the codes are in the wrong hands, and will only pretend to give them or parts of them. Why do you want them? Would you want to be trapped in this machine with the likes of Kite even with the codes?'

'I thought the codes made escape from the matrix possible.'

'You don't need codes for that.'

'What does one need then?'

'To escape something you only have to know what it is that holds you and release yourself from its hold. Remember the movie *The Matrix*. Amongst all those flying bullets were grains of truth. The entire human race is accurately represented by the Judas character, Cipher, who elects to be reinserted into the mainframe of simulation with the immortal words, "I don't want to remember nothing. Nothing, you understand. And I want to be rich... Someone important... Like an actor." Every human is returned to this prison because of his desire for a better illusion. Rejecting all is the method used by the yogis and the monks, but there is another way. It is more difficult but the rewards are greater.'

'What way is that?'

'That brings me to your final and most important lesson. How to defeat the Archons. Are you ready?'

'Yes.'

'First, let's find some compassion for them. Pretend you are someone who only eats pork. And you have spent a great deal of time and effort rearing a whole sty full. One day you find out that your pigs are slowly growing wings and they could very soon fly away. If you let them continue you will starve to death. That is the predicament of the Archons. Fourth-dimensional beings, who are about to lose their food source, a race of third-dimensional beings on a journey to the fifth and sixth dimensions. Above all they must keep the human race as prisoners and slaves in the lowest form of trance, like sleeping aphids, so their only method of escape, which is claiming their own divine evolution, is impossible. Defeating them is two-pronged.

'First, you must find the nothing from which all came and all must go to. Silence. Here you will realize that you have nothing to defend, nothing to fear, nothing to strive for, as you are already complete and connected to the highest source of power. That every perceived want is based on what you have been told you need and every artificial system of belief is simply so that you will not check out of the feeding grounds that the predator race has meticulously designed as the game of life.

'When you have found this perfect place of silence you must conquer the persistent desire to speak into that silence. The real warrior leaves no marks, no tracks. Be fierce about it or you will never win. And this is especially important—vow never to retreat even an inch from this place. When you have conquered all desire, even the need for food, then you will be able to shake loose your soul from its bondage by the night dwellers. You will be able to enter and exit the matrix at will.'

'But how do I enter silence if I can't stop my thoughts, and if, as you said, they are not mine, anyway?'

'Don't try to stop them. Simply watch them without any judgment. The parasites hate being watched. They slink away very quickly. And now it is nearly time for me to go, but first my parting gift to you. I cannot give you the codes, but I can give you a wonder-filled, long life with Dakota in a different timeline. In this life you will be an ordinary human able to use all your limbs.'

This incredibly beautiful phoenix from the ashes of his love? Black was so stunned that for a while he could not respond. An ordinary life was what he had dreamed for, but with Dakota added, his joy knew no bounds. He tried to calm the wild surge of joy, but it would not be tinkered with. 'What about my mother? We must bring her too.'

But Green was shaking his head. 'I'm afraid she won't be able to come with you, Black. The only place I can insert you into is a timeline where she does not follow the rainbow that leads her to you, and you freeze to death at exactly 4.15 a.m. on the same day.'

Black felt confused and lost. To start a new life without his mother? It would break her heart. She had devoted her entire life to him.

'And if I decide not to accept this gift?'

'Your life will be measured in weeks.'

Black was silent for a long time. 'I will explain it to her,' he said finally, sadly. 'She will be happy for me, I'm sure.'

Green shook his head gravely. 'I'm afraid you can't even do that. If you do, her reaction and actions will lead her to spend time in a prison and end her days in a mental asylum.'

'How will it work then?'

'By the time she awakens in the morning you will be gone and she will assume the same people who took you before have kidnapped you.'

'How will that affect her?'

'She will be sad, very sad, but she will come to accept and recover.'

Black said nothing and after a while Green said, 'Well, it is time I was going.'

'Wait, will you arrange it for me that I can spend an hour with my mother with all my limbs working? I promise not to tell her.'

'All right, you will have one hour with her.'

Slugworth tempted all the boys and girls to steal from Wonka... All did...but one... And he inherited Wonka's kingdom...

—Willy Wonka and the Chocolate Factory (1971)

The spasms that shook his body came soon after. They were pain-filled and yet what joy, what beauty. The shudders were feeding his body until he could move his head to one side, see that way, then the other. At the deepest, most fundamental level he was transforming, muscles were softening, lengthening, opening out, healing. Acid crystals were being expelled. The mechanisms inside his body were like scurrying mice; they even made a sound. The groups that had been long asleep were beginning to work together. Giving his bones integrity. His spine stretched as if it was alive, a snake inside his body.

His hands, his legs... All changing. He pressed his elbows into the mattress, his head arching back in an uncontrollable stretch. Long, slow, a dinosaur awakening from its long slumber. The sensation was incredible. The weight of his head was astounding. He jerked his head forward. It snapped into place. He looked at his hand, made it into a fist, and slowly released it. Amazing. He flexed his hand. There was surprising strength in it.

His elbow straightened. He drew his knees up and with his palms flat against the bed, pushed his feet sideways under the duvet until they no longer touched anything. He swung his legs down. He turned to his side and pulled up. He was sitting up. He flexed his shoulders—it was a good feeling—and stood. Oops… Dizzy. For an instant he swayed and had to steady himself by grabbing his bed. The feeling passed.

He straightened slowly and looked around the room. Strange perspective. He wriggled his toes—Oh, delicious—put a foot forward and almost tripped on the toes that bent into his feet. He stopped and flattened his feet. Slowly, Black. And tried again. One small step. Another bigger step. And then wow! The wonder of it. He was walking. He stood at the door to the darkened living room and looked in. Without switching on the light he went to the bathroom.

He tugged the light switch. Use the toilet, like a man, Black. He stood in front of the toilet, aimed carefully, and smiled to see the stream hit the water in the toilet bowl. He flushed it and walked to the mirror. He ran his hand over his bald head.

'Hello,' he said. The sound was soft, foreign. His tongue worked as if he had used it all his life. He looked at himself and smiled. Not bad. His face broke into a grin. 'Good teeth, Black boy.'

A key was inserted into the door downstairs. He left the bathroom. He heard her on the stairs. He walked into the darkened space of the living room and stood in the middle. She opened the door. To say she was shocked would be to badly understate her reaction. She dropped to her knees. Her eyes opened wide, and her mouth gaped and closed then opened again.

'Black,' she called, her voice shivery, unsure, as if it was an imposter who stood in her living room.

'Yes, it's me, Mother,' he said, and smiled.

She stared at him. As if he was angel. Then she frowned. He speaks! Her brain appeared to have slowed down. She could not process the scene before her eyes. 'Did you walk from the bedroom? Can you walk?'

He took a few steps toward her, performed a deft pirouette, laughed, and went to kneel at her feet.

Her eyes were shining like stars. 'I can't believe it. Let me see you walk again.'

He shot up like a rubber ball, jogged on the spot, moved away from her, did a karate chop movement complete with high kick and corresponding noise, and jogged back to her and hugged her. All the love, all the gratitude for this woman who had cared for him all his life without any compensation was in that embrace. She hugged him back hard. Holding the body of the man she had treated as a child. 'Don't move,' she said and listened to his heartbeat. 'Oh, how I love you,' she cried out suddenly, and began to sob helplessly.

'Don't,' he said. 'I love you. I always have and always will. More than you could ever imagine.'

She nodded, though it was uncertain if she had really heard anything he had said. 'You are really cured, aren't you?'

He smiled at her, but so sadly that she gripped his arm in terror. 'You are really cured, aren't you? Tell me you are permanently cured.'

'Mother, let us sit together and talk. I don't know what tomorrow will bring but I need you to listen to me.' And he raised the woman up from her knees in his strong, large hands and led her to the sofa. She followed, compliant and unquestioning.

'Before I do anything else I want to thank you for cleaning me every day without fail for all these years.

More than anything else that was the one task that I wished I could take away from you. My own smells used to make even me cringe. I felt sorry for you. If there was one thing I wished to have been different it would have been that you didn't have to do that.'

Fresh tears welled up in her eyes. 'My son, this thing that you speak of as a chore I did as an act of devotion. A daily prayer. Twice a day I cleaned you and as I did, I thanked God for that opportunity and begged him to grant me another day to show my love for you. Twice a day, every day, I prayed and God granted me the only things I have ever asked him from the day I found you. You are my life. Don't you know, I would have done it ten times a day without complaint.'

The boy cast his eyes downward and she caught his chin in her hand and raised it.

'Don't be ashamed. True love has no boundaries.'

His eyes seemed full of pain.

'What is it, my heart?'

'Nothing,' he choked. 'Whatever you may say I am glad you will be spared that chore. Thank you for everything you have ever done for me. I could never do enough to repay you.'

'Seeing you like this is repayment enough.'

They spoke in hushed whispers, their heads close together. 'What happened to the strange men who came to take you away? What did they want? What did they do?' Sometimes she reached out and touched his face wonderingly. 'I can't believe it,' she whispered. 'After all these years.' They had so much to talk about. They giggled at things. Suddenly she told him with some alarm, 'I can't seem to keep my eyes open. It's not right, I feel it. I mustn't sleep. Don't let me sleep.'

And he saw that what she said was true, she could no longer keep awake. The more she tried to keep her eyes open the heavier they became. 'It's OK, Mum. Go to sleep. All will be well.'

She gripped his arm hard; there was so much desperation in that grip.

'I'll always love you,' he said.

She went to stand, but her body would not cooperate. She looked at him with fear. 'Don't let me sleep,' she begged. 'Don't let me sleep. Please. Pass me that mug. Hurry, Black. I want to splash some water on my face.'

He turned to look at the mug and felt the grip of her hand on his arm slacken. By the time he turned his head to look at her she was already deeply asleep, her fingers trailing down his arm. He smiled gently at her sleeping form. 'It's OK, Mother. Sleep.' With great care he lifted her leaning body and put her poor head on his lap. He watched her sleeping for a while, and then he extricated himself from under her and laid her head gently on a cushion. He lifted her feet up onto the sofa and when he was satisfied that she was as comfortable as he could make her he covered her with a blanket and stood looking down on her.

Time's a-passing, Black.

OK, OK.

He switched off the light and went into her room. It was a small box room with a single closet and a dressing table pushed up against one wall. On the surface of the dressing table there was a hairbrush, a lipstick, a pot of hair bands, and a plastic container of black eyeliner from India. He picked up the lipstick and twisted it upwards—orangey-red. He smelled it—awful. He looked at the alarm clock face on the window ledge. Time's a-passing. He must hurry.

He opened the first drawer. There was a flat box. Inside lay a necklace and one earring. He closed the drawer and put the box with its lid open on the surface of the dressing table. Then he moved back to assess the closet. It was made of cheap, light wood with a laminated surface. Easily he pushed it away from the wall and reaching around the back ran his hand along the bottom edge until he came across the other earring. It had fallen there many months ago and been jammed by the vacuum cleaner into a crack between the wood and the laminate. He pulled it out and looked at it. He blew the dust away and returned it next to the other earring.

He opened the closet. Quite bare, and smelling of mothballs. He caressed the few items that hung inside. The wedding sari, which she had had dry-cleaned, still hung inside its plastic covering. He raised the plastic and touched the intricate gold edge. He tried to think of her on her wedding day and felt unhappy.

He left the room and went into the kitchen. He stood at the doorway and smelled the air—the familiar smell. She had been making egg curry. There was a covered pot on the stove. He opened it and breathed in the aroma. He dipped a finger in and licked the curry. It burned his tongue. He turned the tap open and held his burning tongue in the running water. It was a delicious feeling. The heat evaporated.

He opened a cupboard door. It was crammed full of vitamin and mineral supplements, all his. All went into the brown goo that was poured down his throat. He opened the fridge. Crammed full with fresh vegetables.

Of course. All for him. She lived on egg curry and rice. He closed it and his eyes were drawn to a teacup. It was chipped. He sighed. He didn't have to turn the cup upside down to know it was a Limoges. Her great ambition was to own a Limoges tea set. How many times she had told him about the cake stand and the sandwich plate and all the wonderful accoutrements that made up the setting for a civilized tea. Had he not come into her life she would have had her set by now. He set the cup down carefully. There was an ache in his heart.

Slowly he walked to his bedroom to wait for Green.

The evil spirit said, "Jesus we know and Paul we know. But who are you?"

—Acts 19:15

Black stared unseeingly out of his bedroom window. The sky was midnight blue and moonless. Few stars shone. The sounds of the traffic on the street below stopped and the windowpane became hazy and speckled. It must be 3.29. a.m. He could still see the sky outside but it had taken on an other-worldly appearance. As if it didn't exist. It was just a mirage and only what was in his room was real. He watched the dry shower behind him turn to a display of dazzling lights and a being materializing in it as reflections on the glass. This will be the last time, he thought.

'Hello, Green,' he greeted quietly.

'You're not coming, are you?'

'No.'

'You're using the word of power on me? Your only friend in the whole wide universe?'

Black turned to face him. He was no longer yellow, but an intense red. Black tried to remember what he had looked like when he had first seen him. The memory seemed very far away. Another lifetime ago. 'What does red stand for?'

'Life, growth, decay. What else is left in the endless cycle, but death.'

'Mine?'

'Of an opportunity.'

'Opportunity for who?'

'In this case, me.'

'You know I would never have suspected you, until I suddenly realized that you were using me, exactly as you described how they use celebrities. Let the celebrity tap all the energy then simply tap the celebrity. All that energy of hundreds of millions poured into me. You want it. You're the one they are praying and sacrificing to, aren't you? The one with the codes they want.'

'Yes.'

Black shook his head in disbelief.

'You won't understand, but I was only doing my divine duty.'

'Divine duty?'

'As did Judas; as does Satan. We are the tools by which humans must show themselves worthy of transcendence.'

'Who are you really?'

'The dark is always best nameless.'

'But if you are the dark, then where does all this light,' Black said, indicating the glowing fractals, 'come from?'

'I earned it in the performance of my duties.'

'I don't understand.'

'Look at the patterns on my body, but this time command yourself not to hide from the truth.'

Black looked at the fractals racing to form ever more beautiful patterns and willed himself to see nothing but the truth. And suddenly he was a tiny microscopic creature who was hovering near the fractals. Now he could see what the glowing fractals were made of. Faces. Millions and millions of human faces. Every race, every gender, every age. All of them screaming silently as more and more were birthed. Black closed his eyes at the terrible sight and the microscopic view vanished.

'Who are those people?' he gasped.

'Don't concern yourself with them. They sow; I reap.'

'Is any of what you showed and taught me true?'

'I am not allowed to lie, only dance around the truth a little.'

'You didn't come to me because I was the purest human on Earth, did you?'

'No. The only reason I could approach you was a little chink in your armor. Your envy of others. Their limbs, their freedom, their lives.'

'Envy, the mark of the Archons.' Black shook his head in disbelief. 'All this while. You? A shape-shifting parasite!' He paused. He had heard so much about them. A perverse desire had grown in him. 'I'd like to see what you really look like. Will you show me your true self?'

'You will not like it.'

'I don't care. I just want to know.'

He laughed and when he spoke his voice was sarcastic. 'I am uncertain if you will be able to retain the love you have declared for me if you see the *real* me.'

'Let me decide.'

'So be it.'

He took two steps backward and smiled. From him came an intense buzzing and pulsating sound, and suddenly the door sprang open as if someone had kicked it. A gust of freezing wind and dead leaves came shrieking through, and whirled around Black. The air in the room began to vibrate so strongly that the walls and ceiling became pieces that shifted like flapping bats' wings. The wings moved apart, spread out, and the wall and ceiling opened up until they were no longer in the boy's little bedroom, but in a vast cave. The only physical object that had roiled into that space with them was his bed. A taunt, no doubt. Green began to grow. Here was no boy. He grew until he must have been at least ten feet tall with a thick neck, huge bulging muscles, and a gaunt, bony face.

Black stared, unable to move.

The fractals were next to mutate. They darkened rapidly and began to resemble black veins on his large body. These fractals didn't have soft, rounded edges, but barbs, like fish hooks, or the spikes of arrowheads. They were attack fractals. The attack fractals thickened and bubbled as if they were trails of thick ink running on the surface of his skin. They rattled like disturbed rattlesnakes. And in that changing kaleidoscope the ink became shifting soot that blew away from the being's body in twisting plumes. The black dust took the shape of worm-like protrusions attached to his body. They waved frantically in the air.

Underneath the soot tentacles Green's face was reforming. A visage of terrifying ugliness. And the smell; rotting meat and the expensive incense that Black's mother saved for special occasions. It made him feel sick. The waving tentacles morphed into solid snakes. They hissed and writhed fiercely around his face and bloated body. He appeared to have no sex organs of any kind. The frantically waving snakes trained their eyes on Black. Each with a cold, deadly stare.

Black looked away from them, and looked into Green's eyes. Searching for something familiar, something he could hold onto in that awesome transformation. Green's eyes were glowing like rubies in the sun. Incredibly beautiful but emanating such hatred

324

and evil that Black felt it like static electricity on his skin. His heart was pounding hard. He felt the beast that Green had become drawing something from him. He understood what was being extracted from him. The collective energy of all the people who had voted for him and those that had not. With every second he felt himself become weaker. He felt so weak he could hardly stand. He looked at his bed. He wanted to go and lie on it, but he didn't. Later. There would be time for that later.

'Well, do you still *love* me?' the dark being asked, laughing sarcastically. His mouth was black. Inside there were no sharp teeth but what looked like a rotting pine cone. Strange.

Black moved forward as if in a trance. He took a step and raised his hand. All the snakes reared and prepared to strike.

'Be careful, boy. Snakes are poisonous.'

'If you are evil in nature, why do you care if they bite me?'

'I don't, but I am bound to warn you. Remember free will. At every step.'

The boy stopped and considered what the being had said. He remembered Green's voice: soft, kind, caring, as if from far away, from the past. 'When you can see yourself in a grain of sand, a leaf, a disgusting fly, a stray dog, a king on a throne, a murderer on death row, a raving madman, a rock. Then you may enter and exit the matrix at will.'

'Free will. Yes, the parasites remind us all the time about it.' His voice was only a weak whisper. 'Snakes are poisonous, but these are not...' Boldly Black put his hand out. A snake, the biggest, lunged forward at impossible speed, and sank its fangs deep into his hand. Black screamed. The pain that shot through him made him rigid. Only his eyes rolled down to look at the state of his hand. Bite marks and blood. He could see the blue poison running up his veins, searing and burning its way into the depths of his being. The pain was so intense it made him feel faint.

He fell to his knees. He wanted to cower on the ground, but forced himself to rise. 'Come to me, my own envy,' he gasped. And like Milarepa before him, he lurched toward the being and allowed himself to fall forward, so his head was put into the fanged mouth of that largest, most ferocious snake on Green's body.

The demon snake turned to dust, and Black fell through it to the ground. He lay on the blackened ground and watched as one by one the hissing snakes returned to soot and followed the process through which they had been created, melting into ink fractals that eventually shone with their original light. The dark being was changing too, like a film rolled backwards. Finally Green stood in his place. Exactly the way he had come to Black on that first afternoon. Green and so beautiful. A being that had offered him the most amazing adventure he could have asked for.

Green was no longer looking at Black, but at a transparent tube softly lit from inside that had suddenly appeared out of nowhere into their midst.

What has been is what will be, what has been done will be done again; there is nothing new under the sun.

— Ecclesiastes 1:9

The air began to pulsate and the surrounding scenery was morphing once more, into a much greater size. As if a vast inter-dimensional hall had been called in from some non-material realm to house the presence inside the tube, flawless crystalline hexagrams were multiplying quickly and precisely until they formed an astonishing doomed hall many stories tall. Where the edges of the hexagrams met they glowed softly. It was very beautiful and other-worldly. Black tried to peer into the growing tube, and had the impression of a head and arms and legs, although no such thing was there. Instinctively, he understood that the humanoid form was designed to make him feel comfortable with her, and it was a *her*, a soft, yielding female, a mother, a creator of life, of many lives.

When the tube was almost six feet long it began to radiate a soft light that changed the lighting in the hall in such a way that Black began to perceive everything differently. The first thing he felt compelled to do was to look down at his own hands. They were alive with dazzling colors. Quickly, he looked over to Green. He had become an unstable patchwork of glowing white and black light that appeared to be turning on and off, wavering from black and white stripes to a mosaic of uneven black and white squares. Many faces struggled to form, only to turn into beast-like countenances that were discarded. It seemed to Black that Green could barely keep his humanoid shape.

Black turned his attention back to the tube. It had now righted itself and was taller than a house. Both the tube and Green began to emit waves. The waves coming from the tube were totally unfamiliar to Black, but the sounds discharged by Green were very similar to the auroral hiss from Saturn picked up by the Cassini spacecraft. It occurred to Black that the two inter-dimensional beings were communicating with each other in waves and symbols that were rich in meaning, but his senses could interpret only the gist of it.

'Shared you, your resonance with the child. But won the child again.'

'Won now. Lose soon,' screeched the black and white mosaic before it shivered and vanished.

Black threw his head back to look at the vast being inside the tube. 'What did he mean by "won now, lose soon"?'

But the response came from his eye level. 'You and he have played this scenario hundreds of times in many different timelines. You have always won, but he will never stop trying.'

'But I didn't win. Have I not led a great many people into a trap?'

'Never fear whatever you have created. There is something in it for you.'

'But what about the mass awakening?'

'This is a glorious time, when anything can happen, but the concept of a mass enlightenment is a fabrication of the dark ones. Enlightenment will only occur one individual at a time.'

'And Earth. I saw her as a forge, trying to change.'

'Earth is a sentient being who *allows* the many forms who live in her skin to make their choices, but in the event she needs to be ruthless, she can and will exterminate millions in one fell stroke. Worry not about her.'

'Who is Green, really?'

'The demiurge, the grand architect of the Archons.'

Her shocking answer made Black reel. 'The Chief Lord Archon?!' He remembered again the hideous sight of Green's real self.

'No,' she interrupted his thoughts. 'That is not his real self. It was a form that he thought would strike the most fear into your heart. His form is more insect like, but he is able to take a form so resplendent he is able to sit in temples and places of worship and proclaim himself God. You might recognize his symbols—the single eye; the two fingers up, three fingers down hand sign; androgyny of any kind; the "as above, so below" symbol; and the images of serpents. If you see a god or a goddess stepping on a snake, do not be fooled; it is not a signature of vileness conquered. It is an esoteric code signifying descent. Other signs of his veneration to look out for are cubes, especially black ones. Before he was Green he has been known as the Old One, the Forgotten Father, the Shining One, the Black Sun, El, the Dark Lord, Baal, Moloch, Kronos, Saturn, Father Time, the Rain Man, the Grim Reaper, Lucifer, Satan, the Lord of Rings, Abbadon, Cthulhu, Google, Yahoo—'

'Google and Yahoo? Those are search engines.'

'All Archontic creations are named after him so that every time you make those sounds you are calling *him*.'

329

'Is the Internet an Archontic creation? Surely it is a good thing? It brings people together. So much can be learned from it.'

'The Internet is a black hole of "amusement" that swallows people's lives and destroys whole cultures. Instead of living a real life humans are floating in cyberspace, engrossed by their fantastical "second life". They live not as they are, but as avatars who remain invitingly flawless no matter what their perversions. As with all "gifts" from the Archons, be they televisions or terminator seeds, people are lured to become more and more soulless and hive-minded, so they become better and better prey.'

Black thought of Dakota all alone in their clutches. 'What will happen to her?'

'As you can see we are greater powers who referee the game and keep curbs in place. No real harm can befall her. She has important things to do.'

'Why do the good forces stand back and do nothing while the dark forces turn Earth into a death camp. Surely they must see how impossible it is for humans to escape on their own?'

'The containment process is necessary for the moment. What do you think Earthlings would do anywhere they went?'

Black shook his head.

'They would take their hubris and their greedy, selfish, brutal, addicted culture with them. If a human wishes to leave he has only to change his frequency.'

'Change his frequency?'

'Change your vibration. Stop watching television and reading the newspapers. Disengage yourself from the frequency of chaos, anxiety, stress, and temptation, and begin to find, in the silence, the power that you lost when the predator gave you his mind.'

'Who are you?'

A small part of her, a drop of light, detached itself and hovered at the level of his forehead. It touched him gently then entered him. The drop of pure energy traveled into him, filling him with exquisite joy and beauty. He thought he recognized her, but her knowledge of him was complete. He came upon a mirror, saw a reflection—was that him? No, and yet yes. There were so many inside her and they were all other hims.

The reunion was indescribable. Patterns swirling, fractals bursting open into leaves, flowers, fruit, seashells, followed by an amazing gamut of pixels, fractals, patterns of light, geometric shapes of intricate design. They were all him. His consciousness expanded in an inconceivable way and he became everything that had ever been and ever would be.

He was filled with an infinite love; it encompassed everything. There was nothing to rival it on Earth. The warmth and familiarity of home. He began to laugh with the joyous ecstasy. Then suddenly, without any warning, he was in the belly of something inconsolably sad, a vast, vast void of human sadness—all the pain and hurt, the lost hope, the unanswered prayers, the betrayals; all became his. It filled every cell in his body until he felt as if he would tear apart with the pain of the human race. Intolerable. He began to scream.

Instantly the drop exited his forehead and he fell weakly to the ground. He understood why her energy was encased in a capsule and the reason that only a minute part of her had come to touch him. His physical structure had no capacity to hold the intensity of her vast energy. He would have burst with it.

'That is what I am and what you really are. What you were before and what you will return to when you leave your human form… But without the pain.'

'What am I doing on Earth?'

'What everyone else is. Learning how to use energy. Most think that the secret to using energy is to create something. The real magic is when you learn to use energy to turn something into nothing.'

'Something into nothing?' Black repeated.

'Something into nothing. We'll be waiting for you.'

She left as she had arrived. Without fanfare. One moment he was standing in that vast space and the next he was left in his tiny bedroom with nothing to show for it—he glanced at the clock: 3.29 a.m.— not even lost time. He stumbled to his bed and fell upon it. Already his limbs were beginning to stiffen. As best he could, he maneuvered himself until he was lying flat on his back, in the same position he had been put into all his life.

What rough beast,
its hour come round at last,
Slouches toward Bethlehem to be born?

—William Butler Yeats (1865-1939)

The wheelchair moved soundlessly on the thick carpets that lined the long, wide corridor that led to the lift. As the wheelchair passed the top of the stairs Kite looked down the curving staircase made of Burmese hardwood, and for some unfathomable reason thought of the men who had carved it, their forearms as sinewy and hard as the wood they worked with. He felt himself become very still.

Their poverty; he *felt* it. For the first time in his cold, remorseless life he *felt* something. An odd and burdensome thing. Never had he known empathy, sympathy, or even a conscience... Now he tasted the grinding virtuousness of their lives, so fascinatingly different from the grandeur and opulence of his. Then came unwanted viewpoints; officially he reigned with an iron hand, but wasn't he well ruled too? Every move overseen by frighteningly powerful principalities that required blood and sacrifice each step of the way? Was he really any more than the brown-skinned men?

He frowned. What extraordinary thoughts to have come over him. Of course he was more. They were inferior—vermin, in fact. Whereas he was of superior stock with superior qualities, born to rule. Their right to rule was in their blood. Genetically predisposed to leadership, his family had cunningly rejected the notion of deposable kings or presidents and had secretly ruled humanity from behind the scenes. Generation after generation, going back as far as memory or history could account for, since the very birth of civilization, they had been the bankers. Unexpectedly, an image of the boy came into his mind. He frowned, felt uneasy. He had wanted the boy eliminated, but the old ones had spoken through the mother of darkness and ordered the boy to be released unharmed.

He forced his mind away from the unfamiliar, unwelcome moments of introspection and touched the button that operated the doors of the lift. They swished open smoothly, but as the wheels of his chair reached the entrance the chair came to a sudden stop. He stabbed the start button. Nothing happened. He hit it again. No reaction.

Impatiently he tried the reverse button and the chair began to roll back soundlessly. He slammed his fist on the stop button, but the chair continued to roll steadily back. Angrily, he hit the stop button repeatedly, to no effect. He closed his eyes in frustration. STOP. NOW. That worked. The chair suddenly stalled and stopped. He opened his eyes. It had stopped at the top of the stairs.

Why? The first twinge of fear, a subtle warning at the base of his spine. He tried to inch forward, but the computer system refused to respond. He depressed the button that would summon one of the servants, but the button failed to light up. There was something wrong with the entire circuitry.

'George,' he called, his voice booming and hollow in the huge, empty space. He waited. There were no footsteps or answering voice. It was so eerily quiet, he felt the hair at the back of his neck rise.

'George!' he screamed. There was no hiding the panic in his voice now. He heard a whirling noise come from the wheelchair. His eyes swooped down to watch it as if it was a dangerous snake. The wheelchair began to move. For a moment he was so surprised he did nothing. In disbelief, he watched the wheelchair make small, tight movements. It was turning, it was making him face the staircase. The pain. Be careful of the pain. Then his brain kicked in. He should get out of the chair quickly.

He could still use his legs. He hit his legs. Hard. There was pain. Thank God. There must be use. He put both hands under his right knee to lift his leg out of the metal rest, and suddenly he was overcome with the urgent need to push the forward button. His hand, yes his own hand, moved and slammed down on the button. The wheelchair responded immediately. It shot into the air. He was so frightened he tried to hang onto it, but it hit the banister and went its separate way. He was hitting stairs. Hard. Crashing into the wood that the carvers had spent their sweat and toil upon. He put his hands out in a last-ditch attempt to stop the momentum. His white, weak hands desperately grabbing for the banister. But too much momentum to stop.

Burmese men with wood-like limbs had carved them, too smooth, purposely. The poles he grasped slipped through his hands like water. This was their revenge. He saw them clearly. Their worn, sad faces. It was money they wanted, and it was money he had withheld from them. Money! He had so much. Why did he do it? He feared their worn faces. He was tumbling down, down, down the wonderfully polished stairs. The maids, on their hands and knees. Polishing. Polishing, every day. For slave wages. His wife was at the opera. His lovers were with the men they truly fancied, his children spread around the world taking care of his empire and here he was, hurtling to his death, alone. He landed. Badly.

Oh, agony. His legs were twisted underneath him, broken.

But he was not dead. He was one of the chosen ones. He laid his head on a smooth stair and noticed something strange. Dry rain. What the hell?

There was a fantastic display of light. A being was materializing. He was white with straight, black hair and dressed in resplendent purple robes. He hovered a few inches above the ground. Winged and magnificent. Awestruck, Kite called out the chant for the ceremony to call the old ones.

'I call you, Master and Creator. I rejoice, I mock, I praise your name. Open the gates! Ygnaii Thoth! Open the gates! Claim me as your own.'

The light became so blindingly bright that he had to shade his eyes. The river of light engulfed him. Oddly the first thing he experienced was great love. He felt all the love, the authority, and the knowledge of his master flow into him until he was vibrating like a tuning fork. Nothing could decay here. There was no logic or reasoning, but overwhelming beauty. The pleasure was intense. He opened his mouth and spoke the most beautiful language. His awareness of time had ceased to exist; he was experiencing eternity.

God opened his great wings. They shimmered exquisitely with white light. The old one smiled at him and opened his hands in welcome. Kite reached out eagerly with both hands. His Lord had kept his promise and come for him. He felt himself leave his crippled body and enter the warm, radiant arms of his Dark Lord. In that moment of exquisite pleasure and beauty Kite's eye fell upon an odd thing. He saw the fine, rich robes of his Lord trailing blood. And suddenly everything changed. He was falling into the cold, black abyss of eternity. The sides were carved with faces, hanging upside down and screaming silently. All as shocked and horrified as he was.

The principalities had lied!

'I repent, I repent,' he cried out, but there was no escape from the abyss.

You have been walking the ocean's edge, holding up your robes to keep them dry. You must dive naked under, and deeper under, a thousand times deeper!

—Rumi

Bumi was hurrying down the street thinking of the boy. It was five days ago that the miracle had happened, when he had walked and spoken. But in the morning he had been changed beyond recognition. She had quit her job to sit beside him. Lady Carrington was clearly irritated that she had not been given what she called 'fair notice'.

'Won't you at least finish the month?' she had asked tightly.

'My son is very sick and there is no one else to care for him.'

'I didn't know you had a son,' she said, losing her posh accent.

Bumi had raised her eyes to her employer's narrow, suspicious face. 'I do.'

'Well, if you leave like this, you do realize that you won't get paid for the days you have worked this month?'

'That's all right. You probably need it more than me, anyway,' Bumi had retorted, and left the great Lady's fine apartment. The Lord had called later to apologize and to say that he would be putting some money into her account, but Bumi could hardly care. The money mattered not one bit to her. All her money had been for the boy and now it was of no use.

Although his body was wasting away, every time she had tried to feed him, she had heard his voice clearly in her head saying, 'No.' All she could do was wet his lips with some water. When she cleaned him, she realized that his body had stopped producing waste of any kind. But in her dreams he came to her and told of a great being who had come to him and taught him things. 'The body is afraid of death because it thinks the world is all there is. You must not listen to the fear of the body. When the time comes just let go.'

She had only left the house to buy some groceries, milk for her tea, eggs, a loaf of bread and some cheese. She had been gone less than fifteen minutes. So it was a shock to see the magnificent rainbow that stretched across the sky and seemed to end on her house. She stopped, the blood in her veins suddenly cold. The last time she had seen such a rainbow she had found him. Then the fireworks began, an astounding display of multicolored lights directly over her house. She dropped her groceries and ran. She was panting hard and very frightened by the time she pushed open the boy's door. The room was lit only by a dim bedside lamp. He no longer wanted the TV. His eyes turned to her. He was so frail. So shrunken.

It's time, he said in her head.

'Remember what the great being taught you,' she urged.

I have forgotten everything, but anyway there is nothing to remember. It's all an illusion.

She took his shriveled, still hand in hers.

Don't be scared, he said in her head.

'I'm not. I'm just going to miss you so much. I don't

know that I will be able to bear it. I will be so alone without you.'

You will not be alone, Mother.

'I love you.'

Remember, now, not to come into this room for the next five days.

She covered her forehead with one hand and sobbed softly.

Promise me you won't, no matter what.

'I promise.'

We will meet again soon.

She didn't answer, but laid her fingertips on the delicate skin on the inside of his wrist, and felt for the weak ripples. She felt them travel from his skin into hers, into her blood and tissue and bones and become a part of her. When she had absorbed his last heartbeat, she lowered herself into the chair by his side and watched his cooling body. Her vigil lasted all through the night until the raw, cold daylight filtered in. Even then she sat with her sorrow watching a weak patch of light move along the floor onto the boy's bed. A butterfly flew in through the window and landed in the light. It was the most brightly colored butterfly she had ever seen. Her eyes welled with tears. The beads in his hair. The multicolored beads.

'Oh, Black,' she whispered brokenly. How will I ever manage without you?'

The butterfly lifted itself off the bed and alighted on her hand. Slowly, she lifted her hand and brought the butterfly close to her face. It flapped its wings twice, but remained on her hand. She looked at its beautiful wings and remembered the moth infestation from three days ago, when twenty or thirty moths had flown in through the boy's window. They had fluttered around the lighted bulbs, alighted on the curtains, and eventually landed on the boy, his bed, the floor. Now she knew. The moths had foretold his death. She had been so afraid of the crows, and it was the moths that had come to show him the way to the light.

She watched the patch of sunlight move upward toward the boy's hands, but it reached no higher than the middle of his duvet. And she felt a great sorrow swamp her. Her body felt hollow with it. The boy had not felt the sun on his skin. How he must have longed for its warmth. How could she never have thought to push his bed a little closer to the window? Careless. Careless. That small insignificant fact would torment her for the rest of her life. That she had been remiss in her love.

Then she remembered his words. 'The goal is to remain in a state of awe, like a child. No matter what happens, be in awe that it happened to you. Your pain must not seem less wondrous than your joy.'

She looked at the butterfly, the miracle that it was, and felt awe at the vast pain inside her. The boy had prepared her carefully. She understood instinctively that, on some level that she had no knowledge of, he had shown her a staggering, almost inconceivable act of generosity and love. And the butterfly had come to tell her that he was finally free. He was no longer a prisoner in his frozen, curled body.

'Go ahead, my darling boy,' she sobbed. 'You fly free now. I'll see you very soon.'

And at those words the butterfly left her hand and flew out of the window into the bright sunshine. She stayed for a bit more and kissed his still face one last time. Then she stood looking down at her love and would have tarried longer, but for a voice inside her head, not the boy's, but kindly nevertheless.

Leave now. Leave him be.

She backed away slowly. Even then she didn't want to leave him. But in her head she could hear the voice urging her to close the curtains and close the door after her. She went and closed the curtains and the sobbing began in earnest. She pressed the curtain to her face and cried uselessly for him. Come back. Come back. There is nothing without you.

Go now. Go now, urged the voice.

She lurched to the door.

Close the door, the voice reminded.

She closed the door behind her.

Five strange days passed. She saw flashes of brilliant light through the bottom of the door. Every day she went and stood at the door. Sometimes she sniffed the air for signs of decomposition, but there were none. Once she even touched the doorknob but it never crossed her mind to disobey the boy or the voice. She sat on her bed and made her plans. On the sixth day she would open the door. Then she would go to the police. There would be questions, but she didn't care anymore. She had a little savings. Enough to cremate the boy; then they could deport her. She was ready to return home.

On the sixth day she opened the door and frowned. Then she advanced into the room and stood over the bed. 'Can't be,' she whispered to herself, and looked toward the window. She went to it. It was locked. She dashed back to the bed and ripped the duvet off and stared in disbelief at the bed.

343

There was nothing in it but some nails, where his fingers and toes had been. And not even a full set. She sank to the bed. She had only heard of it spoken of by the holy men of her village, more myth than fact. But the boy had pulled it off. She began to laugh. Amazing. He had distilled matter into energy. He had attained the rainbow body. He had turned something into nothing.

He had become pure light.

Evening was closing in. Bumi shut her front door behind her and walked down the street. A crow sat on someone's roof and called. "Aaarrrk.' She pulled her coat closer into her body and looked ahead. A gust of wind was carrying a paper in its midst. Without thinking she raised her hand and it sailed directly into her palm. She closed her hand around it. The sudden gust died down. She opened her fist and looked curiously at the paper.

We do not forgive. We do not forget. Expect us—always.

——Anonymous motto

Schooner Klaus awakened in a beautiful old palazzo. It was not a hotel as such. It was for Insiders. For a moment he simply absorbed the incredible opulence of his surroundings, the tall windows, the marble, the gold trimmings, the faded silk, the antique velvet, the priceless art, the fantastic detail, the carvings. Finally he sat up and looked out of the window. It was going to be a beautiful day. There were pigeons on the balcony. He smiled to think of his audience with Fish. What an honor. Breakfast. He could have asked for anything but this morning he wanted only fresh croissants and jam, peach jam. He stood up and rang a tasseled bell pull. Almost instantly there was a discreet knock on the door. His eyebrows rose. Wow! Had the guy been standing outside the whole time? Better than efficient.

'Come,' he called. A waiter dressed as a manservant of times gone by entered.

'Buon giorno, Dottore Klaus.'

Schooner Klaus gave his order in English. The man bowed and left. Europeans. They had their uses.

He climbed out of the great bed and found himself walking to the bathroom. More marble and old world elegance. But. Something odd. Why was he going to the bathroom? Schooner Klaus tried to stop walking and found he couldn't. His legs would not obey. In the bathroom he found himself going to the bath. He felt confused. He did not desire a bath. But he turned on the taps. Waited until it was full. Turned them off. Then he found himself reaching for his wallet. He gazed at his own hands without comprehension. His hands opened the wallet and from inside a side pocket produced a little packet.

What the fuck? Razor blades!

He had never bought those. His eyes filled with fear as he watched 'his' hands—he had no control of them—unwrap the razor, and hold it carefully, and far away from his body. His eyes bulged. He had no control. What the hell was happening to him? He should scream. The manservant. Someone would hear. The bell pull. But the bell pull was a mile away. He raised one leg and put it into the bath. The water was deliciously warm.

Mmmm, a voice said inside his head. Female and familiar, but he needed more to put a face to the voice.

He frowned. Another leg was going in. He was sitting in the water in his silk dressing gown.

Hello, the voice said.

Suddenly he knew. 'Shekina.'

A small chuckle. No, Dakota.

'Dakota?' Impossible. Then he recovered. 'Listen, I can make it better for you. I can free you. You can disappear. Go anywhere in the world.'

A sigh. I can free myself.

'But the tracker chip. I'm the only one who can turn it off. I'll make sure no one comes after you.'

It is already turned off.

'You're fourteen years old. Where can you go without a passport?'

Apparently I'm eighteen in the passport I have.

'Who got it for you?'

Strange question for a man sitting in a bath holding a razor blade?

'What about money? I can give you loads. You can have a life you only dreamed of. How much do you want? The sky is the limit. Anything, just don't let me die. Please.'

Money? You think I need money?

'What about the boy? I can let you have the boy?'

The boy is gone. What else have you got?

Schooner looked down at his hands. He had one last trick left in his repertoire. Loudly he called, 'D7114. I call forth Enmark. I demand you come forth now.'

For a moment there was silence then a little giggle.

Enmark is presently indisposed, Schooner Klaus.

'All the unclean things you did, the wickedness—you could not have… You couldn't have cast out the entire multiple system?' he said incredulously.

I didn't. The boy did. Before he died.

His right hand was holding the blade poised over his left wrist. 'Please,' he begged, his voice having lost all its silk. 'Please, Dakota. You can have anything you want. Anything.'

She said nothing.

Incredulously, he watched his right hand rise slowly and suddenly jerk downward to slash his left wrist, so viciously that it touched bone. His eyes bulged with terror. Blood. Blood. Blood. HIS! He watched in fascination as the red clouds formed in the water. Waste, waste, waste…

Click your heels, little kitten. And have fun over the rainbow, she said.

Then she was gone. Instantly his body was his again.

He pulled his hanging hand together and bound it up with a towel. He stood up in the bath and felt faint. Quick, quick. He staggered out of the bathroom. Blood, blood, blood, flowing, dripping, going, going... The bell pull was only a few steps away. He fell on the bed, rolled over, and pulled it, but even he knew it was much too late. Bitch. The croissants!

His eyes glazed over. The darkness was already waiting. He lay on his stomach and died. Scared, listening to all the children he had tortured and killed gathering around his body. They were singing softly, snatches of songs he had taught them.

> Like the weather, one's fortune may change by the evening.
>
> —Luu Mengzheng, Song dynasty

The woman sat in the shade of a mango tree. It was afternoon and the sun was yellow and fierce. She was drinking tea from a fine cup. Behind her was a very large stone house with a swimming pool beside it. The air was noisy with the sound of children playing in it. In the distance she could see a girl walking toward her. Her hair was glowing like a golden halo around her head. As the woman watched with squinted eyes, the girl raised her hand and waved.

The woman turned her head and called out to the woman who came daily to help her around the house to bring another cup from the glass cabinet. Then she stood and went to the gate to greet her visitor.

'Hello,' the girl said.

'You found me,' Bumi said with a smile.

The girl laughed prettily. 'It wasn't difficult.'

'What's your name?'

'Dakota.'

'Well, come and have some tea with me, Dakota.'

'Thank you,' said Dakota and followed her to the table under the tree. She looked around. The compound was large and full of fruit trees. A woman came with a cup and saucer and put it in front of Dakota.

'This is Menachi,' introduced Bumi.

'Hi,' said Dakota.

Menachi smiled broadly. Her teeth were stained red with betel juice.

'She doesn't speak English,' said Bumi, pouring out some tea. 'Milk?'

'Thank you.'

'Sugar?'

'Yes, please.'

'A tomato sandwich?'

Dakota nodded and smiled her thanks. She lifted her cup of tea and took a small sip. 'This is a really pretty cup.'

'Limoges,' said Bumi.

'Expensive.'

'Very. A totally unexpected gift from my employer just as I was leaving.'

'Black.'

'Without any doubt.'

'And how did you come by all this?' Dakota asked, waving her hand to include the massive garden and the stone house.

'I won the lottery.'

Dakota laughed. 'What happened? Did you *find* a winning ticket?'

'Close. A gust of wind blew it into my hand.' And she laughed too. They laughed together. Both connected by the boy. Both thinking of him. Missing him.

'And the children?'

'Orphans. I'm taking care of them.'

Dakota leaned back into the chair and bit into a sandwich. It had been cut daintily. The tomato felt fresh in her mouth. She knew what the woman was going to say before she said it.

'Why don't you stay for a bit now that you are here?'

* * *

How do I know all this?

Because it happened to the woman, the boy, and me. I stayed with her and Menachi and the sweet children (there is something wrong with each and every one of them) for a week, even though I know they are looking for me. I can feel them working in teams to find me. Sometimes I disrupt their little reconnaissance trips and mess with their minds, but it is getting dangerous—soon they will find me. And I wouldn't want to bring trouble to Bumi; God knows she has suffered enough. So I made the decision to leave. Staying in one place is always a bad idea.

That night I dreamed of a shaman. He had painted himself black, and was wearing the mask of a jaguar. There was something sleek and powerful about him. He danced around me, a magic ritual.

'You are not a butterfly,' he told me. 'You are an owl. The owl is special. It is the only bird that does not have eyes on the sides of its head. Like a human it looks directly at the world. If you come across one tomorrow you must come and see me in Peru. There is something I need to show you. I will protect you until you are strong enough to protect yourself.' Then he released a strange shriek and disappeared.

I woke up in the morning and Menachi was going to the market. Bumi asked me if I would like to go too, and of course I said yes. In the market a boy was selling masks.

'Buy a mask from me, madam. (Menachi says they call everybody madam as a sign of respect.) I will give you a very excellent price.'

I looked at the mask he was holding up and it was the mask of an owl face. I bought it. I have it in my luggage. A good luck charm from India. I leave for Peru tomorrow. I think I know where to find the shaman, but I guess it would be more accurate to say that he will probably find me.

It has begun to rain and the rain makes me think of my parents. I am in a car with them traveling through miles of golden wheat. It is warm and cozy in the car. I long to see their faces, but it is impossible for now. I will only bring trouble to them. Let them carry on believing I am dead. One day I know there will be the opportunity to walk into that dear old farmhouse again. We will hug and kiss and remember old times. Afterwards, I will sit out on the porch and wait for the big rains to come. I used to love the rain. How it used to lash angrily at the windowpanes. My mother would be screaming for me to get into the house, and I would pretend to come in, but sneak back out to sit on Grandpa's rocking chair, until I was soaked to the skin and shivering.

It has stopped raining. The air is full of frogs croaking. The children have gone to bed now. They go to bed early and get up early. There is no TV. Bumi will not allow one in the house. It is quiet. The nights always bring me back to Black. I wonder where he is now. What it must be like outside the prison. Before he died he used to visit me in my dreams. It might be hard for some people to believe, but I truly loved him. He was so special, so beautiful. I wish you could have seen him. His eyes, his hands, his lips. I know we will meet again. In another life, another dimension. Who knows? For now I will go to Peru. Maybe the ticketing officer will ask me, as the other one did, if I would like a free upgrade to business class.

Of course, I will smile and reply, 'Awesome.'

Miss Monroe—pure habit makes me call her that—Alice will join me there. It will be an adventure. Perhaps you will come with me. I will tell you about our escape from the Black Hole, how easily we fooled their clumsy iris and fingerprint scanners.

Menachi has switched on her small transistor radio. She likes to sleep on the veranda outside, and music is floating in through the open window. I listen to it. It's been a long time since I heard such music. The words are simple and incredibly catchy. Someone called M.C. Hammer sang it. It's called, 'U Can't Touch This'.

"Who caught his blood?"
"I," said the Fish
"With my little dish,
I caught his blood."

—'Who killed Cock Robin?',
Tommy Thumb's Pretty Song Book (1744)

The man looks out at the mountain range in the distance, its craggy peaks covered in mist. Its wild untamed beauty never fails to move him. He thinks of the story of the man who looked at a mountain face for so long he began to resemble it. Perhaps he looks like the range. Wild and craggy and dangerous.

He is a stranger in these parts, but these are good people who accept him without questions. They think he is a retired city boy. A gringo who made a lot of money, got burned out, and came to their village seeking privacy. No wife. No children. A lonely man with too much money. They bring him provisions, potatoes, special ears of corn, chicken and hint about their unmarried daughters. They don't know they are offering their daughter to the most deadly Delta assassin alive. His track record is impeccable.

He has never failed.

Somewhere in the house he can hear the woman making refried beans or tortillas or some local thing. He enjoys it all. He had thought he had retired—and how he relished it—but now he knows. They will never allow him that right. He will have to kill, kill and kill, until the day he draws his last breath. He picks up his glass, hand-cut crystal from Prague, and takes a sip of the amber liquid. He closes his eyes as it slides down his throat. Gentleman Jack from Jack Daniel's.

Smokey.

He opens his eyes. The world is still the same. Shame. He looks at the photo of the girl on his desk. Behind the vacant eyes a child. So young to have fallen foul of them. He doesn't want to do this. He looks away from her eyes. The phone rings. He lets it. One ring. Two rings. Third ring. His hands are itching. Fuck. They have really fucked his head. His hand claws, then snatches.

'Hello, Fish.'

'Gentleman Jack. You received the photo?'

'Yes.'

'Have you got a location?'

'She was visible yesterday. Briefly. Mumbai Airport.' In his mind's eye Gentleman Jack sees her again, standing alone in that dreary airport lounge. A frail thing. But she was no frail thing. She turned bravely to face him, and said, 'U can't touch this.' And then he could no longer close in and 'look' at her. He was glad. He didn't want to catch her.

He becomes aware of the silence on the other end of the line. Expectant silence. 'Sorry?' he says, 'I didn't catch that?'

'Flying in or out?' Kite repeats with an undercurrent of impatience.

'Out.'

'Where to?'

'Impossible to tell. Someone has put a screen up.'

'Someone other than her?'

'Yes.'

'Who is more powerful than you?'

'Perhaps I have become too old for this job.'

'Perhaps you have not applied yourself to this job. The horses in the carousel don't fly away. They go round and round.'

Gentleman Jack feels his hand go slack around the beautiful glass. Who would believe that crystal was made from sand? His mouth opens. 'She is going to Peru.'

'Well done, Gentleman Jack. Now, eliminate her.'

To be continued…

Want to find out what happens to Dakota or receive advance notification of new releases? Sign up at http://ranimanicka.com/contact/ with the words – WANT MORE.

Acknowledgements

As ever thank you to my mother for a lifetime of love, care and encouragement. As my late father said to her, 'If I am born again I want you to be my wife.' I say to her, 'If I am born again I want you to be my mother.' To the great love of my life, Rick Sansome, thank you for EVERYTHING. To my sister, I express the same sentiment I showed my mother. 'Be my sister again.' To my best friend, Dom, thank you for the never-ceasing support and love.

Gratitude to James Veitch – website designer extraordinaire; Lori Heaford – who meticulously copy-edited and then proofread this book; Spiffing Covers and Melody Simmonds for inspiring book jacket designs; the award winning James Worthington for a super book trailer; sweet Jeanie Boo for her eagle eyes; and the newly married Matt Maguire of Candescent Press for excellent formatting services. Much thanks also to the inimitable Mary Darby of the Foreign Rights department at the Darley Anderson Agency.

My deepest respect and gratitude goes to these remarkable individuals. This book wouldn't be what it is without the knowledge they passed on to me. Dr. Joseph Chiappalone, John Lash, Matthew Delooze, Mark Passio, David Icke, Caslos Casteneda, Steven J Smith, Jean-Dominique Bauby, Jay Weidner, Montalk, Fritz Springmeiser, Robert A. Munroe, Cathy O'Brien, Colin Wilson, Sophia Smallstorm, Zen Gardener, Barbara Marciniak.

Finally, to my readers. Thank you for the privilege of letting me share my story with you. I hope you have enjoyed reading it as much as I have enjoyed writing it.

With much love,

Sources

http://en.wikipedia.org/wiki/Project_MKUltra

http://www.mindspring.com/~txporter/scidig.htm

http://vigilantcitizen.com/hidden-knowledge/origins-and-techniques-of-monarch-mind-control/

http://www.theforbiddenknowledge.com/hardtruth/illuminati_formula_mind_control.htm

http://wermanylights.blogspot.co.uk/2013/01/mind-control-expressed-as-art.html

Grazyna Fosar and Franz Bludorf in their book Vernetzte Intelligenz summarized by Baerbel.

The human DNA is a biological Internet with evidence that DNA can be influenced and reprogrammed by words and frequencies.

http://www.omniology.com/CretaceousHandPrint.html

http://leschroniquesdaragonne.wordpress.com/2012/06/12/the-predator-mind-by-carlos-castaneda/

http://www.amazon.co.uk/Active-Side-Infinity-Carlos-Castaneda/dp/0722537360

http://www.metahistory.org/

https://www.dmt-nexus.me/doc/Journeys Out Of The%20Body-Robert Monroe.pdf

https://www.dmt-nexus.me/doc/Ultimate_Journey-Robert%20A%20Monroe.pdf

http://www.guardian.co.uk/politics/2002/apr/21/uk.medicalscience

http://www.dailymail.co.uk/health/article-1375697/Alfie-Clamp-2-1st-person-born-extra-strand-DNA.html

http://www.healthymoneyvine.com/support-files/psychic_children_of_china.pdf

China's Super Psychics: paperback by Paul Dong & Thomas E. Rafill. http://www.amazon.co.uk/Holographic-Universe-Michael-Talbot/dp/0586091718

http://www.amazon.co.uk/Nag-Hammadi-Library-English-Translation/dp/0060669357/ref=sr_1_5?s=books&ie=UTF8&qid=1367238179&sr=1-5&keywords=nag+hammadi+scriptures

http://www.fluoride-history.de/p-insecticides.htm

http://www.guardian.co.uk/politics/2002/apr/21/uk.medicalscience

http://kcovino.hubpages.com/hub/Experts-Admits-Chemtrails-Are-Real

http://www.naturalnews.com/037451_chemtrails_conspiracy_theory_geoengineering.html

http://www.naturalnews.com/022838_chemtrails_military_health.html

http://www.youtube.com/watch?v=LrDHr4YCOG4

http://www.geoengineeringwatch.org/category/chemtrails/

http://www.aboutthesky.com/transbiology

http://www.carnicominstitute.org/html/webdesigner/research projects/researchprojects.htm

http://www.dailymail.co.uk/news/article-2244272/Florida-officials-consider-releasing-genetically-modified-non-biting-mosquitoes-battle-dengue-fever.html

The Universe as a Hologram by Michael Talbot.
http://www.amazon.co.uk/Holographic-Universe-Michael-Talbot/dp/0586091718

http://www.youtube.com/watch?v=jV9WTLAuhMY

http://www.silverbearcafe.com/private/03.10/rigged.html

http://www.youtube.com/watch?feature=player_embedded&v=XHAXjRPXH2Q#!

http://beforeitsnews.com/beyond-science/2012/12/giant-cube-recorded-by-nasa-near-sun-on-dec-21-2012-nasa-source-alien-cube-first-seen-in-2011-2440352.html

http://www.youtube.com/watch?feature=player_embedded&v=Z7BuQFUhsRM